ICE COLD STEEL

JOHN STEEL
BOOK 7

STUART FIELD

To the readers out there, without whom we could not share our stories.

ACKNOWLEDGMENTS

I want to thank my wife for putting up with my constant disappearance to write.

To the CrimeFest Bristol team for giving me a view of the family of crime writers in the world.

PROLOGUE

London, Whitehall, the Old War Office.

ONCE THE HOME OF CHURCHILL'S WAR ROOMS, IT IS NOW home to MI6 and MI8 of the British Secret Service. A large, white, majestic building close to the River Thames and St James's Park.

The Military Intelligence Section Eight, or MI8, was created during the First World War. It was responsible for signals and communications. It was split into four sections: A, B, C, and D, and during the Second World War, it was renamed the RSS, or the Radio Security Service, where it did a lot of damage, seeking out enemy radio sets and blocking transmissions. Later, Section Eight was absorbed into the Government Communications Headquarters, or GCHQ.

That was until recent world events called for a different approach to how the Secret Service went about its business.

Before, in the days of the Cold War, everyone knew who the enemy was; now, things were different, a whole lot different, and the solution was simple: bring back Section Eight. But their role was different. This would be the Secret Service of the Secret Service, the dirty secret nobody wanted to discuss but needed.

Over the years, whether because of books, TV, or the movies, MI6 had been made public; Britain needed a part of the Secret Service that was just that... a secret.

MI8 was small compared with MI5 and MI6, with only four hundred members and a handful of agents. It had been seven years since its creation. However, the numbers had been kept discreetly short for security reasons. Four hundred was a good number to keep track of its members. In contrast, thousands of employees were more complex and could be easily infiltrated.

MI8 consisted of Army personnel, whereas MI6 consisted mainly of Navy intelligence, and MI5 consisted of Oxford or Cambridge brainiacs. However, regardless of their makeup, they had each other's backs when it came to it.

MI8 shared the seventh floor with MI6. This was cost-effective and tactically efficient because they were just down the hall if MI6 required MI8's services.

It was two in the afternoon when the bad news came.

The head of MI8 sat in his red leather Chesterfield office chair and sighed. The news of the massacre at Lord Steel's residence had reached him an hour ago. An unknown number of assailants had entered the grounds of Lord Steel's estate and proceeded to murder everyone there. The motive and who these mercenaries worked for were yet unknown.

Lord Steel hadn't just been the head of MI8's operations against terrorists and governmental espionage; he had also been a close friend for many years.

The man, known as CO, looked tired and drained. Although he was in his late fifties, he now looked in his late sixties—a drawback of his new job as head of MI8.

He was well over six feet tall, with broad shoulders and the beginnings of a somewhat portly figure, but he held the stature of a soldier. Indeed, anyone who saw him knew he had been a high-ranking officer, possibly a general.

His white hair was styled with a side parting that stood out from his slightly tanned skin. It was the only thing he had brought back from a recent trip to Washington, D.C.

He looked around the office, a large room constructed in the late eighteen hundreds. Tall bookshelves and portraits in gilded golden frames hid its oak flooring and half-panelled walls. He glanced at the telephone on his desk, which had begun ringing. Lifting the receiver from the cradle, he spoke.

'Yes?' His Oxford voice was a deep baritone.

He listened to the person on the other end but remained silent until the man had finished his briefing.

'So, John, he survived. Anyone else?' CO said.

The person continued with the briefing.

CO nodded as he took in the information. 'Heavy death toll, you say, including the Earl and Lady Steel. Bad business. But at least the lad took some of the beggars with him.'

The voice on the phone concurred.

'So, that bloody gardener of theirs came through. Do we know what he injected the lad with? If John pulls through, it might be an idea to get the formula.'

The man continued, and CO listened; his expression changed from despair to hope.

'Where is the lad now?' CO replied, hoping for more good news.

The man on the other end of the line explained the situation and the condition of John Steel. CO's face turned grim with the news.

John Steel was given a thirty per cent chance of survival. He was in surgery, and after that, he would be put in an induced coma to relieve his body from stress as it began to heal itself, and machines would keep him alive.

The man on the other end had been told by doctors that the bullets had missed most of the major organs—whether by the shooter being a lousy shot or by design, planning for John to die slowly or survive but be confined to a wheelchair or even a bed for the rest of his life.

The man finished the call, and CO put the handset on the cradle. Standing up, he headed for the large window at the far end of the room and looked over at the River Thames. He looked down at the brown, murky waters of the river and at the boats; some were moored, and others sped along, their engines roaring and kicking up sprays of water. Beyond, he could see the roof of Waterloo Station as it glinted in the sun.

How had this happened? Who was this damned organisation that kept eluding them?

He turned and looked at the phone on his desk. An idea crept into his mind. They had been looking to recruit John Steel into the MI8 section for some time, but this had put a block on that. Perhaps even worse—he would not be able to join their ranks.

He picked up the receiver and pressed one of the buttons to patch him through to his secretary. 'Miss Dickenson, can you get me the commanding officer of the SAS regiment and the American ambassador here in London? Thank you,' he said, placing the receiver down, walking to a small drinks cabinet, and pouring himself a large whisky. This was not a good day, but John Steel was safe.

CO knew that John Steel was a fighter. John would be back, and if CO knew him like he thought he did, now he would be a force to be reckoned with. All they had to do was control him.

CHAPTER ONE

Seven months later.
Autumn in Alaska.

A BLACK EUROCOPTER SA 360 DAUPHIN HELICOPTER
landed at Ridgeway Creek airport, and several people got out as
the top rotor blades began to slow.

Ken Henning came out of the small building, which was
the airport tower, and rubbed his hands on an oily-looking rag
he had stuffed into the back pocket of his denim dungarees. He
stared at the strange muddle of people: a woman and
three men.

The woman was tall and blonde; she looked more like a
doctor or lawyer. Two of the men were tall and heavy-looking,
military or cops. Then there was a third man. He was tall with
dark hair and ambled as if he was injured. Dark sunglasses
covered his eyes despite the grey skies.

Ken watched as they all climbed into a Range Rover
Discovery that had been waiting for them. It was a used vehicle, probably a rental. The black paintwork was covered in dust

and dirt. Possibly, they had kept it that way so it didn't stand out like a clean and shiny car would.

He thought the whole thing seemed odd, but then it hadn't been the strangest thing he had seen. Ken wondered if it was an actor or some other famous person who had just had plastic surgery and was hiding until the scars healed.

The vehicle took off, spitting dust and small stones into the air as it did so, then cruised along the road until it disappeared from view.

A woman came over and stood next to Ken. She was the local store owner, Maddy Johnson, another person who had lived in the town even before it was a town.

'I guess we got us more rich folk hidin' out,' Ken grumbled. 'I wouldn't mind if they actually brought money to the town. Instead, they hide up in them hills and have the stuff imported in.'

Maddy nodded. She felt the same, but she recognised the man, the injured one with the glasses. 'True, but do you know who that boy was?'

Ken shrugged.

'That was Edward and Elizabeth's boy. You know, the folk that built that fancy place near Edward Lake. The ones that put a whole lot of cash into this place, including your damn airfield.' Her voice was gravelly, and her tone invited little in the way of a reminder of the family he owed his livelihood to.

'Oh, yeah, I thought he looked familiar,' Ken lied.

'Jackass,' she scorned. 'You never met the kid, only his pa, who you badgered with the idea of him investing in your goddam airfield.'

Ken shrugged again and looked shyly at the floor.

'Come on, let's get to the diner; you can buy me a coffee and some pie.'

An hour later, the dusty Range Rover pulled up outside the

Steels' retreat near Edward Lake, parked in the small driveway, and the travellers got out.

The woman looked at the large modern structure and mouthed a 'wow.' On one side was an open plain, on the other a dense forest, and to the front a small lake.

The cabin was not like the typical place that most of the locals had; this was a massive structure made from stone, steel, wood, and glass.

It was a single-storey building with a slanted roof at the back. A large bay window opened onto a terrace overlooking the lake. The cabin was powered by a generator with a secondary as a backup, along with solar panels and a wind turbine. Everything required for several people to outlast a brutal winter in comfort was in place. The roof extended on one side, under which was a smaller building. This was the storage and utility house, which also had a large freezer unit to store meat for the winter.

The view was spectacular, with a forest on one side, mountains in the distance and, down below, the small lake. The retreat had been built when John Steel was a boy and became a permanent holiday home. It was also somewhere Lord Steel would go if he needed some time alone.

A local firm built it using local timber and materials, creating much-needed work in the area. Lord Steel had also fallen in love with Ridgeway Creek and did what he could to help out, whether it was paying for a new road or a roof for the church. Although Edward and Elizabeth were known to the locals, John wasn't. He had been a small child at the time, and when he was old enough, he was sent to Cambridge; after that, he joined the Army.

However, the store owner, Maddy, had babysat John when Edward and Elizabeth wanted some time alone, so when she saw John, she knew it was him immediately.

'You have a beautiful home, John,' the woman said, her voice soft and ringing with a Kent accent. This was Brie Hodgkinson, John's doctor and physiotherapist.

John said nothing; he just stared at the single-storey building as though he were seeing images of the past.

'We had spoken to the storekeeper; she had arranged for the generator to be topped up and the refrigerator and pantry to be stocked,' Brie added.

John remained silent, lost in his thoughts and memories. He looked like he wanted to cry, but she knew he couldn't. It was either an after-effect of the herbal concoction the gardener had given him, or it was psychological; whatever the cause, the effect was the same—John Steel could not cry. This had specialists baffled because his tear ducts were still active, and his eyes would become watery. Still, he was as dry as the Sahara when it came to emotional tears.

'Shall we go inside?' she insisted. 'I don't know about the rest of you, but I need a decent cup of tea.' Brie then went to a small utility house next to the main building and searched for a large blue plant pot, which Maddy had said she would leave a spare key in.

She returned to the side door next to the utility house, holding a key on a small keychain. Brie slipped the key inside the lock and turned it until she heard the click of the lock being disengaged. Then, she gently pushed the door open and stood to the side, allowing John Steel to enter first.

Steel entered slowly and was hit by the smell of cleaning sprays and air fresheners. He imagined that someone had been in to clean just before their arrival. His sunglass-covered eyes scanned the room. It was a long room with a large sitting area and an open-plan kitchen on the left. At the end was a long corridor with six bedrooms, three on either side, and another room at the very end. This had been his father's study; now it was John's. The interior was a mix of modern and contemporary, with white plaster walls and polished wooden floors. The fireplace was made of stone. Wooden beams stretched across the ceiling, giving it a rustic feel. The kitchen was modern but had an old wood-burning stove instead of a gas or electric oven. Wooden glass-fronted cupboards hung from the natural stone walls of the kitchen.

The idea of mixing old and new shouldn't have worked, but whoever the architect was had managed to pull it off.

Brie watched as John Steel walked about, looking at the family photographs on the wall. His movements were laboured as if he were seeing it all for the first time. She watched him move into the sitting area, past a huge L-shaped brown brushed leather sofa and towards a large bay window.

As Steel stared out across the vast wilderness before him, Brie smiled, turned, and headed for the kitchen. 'Right then,' she said. 'I'll get the kettle on, then we can go through your treatment while you're here.'

John Steel didn't move; he just stared at the harsh, beautiful landscape and wished he were dead

CHAPTER TWO

One year later....

It was late autumn in Alaska. The sun was high, but a chilled wind blew in from the east. The land was still green, but TV and radio had announced the beginning of winter and harsh snowstorms.

John Steel was on the wooden terrace doing yoga. He found it stretched his muscles after a good workout. It had been almost a year since the shooting at his family estate—an attack that had murdered his entire family and left him for dead.

Steel winced in pain as he stretched in the Cobra position. He released the stretch and lay on the mat to catch his breath. His wounds to his skin had healed, but the nerves and muscles were still repairing themselves. He rolled over, looked at the perfect blue sky, and laughed.

He recalled his days in the army when the PT instructors would yell, 'No pain, no gain.' Yeah, right. It was okay for them to say as they stood and watched while the troops were run ragged or heaving their tired arses over the assault course after a five-mile run carrying a log.

Days long gone, a life he could never return to—for now. The organisation had seen to that. For now, he was in hiding, but he would be back. He had been with the SAS regiment before the shooting; now, he was on *'administrative leave.'* In other words, he should hide until he was fit for duty or they found the people responsible. In truth, Steel hoped that he could return to his old team and find the bastards himself.

Steel heaved himself up, then began to twist in the middle and pump his shoulders to relieve some of the muscle tension. His muscular frame looked more like an athlete's than a body-builder's. Still, he wasn't surprised, given the training programme a physical instructor friend had given him. He remembered it had taken months before he would even start with the programme. In fact, Steel's lack of motivation had been so bad that the instructor had to stay at the cabin and force him to do something.

The instructor knew that Steel's injuries weren't just on the outside; he was also broken on the inside. He was suffering from survivor's guilt. A special forces soldier who couldn't even save his family! Steel had also seen therapists—or rather, been ordered to. However, none had been much help because it wasn't survivor's guilt; it was something else, something more primal.

Revenge.

Steel walked inside the cabin. It was bright, lit by the morning sun.

As he passed the kitchen on his way to the bathroom, John Steel clicked on the coffee machine and switched on the television using a nearby remote. The news report was about the US Congress and how they would be voting on a new arms contract in the next few weeks.

Steel grimaced at the report. His family's company had also bid for the contract. He found it ironic but not related to the assault on his family. That attack, Steel had found out later, was because of constant operations against the organisation led by Military Intelligence, of which Steel's father had been a part. Lord Steel had been Head of Operations against terrorist organisations and covert ops. Now, it seemed that what had appeared to be several organisations was only one. An organisation they had no idea existed.

When he entered the main bathroom, the slate floor felt cool under his bare feet. It was a long room with sandstone-tiled walls. The toilet and basin were matte black, and the shower was round with stone walls, giving it a natural look, with a rain shower head in the ceiling.

Steel stripped off his clothes and tossed them into a nearby hamper. As he leaned over the sink, he looked up. He stared at his reflection and saw an unfamiliar face. He used to be clean-shaven and square-jawed with blue eyes. A somewhat handsome face, but more rugged than model-like. Now, he only saw a tired man with a long black beard and, most of all, hideous emerald-green eyes. He had seen people with green eyes, and they were beautiful. However, his eyes held a darkness, almost soulless. He shivered at the sight and looked down.

This was the price for saving his life. An old friend of the family, who worked as a gardener, had saved Steel. He had injected him with something to slow the bleeding and start the healing process. In truth, Steel had no idea *how* it had saved his life, but it had taken away the blue in his eyes his wife had loved so much and left him with the cold, soulless green colour.

A year before, he had been a soldier in the British special forces returning home from a tour in Bosnia, and now he was a man in hiding. His family had been murdered at his homecoming party, gunned down by a team of mercenaries for an organisation led by someone called Santini.

Steel had also been shot six times in the back. The shooter had placed the rounds into him from only a few feet away, each one a through-and-through. He hadn't shot randomly; he had taken his time and made a pattern. Somehow, each round seemed to miss vital organs, almost as if the shooter was marking Steel rather than trying to kill him.

Word had spread to his unit in Hereford, and his commanding officer had agreed to say nothing of Steel's location or that he had survived. If someone had tried to kill him and failed, they might try again, and the team could be caught in the crossfire. It was agreed that Steel would move away until he was back on his feet and they had a lead on the people involved. That was a year ago, and the trail had gone cold. They were still out there, so Steel attended the family retreat.

He had trained and hit the fitness room to build up strength and stamina, but his wounds still hurt every time he moved, and the nightmares kept him up.

Steel raised his head to check his wounds in the mirror. Six bullet holes bore their angry scars. The old Japanese gardener had called them *the mark of the phoenix*; Steel had told him he was full of shit.

At the same time, in another part of Alaska, a computer analyst working for the SANTINI organisation clicked a couple of keys on the secure computer of the remote Alaskan outstation. The station was manned by several analysts who had been lured away from their universities by the promise of a lucrative career and a healthy wage. Unfortunately, they had not been ready for what had come next. Each had been selected because of financial or other problems the organisation had discovered and then used against them.

A man had sought them out, going to every major city to

find these students. Then, after giving such an enticing sales pitch they couldn't refuse, they all wanted to sign up immediately. Each of them was instructed to travel to an office in the city, where they would sign their contract and then be given instructions on what came next.

They had all done as they were told, and after signing the many different legal forms, they were given an envelope with a plane ticket, five thousand dollars in cash, and an address in Washington. Two days later, after making their excuses—all of them were instructed that what they were doing was top secret, and nobody could know where they were going—they all met up at the address, and their training started.

This was when the organisation's true intentions were revealed, and the new group realised this wasn't the dream opportunity they had been told about. On the other hand, some accepted what had been presented to them, and it appealed to them more—the chance to do mischief and get rich doing it.

One such person was the new analyst stuck in the Alaskan compound. Still, instead of the nine-to-five job and plush apartment, the agent was stuck in the mountain compound with twelve other people who had fallen for the 'get rich' pitch.

The analyst had been searching the dark web, hacking into government files, and finally, after a week of searching, the agent struck gold.

'Well, well, well. Isn't that interesting,' a muffled voice said.

The agent's task had been to find anything on any of the US President's staff that could influence the bid for the new defence contract.

The agent had no idea why the outstation was stuck in the middle of nowhere in Alaska, but the agent also knew not to question such things. It had been six months since the agent had been sent there. Sure, it was comfortable enough—a large cabin with all the comforts of home and a few extras, such as a pool, sauna, and fitness room. SANTINI had ensured that an agent's stay felt more like a gift than a punishment.

Despite the pleasant surroundings and the comforts that most people would pay good money for, it felt like a prison after a while.

The agent had been alone there on a seven-month rotation. However, with this new information, the agent was going home.

The agent downloaded the data onto a portable hard drive and sent the message to HQ.

To the Chairman... data you required retrieved. Request immediate evacuation. Will bring the data retrieved personally. The file is too large to send over normal means.

The agent smiled and then pressed send. The agent knew the last part was a lie; it would have been simple to send it. But the agent wanted out of this prison, and this data was the agent's ticket. The Chairman would understand the message. After all, blackmail, subversion, and threats were SANTINI's business. The agent was smart enough to leave it at a request to come home. Another agent had once gone too far, asked for ten million dollars, and wound up missing.

No, a flight home was more than enough. Seconds later, a reply came through.

Understood, terms acceptable, job well done. In a week's time, the Glacier tour will be out of Talkeetna. Be on that tour.

The agent smiled, left the computer, and went to pack. The agent would research the tour later, then celebrate with a beer in the hot tub. Soon, the agent was going home.

CHAPTER THREE

Five days later.

THE TOWNSPEOPLE PREPARED FOR ANOTHER DAY IN THE small Alaskan town of Ridgeway Creek. Some drove to their jobs at the lumber yards or up in the hills to operate the massive tree-felling machines. Some travelled to the nearby town of Talkeetna.

Ridgeway Creek was small. What had once been a long stretch of road with a school, a few houses and a gas station was now a small church, a general store, a doctor who also doubled as a dentist, and his daughter, the vet. There was a fire station, a school, a Sheriff's Office, a diner, two hotels and a small airport for the tourist planes.

The town sign boasted a population of a thousand people, which had once been nearly two hundred, but when the logging firm started, that number soon changed. The town boomed.

A hotel was built at the nearby Ridge Lake to accommodate sailors and other water sports enthusiasts, and the river that fed the lake was now home to fishermen. But all that would change; it was autumn, and the weather would change, and then the skiers and the snowmobile people would flood in. Tourists were a new concept to the people of Ridgeway Creek, and at first, it was a welcome change. The town had cash flowing in. However, as with all tourist places, there was the threat of drunks and other troublemakers—something the Sheriff could do without.

A beaten-up green Ford F-150 pulled off a dusty trail and hit the asphalt main road into Ridgeway Creek.

John Steel was on his weekly run for supplies. Winter would soon be there, and because his cabin was fifty miles away, he had to stock up on things like ammunition, fuel for the generators, candles, batteries, canned goods and, most importantly, toilet paper.

He drove past the town's sign and remained on the high street until he found the small parking lot outside the local store.

He paused momentarily and finished listening to the rest of Metallica, who told him, *"Nothing Else Matters."* As the song ended and the local radio presenter came back on, Steel turned off the engine and got out of the truck.

He was a six-foot-two man with broad shoulders that filled his long brown leather coat. His face was hidden beneath a long beard and a pair of glacier sunglasses. He was dressed all in black—cargo trousers, a thick black shirt, a black t-shirt, and military-style boots.

He closed the truck's door but didn't lock it; nobody ever did in Ridgeway Creek. Then, he walked over to the store.

He stood momentarily at the store entrance, then turned. Steel looked a mile up and down the length of Main Street, observing the people going about their business.

John Steel had been in Alaska for a year; in that time, he

17

had come to recognise most of the faces, but two men who had just entered the diner were new. One of them was a tall, shaven-headed man; despite the bulky clothing, Steel could tell this new stranger was heavily built. The man with him looked like a Native American.

He watched the two men with interest as he sat on a bench outside the store, which was due to open at eight o'clock—five minutes later.

The two strangers disappeared inside, and the sun reflected off the diner window, making it impossible for Steel to gaze inside.

Steel didn't like new people, especially ones who carried themselves like soldiers. He flicked through a small notebook containing his shopping list, but his gaze was fixed on the diner. Something about these men was off.

A sudden noise beside him made Steel look at the store door. A woman with fiery red hair, dressed in jeans, a checkered shirt and brown work boots, greeted him.

'Morning, John. You're early,' her voice was husky and had a friendly but firm tone.

'Morning, Maddy, just thought I'd beat the rush,' Steel replied. He was British but had almost no accent.

'Yeah, I've been beating them off with a stick lately,' she said, looking around at the almost empty street. 'Come on, I'll get you a coffee while you see what you need.'

Steel stood, his movement slightly laboured, as if moving hurt.

Maddy Johnson looked back at him and cracked a compassionate smile. 'Still hurtin'?'

'Only when I laugh,' John Steel joked.

The store was around thirty feet long, with a tall ceiling revealing wooden beams and rafters. Like most of the town, the whole building was made of wood.

Two rows of shelves containing everything from canned food to bullets ran down the centre of the store, with a long counter near the door.

There were no surveillance cameras, just like nobody locked their doors. This was a safe town where everyone knew everyone. But the influx of tourists was changing that. There were new faces around town all the time—two of which John Steel had seen and felt uneasy about.

Steel stood at the counter, pulled out his notebook, and flipped the pages until he got to his list. He tore out the page and placed it on the wooden top.

Maddy placed a white mug of black coffee next to the list and looked down at the small piece of paper.

'Stocking up for the winter?' she asked, seeing the large amounts of canned food, boxes of eggs, ultra-high-temperature milk, medical items, and ammunition for a 7.62 rifle, .44 Magnum revolver, and a twelve-gauge shotgun. Batteries for torches, fuel for lamps, snares, and fishing hooks.

'Yeah, thought I'd better get it done now,' he replied before taking a sip of the coffee.

Steel's gaze shifted to the window, where he saw two more strangers head inside the diner across the street.

'Know anything about the new people?' he asked. Maddy followed his gaze just in time to see the two men. She shook her head. 'Not much; they got here a few days ago. Folks have seen them all over town, including the airfield.' She shrugged. 'Maybe they're big city boys who ain't never seen such a quaint town like ours before?'

Steel nodded. His uneasy feeling was getting worse. These were mercenaries, or at least a private army. But why were they there? For him? He couldn't be sure.

'When can I get the stuff on the list?'

'Most of the tinned stuff you can get now, along with the

medical items. Got some ammo here, but I'll have to order the rest of what you want. Can't give you all I've got; you understand.'

Steel shrugged sympathetically.

'I'll have to order some of the other stuff. Depending on when Earl is flying into the city next, I may get everything for you in two days.'

'Sounds good. Like I say, just stocking up, so no rush,' he said.

Maddy shot him an appreciative smile. 'Want more coffee?'

Steel looked down at the half-empty mug, smiled, and pushed it towards her. 'Thanks, Maddy.'

'What for? It's only coffee.'

'No, thank you for taking me in when most of the town shunned me when I arrived here.'

She smiled gently. 'I knew your folks from way back; hell, I used to babysit your little brother and sister—God rest their souls. You and I never got to meet as such; you were in that fancy school and then the Army, and when you were here, you didn't visit town much. Shame, but it is what it is. Besides, you're here now; people have come to accept you.'

Steel cracked a smile, which faded as he returned his gaze towards the diner. His thoughts were full of questions. Who were these men? And what did they want? If it wasn't him, then what was coming?

CHAPTER FOUR

AFTER GETTING HIS GOODS, JOHN STEEL HAD LEFT THE store and stopped at a local diner to treat himself to an American breakfast with extra bacon. On the way, he walked around and chatted with some locals. Ken, who ran the small airfield and workshop, was the man all the local pilots went to instead of going all the way to Talkeetna.

Then he ran into an old man that the locals knew as Old Man Burt, who worked for the logging company. His job was to push the cut logs downriver. They found they could transport more wood for half the cost of using trucks. Despite being in his late sixties, he was still a large bulk of a man, shorter than Steel but broader—most of it muscle from hard labour for around forty years.

They chatted for a while. Burt told Steel he had to go north and get some fresh logs from one of the loggers, but he would push them downriver in a few days.

Even though he was a loner, he thought it best to keep in with the local people in case he needed help.

The sun was high, but a crisp wind replaced the warmth.

As he continued through the town, he observed that there were more strangers. He had seen at least seven new faces. They might have been here for the winter, fishing or hunting, but his gut told him something wasn't right.

He left town and carried on along the asphalt until he reached the turn-off to the dirt track leading up into the mountains. The road snaked through forests and open plains, past waterfalls and small lakes. He was halfway there when he drove over a railway track.

When he first came to Alaska as a child, he soon learned that twenty miles in Alaska differed from twenty miles back home. In fact, those twenty miles could almost feel like a hundred, depending on the terrain.

John Steel was the son of Lord Steel, Earl of Pulborough. Their family home was a fifteen-bedroom mansion built in the 14th century in the south of England, away from the bustle of London.

Steel had never liked the life of an aristocrat, so when he joined the army, despite being offered the chance to be an officer, he enlisted as a private soldier and worked his way through the ranks.

By the age of twenty-two, he had passed selection and joined the SAS regiment. By twenty-six, he was the team leader of his own bunch of miscreants. Life was good. Then, after he had returned home from a tour in Bosnia, it all changed.

An organisation had broken into the grounds of the estate during a celebration party and gone on a killing spree. The group of mercenaries had murdered his father, mother, and wife. Still, he had never learned the fate of his little brother and sister, even though the blood found near their hiding place suggested that they had not survived. Steel himself had been gravely wounded during the attack—shot six times and left to die.

A pothole in the track brought Steel back from his memories. He leaned over and turned the radio up; this time, AC/DC sang about a highway to hell. Steel smiled as he looked at the scenery around him—how wrong they were.

As he drove the twenty-six miles back to his cabin, Steel couldn't help but think about the strangers he had seen. The chances were that it was his paranoia working overtime, but something was not quite right about the group.

As the small lake and his cabin came into view, he smiled. He had gotten used to the quiet and solitude. Steel knew it couldn't last; he would have to venture back into the world, if not for the sake of his family's company, then because he needed to be ready first—mentally as well as physically. If the organisation was coming for him, he had to be prepared. This time, he would take the fight to them. This time, it would be they who would be looking over their shoulders, wondering when it was their turn next.

Steel parked outside the house. After taking the goods from the truck, he would park it inside the barn, keeping it out of the elements.

He took out the groceries and carried them to the kitchen. Then he put away the canned goods in the larder, the ammunition in the gun store—another small building connected to the house—and the meat in the refrigerator room.

After putting the truck inside the barn and locking the door, he went to the woodshed. He brought in an armful of freshly cut logs for the fire in the sitting room and another load for the oven in the kitchen.

The cabin had a traditional wood-burning stove, which was more out of convenience than anything because the cabin was too remote for a gas truck to reach. So Steel had to fetch the required amount in jerry cans and then fill the fuel reserve with those. It took time, but it was necessary. Life in the wilderness was hard, but Steel loved it.

He made a coffee, took a pastry he had bought from the diner, and headed out onto the terrace at the back of the cabin. He sat in one of the wooden chairs and looked out across the lake. Geese flew in formation, and a couple of deer drank at the far side of the lake. The sun was bright in a cloudless sky.

The land before him was a canvas of colour. The mountains were an explosion of yellows, greens, and purples as the mix of trees showed off their autumn plumage. In the distance, a purple blanket of heather clashed with the green of the open plains.

He sipped the coffee and tore the pastry into bite-sized pieces—you didn't rush a pastry from Ma Duncan's Diner. Steel gazed upon the wondrous view before him and sighed.

CHAPTER FIVE

Two days later....

A GROUP OF TOURISTS STOOD ON THE MASSIVE ALASKAN glacier, snapping photographs of the breathtaking scenery. The air was fresh, and the chilled wind burned their throats, but they didn't care. They were a thousand miles from their cares and worries. For one couple, this was their honeymoon.

They laughed, and some tossed snowballs at each other while others took photos of them using their cameras.

Frank Stubbs was the group's pilot, an oldish guy with years of experience, looking on at the group. He felt uneasy, even though this group was like any other he had taken on these tours. Someone in the group had paid a lot of money to get with the group, but the cash was so they would be taken to a different landing site. Four thousand bucks for a detour. But he didn't care; it was easy money because the rest of the group would be none the wiser. And even if someone did question his change in route, he would say he had a package to pick up for one of the people in Ridgeway Creek.

The passengers had learnt that mail in this part of the country wasn't like back home. There was no postman to deliver the mail. It was delivered by rail or by plane to one of the many outposts.

Frank poured himself a cup of coffee from his thermos and sipped the strong brew as he looked up at the cloudless sky. All he wanted to do was get back to the heavens and leave the ground behind for a while, but these people were paying a lot of money for this, so what the heck? He had bills to pay, and his wife was getting on his back about getting a better-paid job, even though she sat at home and watched those damned teleshopping programmes all day.

Frank looked at his watch; it was time for them to leave. He had to have the group back in Talkeetna, but before that, he had to stop off in Ridgeway Creek.

'OK, folks, back on the plane if you please. We gotta get you all back home, but before that, I gotta do a detour to a town on the way, pick up somethin' from the town.'

Everyone groaned, but it was more playful than disputatious, like school kids on an outing.

After the group had retaken their seats and Frank had made sure everyone was there—he didn't want to have that conversation again, and it wasn't his fault someone had wandered off and not told anyone—they took off.

The DHC-3T Otter aircraft had taken off from the Kahiltna glacier without a hitch. The single-propellered aircraft climbed effortlessly through the cloudless sky, the sun reflecting off the gloss signal-red paintwork of the plane. It was full of a group on a flying tour of Denali State Park in Alaska. Now, they were en route from Mount Hunter and on their return flight to the airfield in Talkeetna.

The day had been like any other for the pilot. The skies had been clear, with bright sunshine on a pale blue canvas. It was mid-September, with a good weather forecast until the following week, when it would all change.

Frank Stubbs smiled as he looked out across the expanse of the white-topped mountains and a sky that seemed to go on forever. The tourists behind him clicked away with their cameras and mobile phones at the view from the window.

The passengers were a mix of students, honeymooners, and tourists. They sat amazed at the view below as the single-propellered aircraft climbed higher into the perfect blue. Blankets of fresh powder covered the mountains, giving them a stunning, foreboding look from above. The warm sun reflected on the snow, causing a blinding glare.

All was well. Each passenger smiled and laughed as they took photos.

Twenty minutes later, that all changed.

The plane had gone down into a forest area to the southwest of their last location; for them, it was the wrong side of nowhere. The pilot had been killed instantly, and the rest lay unconscious. All that remained of the aircraft was the main fuselage. A quarter of a mile back, the wings were torn off, and the tail section had disintegrated. The propeller had been smashed to pieces by passing trees, causing one of the blades to break off and be hurled into the pilot's chest.

There was no fire, just small pockets of smoke rising from where electrical cables had been snagged and broken. The white noise from the pilot's radio signalled a loss of communications.

Seven people lay still in the wreck, far from where they should be, lost and alone.

CHAPTER SIX

JOHN STEEL WALKED OVER TO THE DEER HE HAD JUST SHOT. He didn't like doing it, but he needed fresh meat in his larder for the coming winter. This was Alaska, and nipping down to the shops for a steak or sausage was no longer an option. However, here, you killed only as much as you needed, unlike some lands that did it for sport.

As he reached the deer, he knelt beside it, laid a hand on the beast, and bowed his head as if saying thanks or praying for the fallen animal.

A sudden noise made him look up; it was a red tourist plane far in the distance. He had seen many of them before, but this one was way off course—and falling.

'Well, that doesn't look good. What do you think?' he asked, turning to the dead animal. Then he looked back and saw the plane plummeting, followed by a crash but no explosion.

'Think they'll be okay?' he asked the deer, more out of jest than insanity. 'No, me neither,' he said, his gaze locked towards the noise and the flock of birds that had just taken flight from the trees.

Steel grumbled with disappointment, knowing he was probably the only one near enough to help.

He finished preparing the deer for transport to his nearby cabin, tossing the innards for other animals to feast on before heaving the deer onto his broad shoulders. He knew what that sound was and what it meant—that someone needed help and his seclusion was about to be over.

His six-foot-two frame was hidden beneath a hooded leather long coat that added to his bulky appearance. Thick black combat trousers and heavy military-style boots covered his lower half. Worn leather gloves stretched across his large, muscular hands, and black glacier sunglasses shielded his eyes from the sun's bright glare.

A pair of metal dog tags dangled on a beaded chain from his thick neck. The round discs had a rubber silencer with O POS on the outer rim. STEEL. A. J. CE. stamped on each of them.

Even though he was in his mid-twenties, his black beard added several years and gave him an imposing look.

Steel stood up and carried the carcass back to the lakeside cabin. The sun gave off a welcoming heat despite a chilled northern breeze. The landscape was green, with towering yellow cedars and meadows of tall grass as far as the eye could see. It was a postcard view that would soon be a blanket of white. Winter would soon arrive, bringing sub-zero temperatures that would freeze the unprepared.

The cabin was a good half-hour walk from where Steel had started. Still, the weather was beautiful and made for an enjoyable stroll despite the pungent smell of the animal across his shoulders. He smiled as he saw the plumes of thick grey smoke funnelled from the stone chimney. The cabin wasn't the usual self-made shack that most of his neighbours had; this was made from stone and wood with huge bay windows, allowing for a spectacular view of the lake.

The building was around two thousand, two hundred square metres of living space. Its two floors were large enough for eight people to stay in comfort. This had been his family's retreat. Steel stopped walking, looked up at the residence, and a feeling of sorrow washed over him. He used to come here as a kid with his parents and later with his wife. But they were all gone now. Taken from him by the very people he now hid from.

He took the fresh meat into an outhouse built for new kills, complete with a butchery table and a freezer. The whole building was designed to withstand the harsh winters, and with a full larder, eight people could spend many months inside without caring what was outside.

He hung the carcass on a hook and placed it in the freezer, keeping it fresh until he could properly pack it for the long winter. All the while, his thoughts returned to the sound of the plane going down. Every fibre of his being told him to go, but his gut told him to stay out of it.

Letting out a roar, he hurled a butcher's cleaver at one of the wooden joists. The sharp blade embedded deep into the wood, the handle wobbling from the force of the sudden impact. He slammed the heavy metal door and entered the house; the conflict inside his head was too much. All he wanted was to be left alone.

Steel cursed to himself, torn between what he knew he should do—stay put, out of sight—and what was the right thing to do—go and help the survivors.

Inside the cabin, it looked more like a regular home. White walls, a large open-plan kitchen and a sitting room; the floors were polished wood, and a stone fireplace broke up the panoramic windows of the sitting room.

Branching from the large family area was a long corridor leading to bedrooms and bathrooms. As he made his way to the utility room at the far end of the corridor, he stopped at a photograph that hung on a wall. It was a family photograph, taken on the day of his wedding. Everyone looked so happy.

Steel needed to save them all, but one person in particular —a tall, slender woman with hair the colour of straw. It was Helen, the woman he had loved for so long before that day. Now, he only saw her face in nightmares. He had tried sleeping but found he woke up screaming, making his decision to stay out in the middle of nowhere much easier.

He smiled softly as he touched the cold glass of the frame, then turned and headed for the utility room.

Inside were a washing machine, dryer, and racks to hang clothes. There was a backpack that Steel had packed months ago, containing survival items he might need if he had to leave in a hurry. Hanging next to this was a belt with a tactical toma-hawk. The black metal and injection-moulded handle were matte and dull. Taking the belt, he strapped it on, ensuring it was a secure fit.

He turned towards a metal locker and opened it, revealing a selection of handguns, extra clips, and speed loaders. Steel picked up a Smith & Wesson .44 Magnum revolver and a couple of speed loaders, sticking them in the backpack. He took some extra clips for the MK14 and placed them away.

Steel locked the cabinet, turned, and stared at the door.

Was he sure about this?

But then he thought of the alternative. If he didn't bring them to safety, others would come looking, and he would indeed be discovered. No, the best option was to find them and get them off his mountain. The quicker they were safe, the sooner he could return to his quiet life. He wasn't ready to go back to the world. Not yet. He had to be prepared, but his body still hurt from his wounds.

Steel pulled open the door and stepped out into the corri-dor. He knew what he had to do, but his only fear was that there would be no survivors. If that were the case, what could he do? He figured he could go into Talkeetna, the nearest town. People knew of him but didn't know him there. He had gone there to stock up on provisions when necessary, check on places such as the airfield, and ensure the place was still open.

Steel had learned to have an exit strategy in case the organisation hunted him down. He didn't even know if they were looking for him, but he had to be ready.

He then locked the cabin before heaving a black military-style rucksack onto his back. Taking a compass from his pocket and looking to the east, where he had heard the crash, he noted the needle pointing forty-five degrees northeast. Then he took a bearing of his cabin to find his way back, tucked the compass away, and began walking, trying to convince himself this was a good idea.

CHAPTER SEVEN

A MAN SAT IN A GIGANTIC BLACK RV AT RIDGEWAY CREEK. The cream leather seat creaked as he sat back, pulling the mug of strong coffee towards his mouth. He didn't blow on the scalding hot drink; he just took a sip and winced at the strong taste of the brew. He stroked his greased-back blonde hair as if trying to calm himself. It had been too long since the last report said the package was heading into the mountains.

This operation had taken a short time to plan, and now, after all the effort in picking the right people, the man had to sit and wait.

For him, this was torture—the waiting, the sitting around and doing nothing. The man opened the door to the vehicle and got out, revealing his actual height. His six-foot-three frame was dressed all in black: cargo trousers, combat boots, and a thin top that hugged his muscular frame. He was tall and built like a Greek god, an excellent combination for a ballplayer, WWF wrestler, or mercenary. Mr Jones was of East German descent. He had been part of the secret police before the Wall had come down; after that, finding himself unemployed, he had become a mercenary. Now, he worked for Santini.

Mr Jones, or as his organisation knew him, moved to the rear of the RV, where another man sat in front of several monitors. One showed a satellite feed, another was dark and mainly used for video conferences, and the last was hooked to the internet, ready to collect information when required. But all eyes were on the plane leaving Mount Hunter's peaks.

"Let me know when they land; we will do it then," said Mr Jones to the shorter, dark-haired man.

The man nodded and pushed his black-rimmed glasses up the sweaty ridge of his button nose.

Mr Jones smiled; all was going as planned. Santini would be pleased. He returned to his seat at the front of the vehicle and looked out the windscreen. Outside, his men checked their equipment and prepared the three Land Rover Discoverys for travel.

The mission was straightforward: wait for the plane to land and pick up the package from the contact.

The pilot had been persuaded to make a slight detour; cash always had a way of changing someone's mind, and the other passengers would be none the wiser. All the pilot had to do was make up some excuse.

The converted RV had all the usual comforts of a luxury recreational vehicle and a few hidden extras. Hidden in secret compartments were enough weapons and ammunition to take on a small army. But Jones knew they wouldn't need them. However, he was cautious and believed in being prepared.

Each vehicle had also been modified, with strengthened suspension and snorkels for deep water. Under the seats, in hidden compartments, were several assault weapons and ammunition. The team of twenty-seven was ready for anything.

Every eventuality had been prepared for, including a change in the weather. Jones smiled and sipped his coffee. *This was going to be easy*, he thought to himself, feeling confident that nothing could stop them from completing the mission.

CHAPTER EIGHT

After an hour, John Steel reached the first of many patches of forest between him and the crash site. The smell of pine needles and bark filled his nostrils as he breathed in the fresh air. The surrounding trees towered over him and blocked out the sun.

Some of the yellow cedars were over a hundred years old, with trunks the size of large SUVs.

Inside the forest, it was still, except for the cries from birds and the occasional snapping of ground foliage as a startled animal took flight. There was no wind, only the sound of the forest.

He stopped momentarily and took out his compass, ensuring he was heading in the right direction. He was slightly off, but not enough to cause him concern. He looked around, taking note of every boulder, fallen tree, or flat piece of ground, making a mental note just in case he had to make camp on the way back.

To his right, there was a massive fallen tree with flat enough ground surrounding it to make camp for the night if need be. Steel took a bearing on the tree and noted it in a small notebook, along with all the other references he had recorded. Out there, if you were lost, you were as good as dead if you didn't know what you were doing.

After tucking the notebook and compass back into his pocket, Steel headed deeper into the woods, continuing his journey to the crash site.

He walked silently, enjoying the sounds of the forest but keeping his wits about him. He was in bear country, and that was reason enough. He had taken a rifle and pistol with him, more for protection than anything. Still, he had limited ammunition: two ten-round magazines of 7.62x51mm for the Mk 14 Enhanced Battle Rifle and four-speed loaders for the Smith & Wesson .44 Magnum revolver.

He had no idea how far away the crash site was.

The sound of the crash carried on the strong wind blowing from east to west, meaning it could be a couple of miles or fifty miles; there was no actual way of knowing. All he knew was that people needed help.

John Steel pushed forward. His breath formed clouds of vapour as it hit the freezing air. He wore thin layers of clothes but had more in his rucksack for when he made camp. All the walking would keep him warm, so the extra clothing wasn't necessary.

He made his way through the forest. Birds sang happily in the trees above, and deer grazed on low bushes off to his right, paying him no heed as though he weren't even there. Steel smiled as he walked; if he could move unnoticed by wild animals, imagine what he could do with people.

He'd walked fifteen miles before seeing the first signs of the crash. A wing from a small tourist plane lay smashed and scattered amongst downed trees.

A long skid trail led down the hillside, leaving debris from the aircraft and foliage in its wake. There were no signs of smoke or fire in the distance, so there was a good chance the people inside might still be alive; Steel was optimistic.

He stopped at a large boulder and took another bearing, noting it in his notebook before taking a plastic cup of water and sipping.

Steel figured he must be nearing the forest's centre due to the fading natural light. He took another sip, covered the mouthpiece with the neck of the old sock wrapped around the canteen, and then placed it away in his backpack.

Steel followed the aircraft's path while checking his surroundings for predators. They had crashed in grizzly country, and even though the enormous animals would prefer not to mix with humans, it was almost winter, and they'd be hungry—seven feet of teeth and claws, not to mention the beasts could travel at thirty-five miles an hour and smell a carcass from around twenty miles away.

His pace began to quicken as he saw the tail end of the aircraft, which was broken off from the rest of the main body. He checked the surrounding area and found blood on the ground. Only a few spots—meaning whoever it was had been injured but not severely enough for it to be life-threatening. He checked the ground and found tracks leading away towards the north, which he found strange. Why hadn't they gone south, where the rest of the plane would be? He put it down to fear and disorientation, or perhaps something had frightened them into fleeing in the opposite direction.

Steel searched the area further, but there were no signs of anyone there, so he decided to head south towards where the rest of the plane would be.

He pressed on, checking the area for tracks or markings—not just for signs of anyone else, but of animals. He had no doubt that if there were injuries, there was blood, and at this time of year, that was bad. Predators were getting hungry, bears were eating in preparation for the winter, and fresh blood would be like putting out a sign for an all-you-can-eat buffet.

He ventured on until he reached a small stream, stopping to drink from the ice-cold water. The stream was one of the many that came down from the mountains, bringing water from the melting snow caps.

Steel took his half-empty water bottle from his pack, filled it, and placed it back into the side pouch. He paused, looking up at the sunlight breaking through the dense tree cover. He listened to the squawks of birds alerting the others to a stranger's presence. Somewhere, a woodpecker hammered at a faraway tree—the sound of the forest.

In a few months, there would be other sounds—the cries of deer and moose, their strange mating calls. The forest would be alive with new plants and scurrying animals; bears would be fishing in the larger streams and lakes, and eagles would soar high above, searching for a meal for their young.

He wondered where he would be in the spring. Would he be back in Britain, perhaps? Or would he still be here, in hiding?

He was stronger now, in fact, a lot stronger, and he had healed a lot quicker than the doctors had anticipated. Maybe the crap that mad Gardener had injected him with had worked, but the side effects were all too obvious. It had left him with those soulless green eyes.

Sure, it wasn't a super cure; he had no superpowers. It was just a way of speeding up the healing process—or at least that was how the Gardener had later explained it to him. Steel had spent some time at the old Gardener's place before he had come to Alaska. The old man had tried to train Steel in combat, but his heart wasn't in it. Eventually, he had come to Alaska to hide—more from himself than from the organisation.

The physical instructor and the Gardener had also come over to train Steel in martial arts. Steel had picked up a few things, but his interest was lacking. If this had been a training dojo, he would have been lucky to get a white belt.

It had been several months since the old man had been there; he had probably given up on Steel. There was no point in training someone who didn't want to be trained.

The physical instructor had left Steel a training programme. His excuse was more understandable—he had troops to train—but he said he would check in on Steel occasionally to see how he was doing.

CHAPTER NINE

Mr Jones was at Ridgeway Creek's small airport. It was only big enough for one tourist plane or helicopter to land, and he was waiting for a tourist plane. The plane, specifically Frank Stubbs's plane, had been due to land half an hour ago, but it was late.

He could understand cars being late due to traffic on the freeway, a puncture, or any other manner of excuse, but this was a plane. The only excuses he could think of were that one of the tourists had caused the plane to be late or that it had crashed. He was hoping the problem had been an asshole tourist.

A man from the small control room came over to Mr Jones, and his expression was grim.

'Where is my fucking plane?' Mr Jones asked.

The old man shook his head. 'No idea. I spoke to the main airfield at Talkeetna, and they just said it fell off the radar about fifteen minutes ago. I told them that we ain't heard nothin' here, so they are now presumed missing. Unfortunately, we have no idea where they went down. It's nearly dark, so they ain't gonna send search and rescue until tomorrow. They're gonna send helicopters in the hope of catching a glimpse of any wreckage. Unfortunately, the forest is quite dense, and visibility ain't worth shit,' the man explained.

Mr Jones groaned with disappointment. This was meant to be a simple operation, a pickup job, not a damned rescue operation.

He turned without acknowledging the old man and walked to his vehicle. He had an unpleasant call to make, and the Chairman would not be happy.

CHAPTER TEN

JOHN STEEL FOLLOWED SCATTERED BITS OF DEBRIS UNTIL he finally reached the fuselage, which was around half a mile from the tail section. The structure seemed intact except for the missing wings and rear section.

The silence worried Steel; he had expected people to be moaning or yelling for help, but the only sound was a faint white noise from the radio and the birds' chatter above in the trees. Steel moved quickly but cautiously. The last thing he wanted was to stick his head inside the plane and come face to face with a hungry beast.

He circled around to get a good look inside before steadily moving closer. The seven people inside seemed unconscious but not seriously hurt. Then he saw the pilot. Three feet of bent propeller protruded from the man's chest.

Steel stared at the sight momentarily, hoping to feel something for the man, but he felt nothing. Since that day at his home, Steel had lost all feelings of empathy; he was cold inside, almost as if his soul had died. To Steel, the man was just another piece of meat attracting predators to their location.

Satisfied there was no danger, Steel opened the side door and carried the people out. He was happy they were all unconscious because it was simpler to move people when they were not screaming that something hurt. He lined up the survivors on the ground, giving each one some space for when they woke with a start.

Steel began to check the plane for anything useful. Apart from a flare pistol and a packet of spare flares, some energy bars the pilot had stashed in his jacket, a medical kit, and a flight map, there was nothing of use.

He checked the pilot's body for anything to return to the rangers when they came to pick up the survivors. He found a wallet, dark leather and worn. Inside was around a thousand bucks, a credit card, and the man's ID and pilot's licence. There was a shipping company business card, and a picture of a horse's head was on the header. On the back was a telephone number written in biro.

Steel raised an eyebrow, pocketed the cash and business card, and placed the wallet inside the backpack. His gaze fell on the radio set. It seemed undamaged until he picked up the dangling spiral cord and found the handset missing.

He groaned with disappointment. Sure, it would have been an easy way out: call for help, wait for the cavalry, and then disappear back into his world. But he wasn't that lucky.

Steel then turned his attention to the seven people. A sudden bad feeling swept over him. What if none of them could walk? How would he get them to safety before the weather had a chance to break?

A low moan from one of the passengers made Steel turn. It was a woman in her late teens or early twenties. He walked over to her, hoping to get some answers about the crash. The woman looked around, dazed and confused.

She touched her head and winced; her dark skin was damp with perspiration. 'Where am I? What happened?' she said, touching her forehead in another place, but there were no cuts, just bruises. Then she started rotating her left shoulder, checking if it still worked. 'And who the hell are you?' she added, looking up at Steel's bulky form.

Steel didn't speak. He watched as the woman checked herself over for injuries. She sighed with relief that everything worked and was intact. The woman stood up slowly, using the tree behind her as an aid.

Steel stood and looked around at the others in case they all started to awaken.

'You don't say much, do you?' the woman said as she stood upright and tested her balance.

Steel looked back at her but remained silent.

The woman was attractive, with short blonde hair and a face that required no makeup to cover her natural beauty. Her bloodshot blue eyes sparkled with youth.

There was another moan of discomfort as another began to wake. This was a man in his mid-thirties with black hair that had turned red from a slight gash on his forehead.

Steel hadn't bothered to dress any wounds; why waste decent medical equipment on someone who was dying? The woman rushed over to the man and comforted him as he started to shout out for his wife.

'It's OK, Debbra is over there; she is unconscious but alive,' the woman said. She had done it to calm the man, Steel noted.

Of course, she was correct in her bluff; the man's wife was alive, but she had injured her arm, which Steel was setting with a stick and a shirt he had found in one of the backpacks belonging to the passengers.

'What happened?' the man asked, looking into the woman's

eyes for some answer. 'And who the hell is that?' he added, gazing over at Steel.

Steel glared back at the man but remained silent.

'I don't know, but I think he pulled us from the wreckage,' the woman said, looking back at Steel, who was now examining a map he had taken from the pilot.

'He doesn't say much, does he?' the man said.

'The strong, silent type—great, just what we need,' laughed the woman.

'What's with the others?' the man asked.

'To be honest, I just woke up myself,' the woman admitted with an awkward smile. The man frowned at her, but he understood why she had lied.

'So you have no idea about Debbs?' the man asked, hoping for a truthful answer this time.

'The woman who was sitting next to you is over there,' Steel said, pointing to a woman lying next to another tree, a shirt tied around her neck supporting her arm. 'She broke her arm, but she's fine,' Steel said, looking back at the map.

The young woman helped the man to his feet. They waited for a moment before setting off towards the injured Debbra. The young woman left the man to tend to his wife and walked over to Steel.

'How did you find us?' the woman asked with a searching look.

'I heard the crash; I just thought people might need help,' Steel replied, but his mind was elsewhere. He needed to find the best route back to a small town or trading post immediately.

'Well, I'm glad you did. I am Laura Ashwood,' Laura said, extending a handshake. Steel said nothing. He just looked at the map as though Laura wasn't even there.

Laura scowled at Steel's unfriendly behaviour. 'We were

on a glacier tour, just heading home, when we fell out of the sky,' Laura explained. Hoping to get something back from her rescuer, she went silent. She looked at the others and sighed with relief—they had all made it.

'That is Bob and Debbra Norman, newlyweds on their honeymoon,' Laura said, pointing out the man who had just woken up. 'Then we have Natalie Childs and Karen Lee, who were my best friends at university. We decided to get together for a short break, a little catch-up time,' Laura said, pointing to two young women lying beside each other.

Natalie was brunette, and Karen was of Oriental parentage.

'Then we have Clarke Anderson; he's a photographer,' she said, pointing to a large-built man in his forties with brown hair and glasses. 'Then we have Mike Sherman,' Laura said, pointing over to a bald man in his fifties who was leaning against a fallen tree. He had hurt his arm, but it didn't appear to be broken. He had strapped it up using a shirt as a neck sling. Sherman was a good six foot with a sturdy frame; to Steel, his *domina* screamed military or at least a veteran.

'Then we have...' Laura looked around; her expression turned sad as she realised people were missing. 'Where is Alan? Jake?' Her eyes searched the ground before her, hoping there were more survivors. 'Where's Simon and Adam?' she asked, her voice filled with sorrow and despair.

'I found one guy further back; he had been... fatally injured,' Steel said, thinking that telling her about the wolves wasn't the best move at that time. 'The pilot is dead too. Sorry,' Steel said, but his words seemed cold and unsympathetic.

'And the other two?' she asked.

'Didn't find anyone else. They probably woke up before I got here and figured you were all dead—or went for help,' Steel said, tucking the map into his pocket before checking his watch. It was nearly three o'clock; it would be dark soon, and they were in the open, with dead bodies already attracting wildlife.

'We have to go. Wake up the rest of them and leave the dead,' Steel said, tightening the straps on his backpack.

Laura shot him a look of disgust at his lack of compassion.

'We're not going anywhere until we are ready. There are injured people—doesn't that mean anything to you?' Laura asked, shaking her head.

Steel said nothing as he stood up and started walking towards the forest.

'Not very chatty, is he?' Sherman said with a smile.

'Don't take it personally. I figure he's been up here too long —or he's just an asshole,' Laura laughed.

'I'd like to think a little of both,' Steel yelled back. 'And if you are intent on staying, we have to build fires. I suggest four— one on each corner,' Steel said, pointing out specific places. 'We also need to gather wood for the fires throughout the night. I'm off to find you people some food.'

Laura nodded as if taking in the order and looked at Sherman. 'I guess we have our orders,' she laughed and set off to gather the wood with Sherman.

As Sherman followed Laura, he stopped and turned. Something about Steel bothered him, but he didn't know what.

'You comin'?' Laura shouted to Sherman, who smiled back at her and followed behind.

———

John Steel had no use for these people who had invaded his life. However, they needed help, and it was bred into him to assist others. The plan remained the same: find a safe place for the survivors and then disappear once again.

Steel knew his home wasn't far away, but he wanted the location to be kept secret, especially from Sherman. Even though he never said it, Steel knew Sherman was military, and he'd bet money on it. Before, Steel would have stayed with a veteran, but now he was convinced that Sherman was still serving—possibly high up on the food chain. He wasn't private security because he still had that swagger of authority.

As he walked through the thick forest, his eyes darted between the forest floor and the surrounding treeline, looking for tracks or, better still, a deer or something else to cook.

An animal track made him stop and crouch down to examine it. It was a deer—a good-sized one at that. Steel remained where he was for a moment and waited, listening as his eyes scanned for movement. As he remained still, something moved to his left in his peripheral vision. Slowly, he turned and saw a female deer grazing. He raised his rifle gingerly into the aim... and fired.

Steel picked up the carcass and pulled his military knife from a sheath strapped to his right calf above his boot. He began to skin it. The hide would be useful at some point, and now they had fresh meat.

John Steel built a fire and began to cook the meat. He could have done it back at the camp, but there was a problem. The others were there, and he was enjoying his peace and quiet.

Taking out the map, Steel began to look for the nearest safe place. His finger tapped on Ridgeway Creek, but something nagged at him. Those men—the new strangers in town. Was it a coincidence that there had been a plane crash while they were there? Possibly, but even so, he had a bad feeling, so he discounted the town and moved his finger across to one of the lakes.

There was an old couple there; he knew they had a plane because that was how the man entered town. He had been a tour guide, flying people to the glaciers and other sites, and now he was retired.

This was a good option. Steel could bring them there, and then the old man could take them to Talkeetna.

The problem was that it was a good sixty to seventy miles—maybe more—from where they were now to the old folks' place. There were also injured people who could slow them down. And not forgetting the biggest problem—they were city people, and city people don't walk. Sure, they may go to the gym and run, but tell them to walk over hills, mountains and forests, with no hope of a café latte at the end of it? Problem. He could add another day to their travels, at the least.

He figured there was going to be at least one problem child. One who walked too slowly, fell behind, moaned and bitched about everything. His money was on Natalie.

He made a quick mental note to himself: first chance, tie her to a tree and let nature do its thing at the first sign of trouble.

Tucking the map away, he finished cooking the meat and sighed. This might be the last quiet moment he had for a while.

Bugger.

———

Back at the site, Laura and Sherman had collected enough wood for four fires and stacked separate piles to feed the flames throughout the night.

Steel had warned Laura earlier that nobody should be alone when it got dark and that they should stay by a fire. One group member could take turns staying awake to maintain the flames while the others slept. It was a decent enough plan, but everyone was cold, hungry, thirsty and injured.

Natalie had disagreed with his plan, telling him he probably had no idea what it was like to be close to death, saying his plan was stupid. Now that it was getting dark, she realised he wasn't talking crap.

Now she was getting scared as the blackness crept in, and the forest became alive as things began to wake.

CHAPTER ELEVEN

In New York State, footsteps clattered down the long wooden hallway of the grand mansion, an avenue of two-hundred-year-old wood panelling, with priceless artwork hung along it. Ornate brass lamps lit the way to the conference room.

The hallway ended in a grand open space—a marble-floored lobby that branched off to different places: the conference room, an ante-room with a long bar, a winding stairwell to the first floor, and the garden door.

The man stopped in front of the double doors of the conference room and paused. He brushed the creases out of his black suit and straightened his tie. The man, who was in his mid-twenties, took a deep breath and, with a white-knuckled fist, tapped gently on the door. The knock was loud enough to be heard but quiet enough not to annoy.

'Come,' said a commanding bellow of a voice.

The man paused for a second and then nervously entered. The room was long, with the same panelling and beautiful artwork hung in gilded gold frames. Down the centre was a long oak table with French-polished leaves and twelve seats down each side. At the head of the table was a giant monitor. Next to the large screen stood a thin man, the chairman of the organisation, who simply stared at the young man as he approached.

'The boy brings news, and an unhappy one at that, judging by his expression,' came a voice from the screen. With each word, different coloured lines made strange patterns on the display.

'What is it?' asked the chairman, his eyes cutting deep into the soul of the man as he stopped a few feet from his master's chair.

'The plane is down, but it crashed somewhere in a forested area north of the drop-off point. The techs are confident they can pinpoint it to a hundred-metre radius, but it may take some time,' said the tall, thin young man.

The chairman sat back in his seat, his face red with anger. Something had gone wrong; the pilot had been instructed to land in a remote area near Ridgeway Creek, where a team was waiting.

'Tell the techs they have thirty minutes to find that plane.' The chairman paused, a thought bouncing around in his head. 'Where is Mr Jones?'

'Still at the park awaiting instructions,' replied the man.

'Tell him what has happened; tell him to get his team to that crash site,' ordered the chairman.

The young man nodded and rushed off, all the while thanking every god possible that he was still alive.

'This is disappointing to hear, Chairman,' said the voice as blue, yellow, and red streaks danced across the black background of the display. 'I want that package found,' said the voice before the screen went still, and communication was severed.

The chairman stood up, revealing his six-foot-one frame,

donned in a blue pinstriped suit with a white rose in the buttonhole. He was in his late fifties and had held the position for seven years. The chairman strolled out of the room and across the marble floor to the gardens.

The sky was now a deep purple with streaks of grey clouds tinged with orange. He walked over to an impressive bronze fountain. The multi-tiered structure was lit by several underwater lamps, enhancing the beauty of the green metal. The chairman reached into his pocket, pulled out a single coin, closed his eyes, and flicked it into the water.

'I never took you as a superstitious man,' said a voice from behind the chairman.

'I figured it couldn't hurt,' replied the chairman without turning around. 'What are you doing here anyway? I thought you had things to attend to?' the chairman asked, feeling a sudden chill run down his spine at every word the other man said.

His voice was a symphony of vocal chaos—highs and lows with each word—like a violin played by an amateur... or a madman.

'Oh, plenty of time for that, I assure you, Mr Chairman. However, this is too delicious to miss—a hunt, no less. Can I play too?' asked the man from the shadows.

'You have your assignment; see to it,' ordered the chairman, feeling his spine tingle with discomfort at just being in the man's presence.

'As you wish,' the man replied before turning and walking away. The tap of his shoes on the tiled floor echoed through the corridors, and the faint sound of music from a pocket watch faded as the man left.

The chairman shuddered and wiped his sweaty brow with a handkerchief.

'Can't believe that goddamn psycho works for us,' the chairman mumbled to himself.

His gaze returned to the running water of the fountain. He was gathering his thoughts on what to do next. The plan was still in play. If they didn't know anything, then neither would the target.

The chairman took out his cell phone, pressed the speed dial number, and waited for someone to answer.

'We have a situation, but nothing we can't handle. We have people there.' He paused while he listened to the person on the other end. 'Don't worry; the package will soon be in our hands. Just make sure you are ready.'

CHAPTER TWELVE

When John Steel returned to the camp, all the survivors were awake. They were bruised and battered, some of them much worse, but they were alive. Four fires burned brightly, breaking up the pitch black of the night. He was glad she had followed his instructions—not too high or large, but just enough to ward off any beasts and give warmth.

Steel felt the wary eyes upon him as he entered, making him feel his presence there was more than a rescue mission or act of kindness.

Steel laid down the fresh meat and began to cut it into more manageable pieces for the fire. Each piece was then stuck through with a sturdy stick and placed over the fire to cook.

'Who is he?' asked Karen Lee, her voice almost a whisper.

'You know, I have no idea,' Laura said, suddenly looking at this mysterious stranger. She had to admit that his dark clothing and the reflection of the light from the campfire gave him an aura of something evil.

'So, where is he?' Karen asked, looking around.

'Off getting us some food, he said. God knows what there is

to eat around here, though.' Natalie scowled, listening to her belly make a disagreeable sound.

Sherman smiled and shook his head in disbelief. 'God damn civvies,' he said under his breath.

Natalie was just about to say something when a piece of cooked meat landed on her lap, causing her to yelp and jump briefly.

Natalie looked over to Steel, who was smiling to himself.

'Eat,' Steel said, standing up and passing the food to the others. 'You'll need your strength.'

The survivors took the food and gingerly picked at the mystery meat.

'What is it?' Natalie asked as she sniffed at it.

'Chicken,' Steel lied, causing Sherman to smile to himself.

'Doesn't look like chicken,' Natalie replied, shooting Steel a suspicious look.

'Just tell yourself it's chicken,' Steel grumbled, feeling somewhat unappreciated.

'Is there another option?' Natalie asked as she was about to give Sherman her piece of meat.

'Sure, eat and live or starve and die and become dinner for these,' Steel said, pointing to the meat on the fire.

'So, what is it?' Laura asked, sniffing suspiciously at the meat.

'Venison,' Steel replied, tearing off a piece of the meat and chewing it.

He looked around at the blank expressions. 'It's deer,' he clarified.

The group's expressions didn't change except for Sherman and Clarke, who ate happily.

Steel sighed. 'It's Bambi.'

Suddenly, their expressions changed to horror. 'It's Bambi? You expect us to eat Bambi?' Natalie shouted.

'No, we are eating; you're just bitching about it,' Sherman said, taking another bite of the meat. Sherman and Steel exchanged nods as though words were not necessary.

Natalie slowly picked at the meat, turning her nose up with every bite.

Steel said nothing. He just stood up and took out a flashlight to check out the plane and what was practical.

'What's the CAS-REP?' Steel asked, turning to Sherman.

'CAS-REP?' asked Bob, somewhat puzzled by the question.

'Casualty Report,' Clarke responded. 'I heard it a lot when I was doing photo shoots in Afghanistan, Bosnia and the Gulf. It's a way of asking how everyone is and what injuries are present,' Clarke added, leaving everyone nodding at him as though he was someone to be admired.

'So, who is slightly hurt, hurt, and badly hurt?' Steel reiterated.

'All have cuts and bruises, two broken arms that you know about, Karen has a sprained ankle; apart from that, we are all lucky to be alive, thank you,' Laura said with a smile.

'Med student?' Steel asked.

'I started med school but bailed; it wasn't my thing. Then I went to Hudson; that's where I met Laura and Karen,' Natalie said, chewing on the meat.

'So, tell me, Mr....' Laura started, hoping to drag a name out of Steel but got nothing but a stone-faced stare. 'What's a Brit doing all the way out here?'

'It was quiet,' Steel answered as he sauntered to one of the furthest fires and removed his sunglasses as he sat. He figured his soulless eyes would be hidden by the dim light or at least the shadows cast by the fire. He just had to remember to replace the glasses when he woke the next day.

'Was?' Bob asked.

'Yeah, you lot showed up,' Steel said with a shrug, making Sherman laugh aloud.

'I love this guy. Sure, he's a Brit, but you gotta love him,' Sherman laughed.

Laura looked around at this group of perfect strangers. Sure, they had been on the plane and seen some sights together, but she knew nothing about them apart from their names.

'So, what brings everyone here... on the trip, I mean... not... well, you know what I mean?' Laura asked, correcting herself.

'It's our honeymoon. Thought I'd book a trip to remember,' Bob laughed at the irony. 'Boy, we ain't gonna forget this trip in a hurry, that's for sure.'

'I was here on holiday,' Sherman started. 'You know, do some fishing, see some sights,' he laughed and shook his head. 'Do some adventuring in the woods.'

John Steel remained silent; he just tended to one of the fires and observed the group.

'What about you, Clarke? On some big story?' Laura asked.

He shook his head. 'No, not really. I was here doing some research for a friend—nothing big, just a... favour. I also thought I'd take some trips while I was here and probably look up some old friends.'

'And what about you three ladies?' Sherman asked, directing his question to Laura, Natalie and Karen.

'We are on our break; we thought we would do something special instead of doing the usual and flying back home. In fact, it was Natalie's idea. She was up here doing some studies on her major and thought it would be fun,' Karen replied.

'So, what are you majoring in, Natalie?' Clarke asked.

Natalie stopped rooting around in her pack for a second before looking at Clarke with a neutral expression. 'Two majors—computer studies and environmental change.' Then she returned to her search, pulled out a white pill bottle, opened it, and shook one out. She slipped it into her mouth and drank.

Steel looked over suspiciously.

She caught his gaze and shrugged. 'Magnesium tablets. I get cramps in my muscles a lot, and my doctor says I have to take them.'

Steel said nothing, just gave a quick nod.

'I'm majoring in business and government,' Laura interjected.

'Administrative information management technology. It's a study on how the office environment affects workers or something like that. I sleep through most of it,' she shrugged. 'It's my dad's idea, not mine, but he says I have to go to university, so here I am.'

'Her dad is loaded but won't give her handouts. He says she has to make her own way in life,' Natalie groaned as though she disapproved of the concept.

'Nothing wrong with trying to be your own person,' Steel said before biting into a piece of the cooked meat.

'Spoken like a person who has nothing,' Natalie sneered. 'Don't tell me, Momma and Poppa made you work for your pocket money and appreciate the money you got?'

Steel looked over at her, his features distorted by the light of the flames. 'Something like that,' he grinned. He put his glasses back on before placing another piece of wood on the fire, picked up the rifle, and then stood up. 'Get some rest; I'll take the first watch. Make sure you sleep next to someone for warmth,' Steel said as he passed the packages of thermal blankets he had taken from the plane. 'We take an hour each and ensure the fires don't go out,' Steel added.

Everyone nodded and picked a partner to sleep with for warmth.

The people fell asleep from exhaustion, their backs against

the plane for shelter. Steel stood up, topped up the fires, and threw more bits of wood on each before sitting on a large rock at the centre of the camp. His senses were alert; the fear of attack by something made the hairs on his neck stand up on end with excitement. His blood raced through his veins; his heart pumped so hard he thought it might come through his chest. He felt alive again.

CHAPTER THIRTEEN

NATALIE WOKE TO BIRDSONG AND THE SMELL OF THE forest. The dense blanket of foliage above blocked most of the sunlight, but there was enough to see by. She sat up and looked around. Everyone was still asleep, and the fires were still going strong. Natalie stood up and stretched out her weary muscles and bones.

The trauma of yesterday and the uncomfortable sleeping arrangements made her feel a thousand years old.

She reached for her backpack and searched for something. Then, after looking around to ensure nobody was watching, she popped a tablet into her mouth and took a sip from her water bottle to wash it down. She took another mouthful of water, then replaced the lid before placing it back into her pack.

She yawned, pulled the metal foil blanket around her, and walked to the closest fire to warm up. Despite the situation, she had to admit that this was a beautiful place to camp. Natalie turned to speak to Steel, but he was nowhere to be seen.

'He's gone; the son of a bitch has left us,' she mumbled loud enough to force Sherman awake.

'What's up?' Sherman asked, forcing himself up off the ground.

'The stranger, he's gone,' she replied, flapping her arms angrily.

'What did you expect him to do?' Sherman asked.

'Well, get us out of here for one thing,' Natalie shouted, forcing the rest of them awake.

'What's up, what's wrong?' everyone asked excitedly.

'The stranger, he's just up and left us,' Natalie said, pointing around at the camp.

'Are you sure? He could have just gone to take a leak or something?' Bob asked in disbelief.

'His stuff is gone. If he had just gone to piss, why take that?' Natalie shouted.

'In truth, I'm not surprised he left us; I think I would have done the same,' Sherman said with a shrug.

'What the hell are you talking about, old man?' Natalie barked.

'Did anyone thank him for rescuing us, for pulling us out of the aircraft? For even turning up to help us? Did anyone bother to ask his name?' Sherman said with a low growl. 'We all expected him to get us to safety, look after us, even feed us. The man left his home to help, and we did nothing but show the fella what ungrateful assholes we are.' Sherman looked around at the group, who stayed silent, contemplating what he had said, their eyes fixed to the ground like punished children.

'So tell me this: Who restocked the fires last night if he has taken off? Nobody woke me for a turn. If that's the case, then this fella stayed up all night and watched our backs, and you're gonna come out with that shit?' Sherman barked at Natalie, who just stood with her mouth opening and closing with no words coming out.

Suddenly, from behind them, Steel brushed past, holding another skinned animal ready to cook.

'God, this place was so quiet before you lot turned up. Do you do anything but argue? The sooner I get you to a town, the better,' Steel said, sitting down and preparing the meat on the sticks they had used the night before.

Sherman burst out laughing at the dismay of the others.

'Oh, you gotta love this guy,' Sherman laughed and sat beside Steel, helping him to skewer the meat. 'Right, you lot, we need more wood for the fires, and we need to find water. Break yourselves down into teams,' Sherman ordered.

The group stood open-mouthed and shocked at the commands.

'Now, people,' Sherman barked, making the survivors organise themselves into finders and carriers. Sherman laughed and looked over at Steel, who held his stone-faced expression.

'You don't say much, do you, fella?' Sherman asked.

'No point talking unless you have something useful to say,' Steel replied.

'Ain't that the truth,' Sherman agreed as he stuck the pieces of meat on the sticks. From then, the two men sat in silence. No talking was necessary, only the sound of the forest.

Steel had spent most of the night formulating a plan that didn't include returning them to his cabin. If the pilot's map was to be believed, there was a small settlement near a lake not more than sixty miles away.

This meant they had a plane or some form of communication with one of the larger settlements. It was out of his way, but then he couldn't tell them which way to go and leave them, even though the thought had crossed his mind several times. The only two who might make it were Sherman and Clarke.

Steel felt Sherman was special forces, possibly Navy

SEALs or Delta. Clarke was a photographer, but Steel knew the type—combat journalist—a tough breed of people who were more nuts than the soldiers they were inserted with. He had seen a couple in Bosnia—his last tour with the British special forces before his world was torn apart.

He hadn't slept. He couldn't. Steel knew his nightmares would make the people even more afraid of him. Instead, he studied the map, planning routes where they might find water, food, and, hopefully, shelter.

It was seven in the morning. They would eat and carry the rest of the provisions. In Alaska, sixty miles would feel like a thousand, and that was with everyone feeling fit. He had injured people in the team, and that would slow them down. The two men looked up as the gatherers returned, holding arms full of wood.

They refilled the reserve piles next to each campfire and went to stock up the fires, ready for the day, before Steel stopped them.

'We only need one fire,' Steel said, placing the meat spikes at an angle so the meat could cook on the blazing fire.

'We leaving?' Sherman asked.

'After we have eaten,' Steel replied to the disappointed looks of the gathered.

'Are we having deer again?' Natalie complained as she turned her nose up at the sight of the meat cooking on the wooden stakes.

Steel looked up and just stared at her. Even though the sunglasses shielded his eyes, she still felt his glare burn straight through her.

'Now everyone is here,' Steel said, laying out the map flat on the ground and holding it down with four stones at the corners.

'We are here,' Steel said, pointing to a green-shaded area on the map showing a forest. 'Over here is a lake—Twenty-five Mile Lake, to be precise. There is a small settlement, and they have a plane,' Steel explained. 'The problem is it's around sixty miles between here and there.'

'Sixty miles, no problem, we can do that in a day and a half,' Bob said confidently.

'If anything, I would say two and a half—two if we are lucky,' Steel said, shaking his head. 'There is rough and unknown terrain, and we have wounded people.' Steel explained, 'This won't be a simple pop to the shops; this will be hard work.' Sherman nodded as if in agreement.

'We move at the slowest person's pace, we stick together, and you do exactly as Sherman or myself say,' Steel said, standing up and leaving the map on the floor for everyone to look at.

'Why Sherman?' Debbra asked suspiciously.

'Because I think he has been in situations like this before, and he probably has more of an idea what lies ahead than all of you,' Steel answered, purposely avoiding mention of Sherman's involvement with the special forces. If Steel's time in the SAS had taught him one thing, it was *If you are with the Regiment, you don't advertise it.*

Steel looked around at the varied expressions on their faces. He knew he should be more sympathetic to their situation, but then cuddling them wouldn't get them to safety.

'Eat and rest; we leave in an hour,' Steel said, walking over to the freshly retrieved wood, sorting out the best ones to carry and making two small bundles for the able-bodied. He found one piece of branch that could be cut away to act as a crutch for Karen and her ankle. Finding a spot on a fallen tree, Steel sat and got to work using the large knife.

'You could be a little nicer,' Sherman said as he sat down next to Steel.

'They don't need me to be a friend; they just need me to get them and you to safety,' Steel said with a cold expression. 'When you all get to your warm beds, I won't be a second thought—just how I like it.'

'Is that why you haven't told us your name?' Sherman asked.

'Names are of no consequence, just ways of individualising everyone,' Steel said, smoothing the U-shape of the piece of wood. 'But if you feel it necessary, you can call me... John.'

'Pleased to meet ya, John; I'm Mike,' Sherman said, extending a handshake.

Steel didn't react; he just kept smoothing the wood with the blade.

'We aren't the enemy, John; we're just people who need help, and you're here because you are a good man,' Sherman continued.

Suddenly, Steel looked up and stared at Sherman with a chilling glare.

'No, Mike, the only reason I'm here is to get you people away from me. The sooner you are in a town, the better. If I'd left you, that would have meant search parties and helicopters. I'm here so everyone will leave me alone,' Steel said, standing up and resheathing his blade. 'Oh, and one more thing, Mr Sherman, I'm far from a good person.'

Steel left. Sherman sat on the tree; his interest was now buzzing. He wanted to know more about this John—if that was his real name. One thing was certain: he was running from something or someone. Not out of fear—he doubted the man knew what the word meant. No, this was survival; someone was hunting him, and Sherman wanted to know why.

Steel walked back to the group as they tucked into the cooked meat. He spied Karen sitting on a seat removed from the plane. He silently placed the newly constructed crutch beside her and headed for the fire.

Karen picked up the length of fashioned wood and turned her nose up at the lack of padding under her arm. But she knew it was best not to complain, just in case the walking aid ended up in the fire.

'Thanks, it's very kind of you,' Karen said almost honestly.

Steel nodded in response and tore a mouthful from the meat.

'How long have you lived out here, mister?' Debbra asked inquisitively.

'Long enough to be forgotten about,' Steel replied, leaving everyone with confused faces.

'What do you mean... are you a criminal or something?' Bob asked, somewhat scared at the thought.

'Are you a murderer?' Natalie asked in an eerie, excited tone.

'Not yet, but I'm getting close,' Steel replied angrily, sick of all the questions. He finished off the meat steak and headed back to the fire to start packing away the other pieces of meat ready for the journey. The others sat quietly as they watched Steel divide the meat so each person had one and handed them out.

'What about you?' Laura asked, noticing Steel went without.

'I can always find something to eat. Besides, you lot need as much protein as possible,' Steel said, walking over to Laura and picking up her backpack.

'Hey, that's mine!' she screamed in panic. 'What the hell do you think you are doing?'

Steel went through the backpack, tossing out what he considered useless.

'Hey, that's my stuff; you can't just do that,' she yelled, gathering up the items Steel had discarded.

'We have to travel light, we have a long way to go, and this crap is extra weight you don't need,' he explained as he dropped the pack and headed over to Karen, who was hugging her pack. 'Give it up,' he said.

Karen shook her head and hugged it firmly.

'Look, people, I don't really care; you have to carry this shit, not me, but believe me, all that extra crap you think is important will soon make you hurt.' He watched as Laura stared reluctantly at the heavy books and things from the gift shops, then let them fall to the ground before pulling on her backpack.

The others began sorting through their possessions, discarding heavy items and deciding whether the phone charger was light enough to hold.

Steel grabbed his pack and swung it onto his shoulders, then jumped up and down, testing the weight distribution and if the pack sat correctly on the small of his back and shoulders.

He tightened the straps and then pulled out his compass and the map. Taking a bearing, he scribbled the figures in the notebook and then packed them away.

'We have to go through the wood to a clearing. From there, we head north,' Steel gazed upon their clueless expressions and rolled his eyes behind his sunglasses. 'left,' he said and was returned with nodding heads and smiles. 'We travel until dusk, and then we make camp.' Everyone nodded as if taking in the briefing, but Steel knew that most hadn't even listened to a word he had said. All they needed was a guide; they didn't care which way was north or east as long as he did. City folk on a trip searching for adventure suddenly stuck in more of it than they could handle.

Sherman looked over at Steel and smiled. *He thought that this guy knew what he was doing, and he sure as hell wasn't a bushman.* Then he remembered Laura's question: 'What was a Brit doing out here?'

As they set off in single file, a small metal cylinder hit the ground and was soon lost underfoot. As they left the clearing, a tiny red LED blinked on top of the inch-long metal tube.

CHAPTER FOURTEEN

It was almost dawn when Mr Jones got the call on the Satphone, informing him of the new mission objective. He grumbled under his breath, disappointed at the lateness of the news.

'We should have been informed straight away,' Jones growled at the poor messenger before hanging up.

'Gear up, we are moving,' Jones barked the order.

'What do they want us to do?' asked Jones's driver, a huge man with muscles on his muscles—an Austrian ex-special forces reject who was kicked out for excessive force.

'Find the crash site, retrieve the data, and the agent,' Mr Jones growled, annoyed that it had taken the powers that be so long to come up with a decision. 'Get the rest of the boys, Eric, and let's go huntin'.'

Eric Krugger nodded with a smile and pulled his leather combat gloves tightly over his massive hands.

Mr Jones headed over to his lead vehicle. He opened up the back, revealing the arsenal they had brought with them: 5.56

assault rifles, .338 Winchester Magnum sniper rifles, and assault shotguns with tumbler magazines.

Mr Jones grabbed an electronic tablet and opened the maps application. Then, he began to search the area where the plane supposedly went down and plotted a route to it.

If one of them could read a map, there were four possible locations where the survivors could head. So, he broke his men into four teams. Each team would take a location and report back on target confirmation.

The information HQ had given was thin to the point of being translucent. The transponder had failed just after they left, going over the glacier from Hunter Mountain. So, in truth, it could be anywhere. It wasn't much to go on, but then what choice did he have?

The thought of the pilot taking the money and running had crossed his mind, but would he really leave his family to suffer the consequences? He'd have to be a real bastard. However, their research had shown the man had no spine and a massive gambling problem. He could run, but he would almost certainly reappear again.

Mr Jones had met the wife and kid; they were friendly. He didn't want to hurt them, but that was the job. That's if the pilot ran, of course.

'The men are ready; what do you want to do?' Eric said as he approached.

Mr Jones picked up the tablet and nodded for Eric to follow. The two men walked to where the others were waiting for their new orders.

'A couple of hours ago, the plane went down, and we have little light left, so I suggest we hurry. I sent the locations and your orders to your devices. We will split into five teams. Team Charlie, led by Sven, will locate the plane and recover the package if possible. Team Bravo, led by Lenny, you will go to this lake; there are reports of an old couple who have a plane—secure the property just in case the survivors make it there.'

Lenny nodded and noted down the grid on his small tablet.

'Lockwood will lead Team Delta, and you guys will pick up the rear in case someone doubles back. Alpha, led by myself, will remain here with the vehicles as a command post until required. And Echo, led by Finch, will run to the east of Sven and Lockwood, making sure nobody slips through the net.'

Everyone nodded to confirm their orders.

'Right, let's go,' Jones said with a smile.

As Jones and Eric headed back to their vehicle, they could hear the roar of engines and the spinning of tyres as the teams took off. They climbed inside the four-by-four, and Eric started up the mighty V8.

'Do you think we'll find any survivors?' Eric asked as he put the lever into drive and moved out.

'Well, if there are, there won't be for very long,' Jones smiled.

The thought of a hunt in a massive wilderness excited him. Unfortunately, there was no sport or thrill in going after dumb tourists, but he'd make the most of it. Mr Jones was a cruel man who took great pleasure in his job—possibly too much pleasure, some would say—but he was good at what he did.

The Chairman sat at his desk back in his office. This was a twenty-by-twenty square foot space of oak flooring, side panelling, and furnishings. A grand desk sat in front of a leaded set of windows. Against the right-hand wall was a black marble fireplace. Along the opposite wall was an ornate oak bookshelf that took up the entire wall, filled with works from various authors on various subjects.

A Persian rug stretched across the polished wooden floor, held steady by two Chesterfields. The green upholstery matched the desktop leather and the high-backed vintage office chair. Oil paintings hung in gilded gold frames, adding colour to the dark surroundings despite an array of polished brass fittings and fixtures.

The building was a turn-of-the-century stately home tucked away in the rural settings of New York State. This was one of the safe houses of an organisation bent on achieving several goals: money, chaos, power, and inanimate. They worked on blackmail, gun-running, assassinations, theft, and smuggling. However, despite all this, they did not want world power or anything that would put them in the limelight. They worked in the shadows and kept things small and discreet. Even their real names had been lost along the way.

The Chairman rocked in his chair. The brandy swirled around in the brandy bowl in his hand. The plan had not gone well, but Mr Jones was already underway. It was important that the package was recovered by midnight in two days' time, or the leverage would be lost. Unfortunately, there were no contingency plans—this was not the case this time.

The tape to the target was en route and would be there sometime in the day. Delivered by the daily post, making forensics almost impossible once more people had touched it, the fumes from the sorting office contaminating it—the perfect delivery system.

The Chairman looked at his computer screen. There were several emails from different sources, but nothing of consequence. There wouldn't be any updates for some time, but he still felt impatient. He looked at the second monitor and the long list of operations underway or due to occur soon.

Each one was devious and risky but, at the same time, a profitable venture. He took a sip of the brandy and smiled. Despite this one upset, things were moving as planned in other quarters. He stood up, walked to a large bay window, and looked across the gardens. The sky was full of towering white clouds, which blocked out the sun occasionally. It seemed like the perfect day.

He hoped the good weather and good fortune would continue. The Chairman took another sip and sighed. Now, all they had to do was wait.

CHAPTER FIFTEEN

AFTER AN HOUR AND MUCH WASTED TIME WAITING FOR Natalie to catch up, Steel ordered a quick break. He needed time to orient himself using the map and compass. Sherman joined him.

'Are we on track?' Sherman asked, watching as Steel used his finger to track their route.

'If you mean we are heading in the correct direction, then yes. I am unsure if you mean we will get there before next Christmas. Maybe if we left some people behind,' Steel smiled.

Sherman was unsure whether Steel was joking or not.

'There should be a stream over there, possibly in half a mile. We can stop and take on some water,' Steel said, pointing to a blue line on the map.

Sherman nodded. 'Sounds good.' He looked back at the tired group. These were city people whose idea of the outdoors was a local park. They weren't just fish out of water; they were completely lost, unprepared, and, in some cases, unreasonable.

'Natalie seems to be struggling the most. Luckily, Bob and Debbra are looking after her,' Sherman said, nodding over to the three sitting together. 'Maybe we should move her to the front, the slowest person's pace?'

Steel looked over at the troublesome woman; she was constantly irritated, but he had said he would get everyone to safety. Perhaps he should make a clause in that statement, like fall behind, and you are alone. Good luck. He shook his head. 'Wouldn't do any good. It isn't fatigue—she's just being a dick.'

'Solution?'

'Apart from tying her to a tree and covering her in peanut butter? Carry on as we are and hope she irritates the others enough that they kick her arse,' Steel exclaimed with a shrug.

'OK, time to move,' Steel said, pulling on his backpack. 'We need to go before we lose the light. I don't feel good about traversing these woods in the day, let alone at night.' However, what Steel wanted to say was With all of you, but he thought it best not to.

He heard the moans and groans of the others behind him. Their bodies hurt from the bad sleeping conditions and the cold, but most of all, they were bruised from the crash and were on the mend.

Steel smiled as he knew that pain from doing exercises in Wales. They carried over a hundred kilogrammes in a bergan and webbing while marching for miles in all kinds of weather. Sleep was when you could get it, and eating and drinking were sometimes on the move.

Steel turned to see the mixed band of people behind him. All of them were eager to get home, away from all this nature and into the comfort and security of their homes. He looked over to Sherman, who was taking up the rear guard—or tail-end Charlie, as some liked to call it—making sure nobody got left behind. The two men nodded to each other as if confirming that each was ready.

'We move steady and to the slowest person's pace,' Steel

beckoned Karen forwards. 'If you need to stop, say something. If you need to piss, say something.'

Steel looked around at the frightened faces before him and nodded. 'Do what I say, and everyone goes home,' causing everyone to return his nod of reassurance.

Steel turned and walked off in the direction the compass had given, making sure to keep up with Karen, who was next to him.

CHAPTER SIXTEEN

Mr Jones's men had set off at first light. Most had camped out overnight due to poor visibility and driving conditions. But now, the sun was rising and bringing with it a perfect sky.

They had a good time finding the locations, but there was no aircraft. The fourth group had moved past Swan Lake and up towards the wreckage. The seven highly trained mercenaries moved slowly through the forest in a straight-line formation, five metres apart, with weapons on their shoulders and safety catches applied.

The leader was a six-foot-three monster named Sven. He was a Swede with short blond hair, blue eyes, and a chiselled jawline. He had served in the special forces but had left after failing his psych analysis.

He carried his 5.56mm M4 custom assault rifle with a Remington 870 shotgun attachment high on his shoulder and across his chest, ready for action. Not that they were expecting trouble from the survivors, if there were any. One of the men who had taken point called out on the radio that he'd found the aircraft—or what was left of it.

Sven called for the men to advance double-time and form a perimeter around the site. He rushed forward; his long legs carried him at speed towards the waiting scout.

'What have we got?' Sven asked, looking at the tree line before he spotted the red paint of the aircraft. Both men raced forward, ready for the cries of thankfulness from the passengers. As they approached, the eerie silence halted them. Slowly, they moved closer, this time waiting to find the bodies.

'The boss ain't gonna like this,' Sven said, taking out his cell phone and pressing the speed-dial button. After a couple of rings, Jones's voice came over the speaker.

'Yes, what you got?'

'We have the plane; it's empty except for the pilot. We have campfires and what appear to be animal bones,' Sven answered.

'Well, ain't they resourceful? Saw too many survival documentaries, I take it,' Jones said. 'Keep trackin' them; let me know when they make camp.'

Suddenly, something caught Sven's eye—a blinking red light from the ground underneath some bark chips and sticks.

'There's something else,' Sven said, bending down and picking up the small cylinder. 'I think the contact just left us something,' he said with a smile.

'Is the package there? Did the asset hide the package on the plane?' Mr Jones asked.

'Negative, no sign of it or the asset. They probably thought it might be best to keep it on them, just in case the plane caught fire or something,' Sven replied.

'Track them down and bring the asset and the package to the exfil. Let me know when you have both, or at least the package,' Mr Jones said before hanging up.

Sven had his orders: track them. But Mr Jones never said

not to engage. Sven whistled loudly to draw his men's attention and told his scout to track them.

The man was smaller than the others at five-nine, a mixed-blood child of a Sioux Indian and a French Canadian soldier. The others followed close behind, unaware of any new plan; that briefing would come later. All they had to know was to stay close to the crazy Indian.

George soon picked up the trail and could tell how many people had passed and how many of them were slow movers. Sven and the others gave George a wide berth of around ten feet, not wanting to disturb his concentration. One guy had done it once, and it ended with a knife in his head. George crouched down and moved his hand over the disturbed ground as if he were picking up a signal from it. He looked around at the thick forest and then closed his eyes before inhaling a lungful of air through his nose. His eyes opened, and he stood up.

Sven looked at the man with a curious gaze. He wanted to call out if anything was wrong but thought it best not to.

George moved off without a word.

Silently, the others followed in a single file with ten feet of spacing between them. Sven took out his tablet and checked the location of the other teams. Each had been relocated to places where the group might head. One of them was Twentymile Lake.

CHAPTER SEVENTEEN

THE CHAIRMAN WAS SITTING IN A CAFÉ. THE SUN WAS warm despite a chill from an easterly breeze. He chose to sit outside. He didn't care much about the inside of cafés; he had reservations about restaurants.

He felt his mobile phone vibrate in his overcoat and retrieved it. Checking the caller ID, he saw it was Mr Jones.

'You are calling with good news, I hope, my boy?' he asked in an optimistic tone.

'Negative, sir. Charley's team found the plane; two were found half a mile from the main crash site. Animals had been at them, and the plane, what was left of it apparently, was empty except for the pilot, who was dead,' Mr Jones replied in a neutral tone.

'And the package?'

'Also negative. Charley's leader suspects that the asset held onto it either because they were not able to conceal it or they felt the aircraft might catch fire.'

There was a pause while the Chairman thought for a moment. Either theory was possible, but he preferred the more straightforward explanation. 'Or the asset wants to hold all the cards, ensuring we extract as agreed.'

'It's also possible, sir. At the moment, Charley's team is tracking the survivors. Due to them being civilians, there shouldn't be too many complications,' Mr Jones said.

'True, but you sound uneasy. Is there a problem?'

'The only problem we have, sir, is, as you know, when you think it's going too well, that's when the shit hits the fan.'

The Chairman smiled and nodded in agreement. 'So true, Major. Just keep me apprised, and don't forget we have less than a week to get this done, or I'm calling abort. However, we will continue as planned. My flight to Washington is in an hour. I'll contact you when I'm there. Just get that bloody package.'

'Understood, sir. Alfa leader, out.'

The line went dead, and the Chairman returned his mobile phone to his pocket. He felt uneasy. He had felt that way ever since he had heard about the crash. This was meant to be a simple operation, and so far, it had gone spectacularly wrong. Someone else was playing; the question was, who, and what did they want?

The waitress came out to see if there were any dirty dishes to clear, and he gestured for a refill. She nodded, and after clearing a nearby table that had just been vacated, she headed back inside.

The Chairman sighed and closed his eyes, taking in the sun's warmth, when his mobile phone vibrated in his pocket. He retrieved it, saw the caller ID, and froze. It was the boss.

He swallowed, clicked the green call button, and said, 'Yes, sir.' Then, he listened in silence until it was his turn to speak. He told the person on the other end everything they knew about the situation at that time.

The caller said they wanted the Chairman to keep them

informed. The voice was distorted, giving it an electronic tone. Then the phone went silent; the caller had ended the call.

The Chairman blew out a lungful of air he didn't know he had been holding in.

At that moment, the waitress returned with a fresh cup of coffee, placed it down, smiling as she did so, and then took his empty cup.

'Bad day at the office, sir?' she asked.

'What?' he replied, still shaken up by the call.

'Bad day at the office? I saw you were quite happy until you got that call,' she replied.

The Chairman shook it off, and the smile returned to his face. He picked up the fresh cup. 'No, just my wife reminding me we have unexpected guests coming. Nothing we can't handle.'

'That's good to hear. I hope you have a good day, sir,' the friendly waitress smiled and left.

He wondered how much of that conversation was genuine and how much was buttering him up for a good tip; after all, many of the people working in such jobs lived off their tips. He remembered the sign on the door: 'Don't forget to tip your waitress.'

He returned his attention to his coffee and watched the world go by. *Yes, nothing we can't handle,* he thought to himself.

CHAPTER EIGHTEEN

THE GROUP HAD MADE A QUICK STOP NEXT TO A SMALL stream they had found. Steel had told them to fill any water bottle they had. He filled several travel water bottles and the canteen on his belt. He had learned that just because you have found water once, it doesn't mean you'll find it again when needed.

He looked over at the group and saw they were already feeling the effects of the march. He was used to it, but these were city folk who more than likely worked in an office all day. Their clothes were all wrong for hiking. They had ski suits and thick jackets—perfect for play but not for what they were doing. Most had nothing underneath apart from long johns, so stripping off wasn't an option. Their boots weren't made for hiking, only for keeping off the snow.

Steel knew this would soon slow them down, as they would begin to sweat with all the extra layers and blister their feet. They had done eight miles, and Steel feared this was how it would continue: walk for eight and rest for half an hour. He looked at his watch. That distance had taken them nearly an hour. He hoped the open ground would be kind and the weather would hold.

Steel put his water containers away and swung the pack back onto his back with a sense of urgency.

'Let's go,' Steel said, hoping the edge of the forest would appear soon.

'Can't we rest a little more? It's such hard work,' Natalie complained.

'Sure, you know which way you're going?' Steel said, causing them all to smile—until they realised he wasn't joking.

'We have a long way to go; the more you rest, the less daylight we have, and the sooner we are out of the forest, the better chance a plane will see us,' Steel explained. 'So you can stay here and feel sorry for yourselves, or you can get off your arse and start walking.'

Sherman smiled as he stood up. He had to admit Steel's approach was novel, if anything, but effective.

The group stood up and began to follow as Steel led Karen onwards. They had minimal food and water, but they had the means to get more. He worried that their stamina would leave them earlier than he anticipated. It would eventually happen—something that could finish them sooner than starvation or thirst would.

'Look, the settlement will have beds, running water and probably booze,' Sherman said, hoping to boost the people's morale.

Steel frowned at the man's attempt to jumpstart their motivation. A few cracked a hopeful smile, while others remained sour and sore.

'Sherman, if you suggest they sing a walking song, I'm leaving and going home,' Steel said in Sherman's ear, causing the man to smile.

'I know! Let's sing something,' Sherman shouted, causing

Steel to groan with disappointment as Sherman led the group off, leaving Steel guarding the rear.

Steel smiled and shook his head while swearing under his breath at the stunt Sherman had purposely pulled. As he went to set off, Steel stopped and turned slightly.

The sound of a large flock of birds flying away echoed through the forest. The hairs on the back of his neck stood on end as if a bad feeling had rushed over him. Something was wrong.

They weren't alone.

CHAPTER NINETEEN

For hours, they had wandered through the mountain forest, taking small breaks so the wounded could rest. As they did so, Steel used the time to check the map and the compass with Sherman to ensure they were heading in the correct direction. He figured Sherman needed to know where he was taking the survivors in case something happened.

Natalie's constant complaining and lagging behind were beginning to get to Steel and the others. On more than one occasion, Steel had thought about just carrying on when she had fallen behind, but some of the group had insisted he wait for her to catch up.

The forest was thick, and the ground was full of broken branches and tall undergrowth. They were far from the usual paths created by constant use.

Occasionally, a break in the forest revealed mountains and waterfalls. Sometimes, an eagle would fly overhead, or a moose herd could be seen grazing in a valley. Steel and Sherman would stop momentarily to take in the majestic views, giving the others time to steal a quick break. They were heading down at an angle but still had some way to go.

Steel had shown the group the route on the map, using his finger to track the way. They would be passing massive waterfalls and caves. He needed them to know the route—not just to give them a small piece of mind that he had a plan but also so they had a slight chance of catching up with the group if they were to get lost.

At one clearing, Steel stopped to check his bearings, using the land's features to orient himself. Down below, in a small open valley, he noticed something. Taking out his binoculars, he zoomed in to find a group of eight men travelling along the valley in the same direction he was taking the survivors. They wore all black, had medium-sized military backpacks, and carried automatic weapons. This was no hunting party or rescue team.

He wondered who they were and what they wanted. His gut told him something was off about these men. Still, after the incident at his home, he had massive trust issues regarding people dressed in such a fashion.

Perhaps he was wrong, and it was American special forces on some training manoeuvres? But he couldn't shake the feeling. Was it a coincidence that a plane had crashed, and instead of a rescue team, armed men had arrived?

He knew he had to leave the group and track the armed men—watch them for a while, just for his own peace of mind. Perhaps they were an army unit looking for Sherman? But the timeline was off; it was too soon. Plus, how did they know where the group of survivors was?

He looked again. Was the team heading for the lake, not up the mountain? Perhaps he was wrong after all. If they knew where the survivors were, they would be travelling up, not across. Steel lowered the binoculars and looked behind him, deep into the forest. Was there a second team? Had they come up from the plane and pushed the survivors towards the team he had seen? A classic pincer movement—push the prey into a killing zone.

Steel shook his head. Was he overthinking things? Were these just random people off for a fun weekend in the wilderness? Possibly bored businessmen playing soldiers.

He was just about to tuck away the binoculars when he decided to take one last look.

The lead man stopped and held up a fist. As he did so, the others dropped to one knee and faced outwards in a tactical fishbone manoeuvre. Then the man spoke into a radio on his shoulder, and as he did, he looked up at the mountain and then back at the way they were travelling. He nodded, then stepped off, and the others followed in a single file. At that moment, Steel knew two things. One, these weren't soldier wannabes, and two, another team was coming up from behind the survivors.

It was another four hours before they reached the final clearing. Bright sunlight and a cloudless blue sky greeted them.

Steel let them rest momentarily while he took out the map and got his bearings. To the south, there was another lake— Swan Lake. But it was farther away; all the cabins were located on the far side, and it was a big lake.

TwentyMile Lake was much closer and smaller, plus it had a marking on the map denoting that there was an aircraft there. No doubt, it was something the pilot had marked for reference.

Steel took note of the markings the pilot had made on the map—dots in different colours in various locations. He put it down to places of interest he often flew past on his tours. Normally, he would think nothing of it, but he didn't believe in coincidences. Everything had a meaning.

Happy with the route they had to take, Steel tucked away

the map and compass into his pocket. A strong breeze carried a chill and made Steel's long coat flap like a flag on a mast.

'What are you thinking?' Sherman asked as he moved up to Steel's side.

'I think you need to take these people east to the lake. It should be easy from now on,' Steel said, taking out the map and a second compass.

Sherman gave Steel a confused and disappointed look as he took the navigation items from him.

'I've done my bit. Besides, they've already made it clear I'm not needed,' Steel said, unstrapping his boot knife and handing it to Sherman.

'You're just gonna leave us?' Sherman growled.

'We both know what you are and that you probably do this on weekends for fun. And no, I'm not leaving. There's something I need to go back and check out. I can't be sure, but I think we're being followed. Now, it could be a rescue team, in which case I'll bring them to you,' Steel added.

'But?' Sherman asked, a frown crossing his face.

'But the way they were dressed suggested something else.'

'You mean those guys you spotted in the last clearing? I couldn't make them out too well with my binoculars, but I get what you mean. I've never seen a rescue team wearing all black before,' Sherman agreed. 'They could be hunters, I guess?'

'Yeah, I thought that too, but I saw some similar people in town just a couple of days ago.'

'So what, you're going to find them, and then what?' Sherman asked.

Steel shrugged. 'Like I said, if they're a rescue team, I'll bring them to you.'

'And if they aren't?'

Steel shrugged again and tapped his hatchet. 'Then we'll have another discussion.'

'Take my pack; it has enough supplies to help you along,' Steel said, pulling it off his back and handing it to Sherman, who said nothing.

'Oh, one thing, Sherman. Where were you heading before the crash?'

'Back to Talkeetna. Why?' Sherman answered curiously.

'No reason,' Steel said with a shrug before turning towards the forest.

Sherman watched Steel disappear back into the wilderness until he had blended into the shadows.

'Where's he gone?' Laura asked, only now realising Steel wasn't just going to take a piss.

'It's just us now. He's left us with tools, weapons, and water. I've got the map, and I know the route we should take,' Sherman barked.

'I knew he'd quit,' Natalie scoffed.

'Is it any wonder? You've been on his case ever since we woke up, as though it was his fault we're in this mess,' Bob growled.

'Look, it ain't ideal, but that's how it is. So suck it up, and let's get to that lake,' Sherman said with a commanding roar.

The rest nodded, though their faces were saddened. Sherman went through the pack and gathered the others around him. He knew there was still a distance to travel, but he was confident they would reach the correct spot before dusk.

As they moved off, Steel watched from a crouched position. As the last person disappeared from view, Steel's gaze shifted. Looking deep into the forest, he pulled out the hatchet from its sheath, his expression hardening.

'Right, let's see who you are, shall we?' he said, skulking off into the dense forest's blackness.

CHAPTER TWENTY

THE MERCENARY CALLED GEORGE HAD FOLLOWED THE trail for a distance before stopping to take on water. Despite the cold temperatures, it was thirsty work.

Behind him, Sven was having trouble with his tablet due to all the interference from the trees.

George smiled. Despite all the technology, they still required the human touch—something that never broke down, had to be plugged in, or required a satellite. He took another mouthful of water and placed the canteen back into the pouch on his belt. The others were waiting for him to take the lead, eager to begin the hunt.

George watched as one of the men, Stephan Kruger, took out a large knife from a leg sheath and began to chop at the vegetation. He wore a sadistic smile as he did so.

Kruger was of average height and had a muscular build. A black baseball cap covered his short red hair. His tactical vest was full of ammunition pouches and knives. A nickel .44 Magnum Desert Eagle pistol was holstered on his left leg, and a custom AK-47 assault rifle with a grenade launcher attachment slung down to his side.

George looked around at the others. Killers for cash, an army with no other oath but their own—none of them could be trusted. Each one would change sides if the price were right—all but the other team leader, the man known as Sven, who was as loyal as they came.

Besides, nobody was foolish enough to mess with the organisation; if they did, Mr Jones would be tasked with hunting them down and killing them. If not, they'd end up with the new guy, and nobody wanted to end up on his table. George had heard the guy's name once but had forgotten it or just chosen not to remember; Wilson or Williams, he thought it was.

George turned back to the trail. The marks couldn't be more apparent—drag marks from a walking cane or crutch. But most of all, there were the broken twigs or a stacked pile of bark or stone. The asset was leaving a trail, one even a blind man could follow.

He smiled again and followed the trail but ignored the obvious markers. He preferred to use his own way. It was more reliable. Anyone could have created the piles, including the one guiding them.

Every ten or so paces, George would stop and check the trail, searching for anomalies such as a change in stride or signs of fatigue in survivors.

To his disappointment, they all seemed to be holding a steady pace and stopping every so often. This was undoubtedly good news for the mercenaries, as they would catch up sooner. On the other hand, it meant whoever was leading them was organised—possibly ex or serving armed forces. If that was the case, he could be in trouble, but it was nothing they couldn't handle.

'Problem?' Sven called up as he saw George holding on to one spot longer than he had with the others.

'The tracks are constant,' George said, picking up a piece of bark and smelling it.

'Meaning?'

'They are moving at the slowest person's pace, taking regular breaks,' George explained.

'So?' one of the other mercenaries said with a shrug.

'It means they are organised; someone is leading them,' Sven said with a growl of disappointment.

'You think they're Army?'

'Hard to tell. Could be,' George said, standing up.

'Ain't killed an army boy for a while. Bring it on,' laughed another mercenary.

'With any luck, it's a woman; we can have some fun before we kill her,' grinned Stephan.

'We don't know what we have here, so stay frosty and watch your arcs. It could be a local who just knows their shit, or it could be something else. Either way, don't get complacent,' Sven ordered, pulling the weapon close to his chest. He suddenly had a bad feeling, mixed with excitement. This was no longer just a hunt for lost survivors. This was a hunt for a possible worthy adversary.

'George, move out,' Sven ordered. George nodded and resumed his tracking. Several feet back, the men followed—this time in a staggered formation. Weapons were pushed into shoulders, ready for anything. The men inched further into the forest, hearts racing and adrenaline pumping. This was going to be a good hunt.

George followed the trail for another mile before stopping and raising a fist to signal to the others to hold position. He crouched down and checked the ground for the usual signs that the group had left. He smiled as he saw more drag marks.

People were starting to get tired. He looked for the markers the asset had been leaving but found none. It was possible he didn't have time to leave any, or with so many people lagging behind, he may have feared they would be seen.

'Anything?' Sven called up.

'They are getting tired, but the asset has stopped leaving markers,' George explained. 'He may have stopped just in case someone discovered them.'

'If they're that tired, they may decide to make camp,' one of the mercenaries said hopefully.

Sven looked at his watch. The luminous dials pointed to three o'clock. He knew they would have little chance of getting to a clearing before dark, but they could catch up to the survivors if they had made camp.

'Okay, I suggest we camp now and rest. Those survivors aren't going anywhere fast. Besides, I have a plan,' Sven ordered.

'Make camp? We should push on. Can't we use the night vision equipment?' said Stephan.

'They won't be going anywhere; it gives us a chance to rest up and get some grub. We can catch them up in the morning. Besides, I don't trust the NVGs with all this undergrowth. I'll get Lockwood and his idiots to go on while we rest. Possibly, leapfrogging is the best thing in this situation,' Sven explained, looking at all the loose bark chips covering tree roots, stones, and other trip hazards. The last thing he needed was a team member down because of a stupid accident.

'Tomorrow, first light, we move out. We need to double-time it, close up the gaps, and George,' Sven said, looking at the tracker, 'no more stops. Quick, easy, and just use your eyes.'

George nodded and turned. He wasn't happy with the order but understood the pressure of pressing on before dark. George looked around as if checking the trees for something.

'Anything wrong, George?' Sven asked.

'No—it's nothing, just my mind playing tricks on me,' George said, turning around and picking up the trail before heading off as quickly as his tracking skills would allow, the others close behind.

All the while, George felt they were being watched—and hunted.

CHAPTER TWENTY-ONE

AFTER LEAVING THE GROUP, STEEL HAD DOUBLED BACK. He didn't know how far the pursuers were behind them or what they wanted. It was too soon for a rescue team to be so close, and it would have been hours before they could have mustered so much manpower so quickly.

That's if anyone was looking for them at all. Had the pilot had time to call in a *Mayday*?

Steel had covered the tracks the group had made and decided to make some of his own, leading off to the south.

He'd already got a bearing on the lake, so all he needed to do was follow that; he didn't need the track. Steel knew the people tracking them weren't a rescue team because he'd heard no helicopters or barking dogs.

This was deep Alaska; no helicopters with thermal imaging for miles existed. Whoever they were, they were moving silently and not calling out to let someone know they were there.

He had noticed the markers and put it down to Sherman leaving a trail, just in case a team did show up, giving them something to follow. It was a useful trick, but in this case, deadly.

If Steel were wrong about the mysterious guests, he would, in fact, be leading them to the others. But for now, they were unknown hostiles and should be treated as such until proven otherwise.

Steel had made the tracks quickly, ensuring they led to a stream he had seen on the pilot's map. It was an excellent place to camp if ever there was one. He knew they would make camp at last light, but he was under pressure to make the trail as convincing as possible. He had no idea how far back they were, but he figured they were far enough away for him to finish the fake trail and then find a good vantage point.

Steel checked his watch. It had just gone three o'clock. He had led the group out in good time from when he had first felt they were not alone.

He'd always had good instincts, especially the sense of when something was wrong. It had saved his behind on more than one occasion, and this was no different. Steel finished off the trail, ensuring he'd added a few false tracks, making it appear as though people were dragging their feet.

The place by the river was perfect, with a flat plateau next to a fallen tree, ideal for wind cover. But most of all, it was full of trees that were perfect for use as a lookout nest.

Steel doubled back, ensuring his new path would remain undiscovered. Where he had created the new path, he had found an old tree that had split in half, leaving a hollowed-out dead trunk reaching out of the ground, with room enough for a person to fit into. The dead tree looked ominous, so nobody would think twice about having a bad feeling about it, making it a perfect place to observe.

He needed to know how many there were, how they were dressed and, more importantly... how they were armed. He hoped he was wrong and that it was just a couple of hunters stocking up on meat and fur for the winter reserves.

At four o'clock, Steel saw the first of them. A small man compared to Steel, he was a blond man with a ginger beard, dressed all in black tactical gear.

As Steel watched from his hiding place, the man crouched down and waved his hand gently over the grass, bark, and broken branches.

Steel smiled to himself. The hunters had themselves a tracker.

He watched and listened to the conversation. The tracker told a huge man about how the group was moving and how they were organised. Then he watched as they moved down the fake trail he had created.

His plan was working; he just hoped it would take some time before they realised it was fake. Deep down, he was anxious to see if he could fool a tracker. The last of the team members moved out of sight. That was Steel's cue to vacate the hiding place and track them as they travelled.

Steel kept far enough back not to be seen, but he knew where they were heading; he just hoped they stayed on course. He stopped near a group of large rocks that jutted from the ground. Crouching for a moment, Steel took a deep breath, inhaled a lungful of fresh air, and listened to the birdsong, waiting for it to stop and for the birds to fly away. Steel had used the path he had doubled back on and had overtaken them by a few minutes. From his perch, he had a perfect view of the fake path and the approaching men, but he was invisible to them; his form blended into the rock as though he wasn't even there. He remained still, his breath shallow to hide the rise and fall of his chest and shoulders.

Steel watched as the men moved past. The tracker stopped to recheck the trail. The big man asked the tracker if anything was wrong, and the man explained the group's problems and failing strength.

Steel smiled. His plan was working.

The leader ordered the men to make camp—something Steel had envisaged would happen because they would be losing light.

Steel watched the tracker look around as if something was watching them, but his gaze fell on a group of trees to his right. Steel closed his eyes, as if not seeing the man would help with his camouflage. Then he heard the order to move out. His eyes opened, but the sunglasses still shielded him.

As the team disappeared once more from view, Steel stared down the path they had taken. He had two options: leave the mercenaries and hope they didn't pick up the scent, or sneak near the camp and overhear what they had planned.

Steel had no idea what they wanted from the group. They were nobody special—a married couple, some students, a war photographer, and a soldier. If anything, they were after the soldier, but that would mean he was way up there on the food chain for someone to send mercenaries to extract him. The problem was that if that were true, it would mean that everyone else was expendable, and he couldn't allow that to happen.

Steel was about to leave when he watched the big man get onto his radio and call for Charlie's team. He then told the team leader about a leapfrog plan—how his team was getting some rest now and that Charlie's team was to keep moving until the last light, then get some rest. Then, at first light, the Bravo team would move on while they rested, and so on.

The team leader on the other end of the radio said, "Roger that," and then Sven placed the radio back in his pack.

CHAPTER TWENTY-TWO

SHERMAN WALKED ALONGSIDE KAREN, WITH THE OTHERS not far behind. No one had questioned why the stranger wasn't with them. Sherman had lied. He'd said Steel had felt he had taken them far enough and that the way from there was easy. For some, it was a welcomed departure. Natalie, for one, was glad to see the back of the man. He had treated her like a dog when she was from a wealthy family and required to be treated as such by those below her station.

It seemed to Sherman that the only person who cared was Laura, but it didn't matter. He was gone, and Sherman was left with the human baggage. Sherman was still convinced that Steel had made up the whole 'We've been followed' routine and had just fled. But then, who could really blame him? The people had been ungrateful and demanding. Hell, Sherman had thought about leaving them several times on the route.

Sherman pulled out the map and checked the compass Steel had given him. From his reckoning, they were on the correct path. The map showed there was another small forest between them and the lake. This would be a perfect place to camp out. The trees would give them cover and plenty of wood for a fire. They had minimal food and water but enough to see them through to their destination if they rationed it properly. Everyone was tired from walking but, despite this, in good spirits.

Sherman placed the compass and map away and pointed to a tree line in the distance, some two to three miles in front of them.

'That's where we are heading, folks,' he said in a cheerful voice. 'We'll make camp and then head to the lake in the morning,' he explained.

The news was greeted with many moans and groans of disappointment, especially from Natalie.

'We need to get there before nightfall if possible, so no rest stops until we get there.'

Sherman could feel the looks of hate and disappointment, but he didn't care. They had an objective: to reach shelter before nightfall. For Sherman, it was essential to know the lay of the ground, what resources were available, and where the best shelter place was. For the rest of them, it was another long walk with no end in sight.

Sherman ushered them on, giving words of encouragement.

Before them, a wave of green met a pale blue horizon and distant snow-topped mountains. The sun was bright, but a cold breeze from the west dulled the warmth.

Sherman knew he couldn't push them too hard, or they would sit where they fell, more out of disobedience than anything. He had to be firm but with a gentle touch, unlike Steel's brash but effective approach of threatening to walk off and let them fend for themselves.

This tactic seemed to work, but Sherman couldn't do it; he was in the same situation as the rest.

The group moved slowly but at a steady pace, each one

feeling fatigued, hungry, cold and bruised. In any other circumstance, they would stop and take in the harsh beauty of their surroundings, but all they wanted to do was get to the wood line and make camp. Sherman knew there was a bear problem, especially from the grizzly. Using several fires from the night before might fend off unwanted predators. He reached to his right shoulder and touched the sling of the assault rifle for a sense of comfort. If this were one of his operations, he would have trip flares set out and sentries with night vision goggles.

Sherman smiled. He had done many training exercises in his career, but this was a harsh reality. He was starting to realise that you can train for anything to do with combat, but when it comes to survival, you are facing a much deadlier foe—Mother Nature. As a combatant, you train to work with other similarly trained personnel or by yourself, but here he was with unwilling civilians, and that was something he had never trained for. He smiled as he made a mental note.

Next training plan: working with pain-in-the-ass civic in survival situations.

As he moved along with the group, Sherman's thoughts returned to the stranger who had saved them. He wondered about who he was and what had forced him to seek out a life of utter solitude.

The man had skills, possibly enough to match his own. Sherman thought this John character had been, or still was, in the British Armed Forces: SAS, SBS, one of the Marine regiments or Parachute Regiments. Sherman wasn't even convinced that the name he had been given was real or made up. *John. What was his last name, Smith?* Sherman laughed to himself.

The stranger was mysterious, if nothing else, but at the same time, there was something familiar about him. Possibly someone he had read about or someone they had met once.

Sherman shrugged it off and powered forward past the rest to ensure Karen was OK. The group started to sing a joyful song he hadn't heard for a while. He feared the stranger was right and that their pursuers would hear their voices. But their spirits were beginning to lift, so he dared not stop them. Sherman figured it was worth the risk. Besides, whoever they were was probably deep in the forest and unable to hear them. At least, that was what he was convincing himself of.

The sun began losing its brightness, but the sky remained clear. Sherman checked the tree line to his far left and the open ground to his front and far right. The countryside had a harsh beauty, but it would kill you if you disrespected or underestimated it. They were hundreds of miles from anywhere but had good spirits and hope. Sherman just hoped that was enough to see them through until the end.

CHAPTER TWENTY-THREE

Steel left the big man and headed on; he needed to get to this Charlie team as they were the closest to the survivors. He would track them until they made camp, then try to interrogate one of them.

He waited and saw the two teams converse with one another. Then, the second team moved on. The team leader was a smaller man than the other team leader. In fact, the two teams were completely different. The big man's team looked more professional; the mercenaries looked tougher and more worn, whereas this team was obviously the cannon fodder of the group. Each man looked tired and distracted. If he were going to get anything, it would be from this group.

Steel followed them for another five miles. Then the leader stopped, looked at his watch and the sky, and tossed his pack down.

'Right, we'll rest up here until morning, so get your shit in order. Trent, you got first stag, then Morgan. Get to it, fellas. It will be dark soon, and we need to set up a fire by then. Move,' he ordered, and the men split off to set up the camp.

Steel watched the men make camp. Each man had a sleeping bag and bivi-bag to keep off the elements. Two of the men went to get wood, and the others stayed to finish the camp and fortifications. Steel watched angrily as the three remaining men placed claymore mines in a circle, creating a perimeter around the camp.

When the wood arrived, four places had been set out for fires. Unlike what Steel had done back at the plane, these outlined a square, marking their boundaries.

This was a ten-by-ten encampment—large enough for sleeping and moving about without leaving the site. But it was also too enclosed for Steel to sneak in and take them out if necessary.

He had hoped they were a rescue team, but they had all the hallmarks of mercenaries. The question was, why were they here, and what—or who—were they after?

Steel decided to observe for now and learn more about the men before making a rash decision.

Killing a rescue team wouldn't win him any bonus points, given his non-existent popularity with the survivors. Steel knew the response time out in the bush, and it was nowhere near as quick as what these men had been.

First, they would send a search plane to fly over to look for any signs of wreckage. Then, they would send in people on foot to assess the situation. Of course, this was only possible if they looked in the right place.

Steel remembered the markings on the pilot's map. They were, of course, to return to the town by a hundred miles at least, and if they were purposely off course, that meant the plane's transponder had been turned off. The crash was an accident, but their change of course wasn't.

Steel took stock of the men, assessing their height, build, and the types of weapons they carried. He also assessed each man's personality. There was no doubt they were muscle for hire; the question was why they were here and who was footing the bill. As he watched, the men had already set up camp with a roaring fire in the centre and four outer ones.

Each man had a mini tent the length of their sleeping bags, with a side zip for those brief encounters. The men were set out in a circle, so each arc of fire was covered. Steel smiled as he watched the professionals lay out their encampment.

There was one man on guard. He sat on a huge fallen tree with a perfect overwatch of the site. A pair of night vision goggles was strapped to his head, ready to be brought down over his eyes when required.

Definitely not a rescue team, Steel thought as he bit into one of the dry meat sticks. These men had weapons, shelter, rations and, more importantly, the likelihood of a vehicle waiting for them back where they had found the trail to the plane.

One of the men started to break out his MRE, or *ready-to-eat meal*, and began to prepare the chemical cooker. The men were complacent. The guard and the mines made them feel comfortable enough to let their guard down. Steel smiled—bad mistake.

One of the men, possibly the leader, was smaller than Steel and had an intent look about him. He had short blonde hair and a ginger beard. He was in his mid-forties, with a stocky build. The man was walking around with an electronic tablet, but Steel couldn't see what was on the display.

Steel knew he couldn't risk changing position just to satisfy his curiosity. The leader was walking about, looking for a good reception for the device. As he grew near, Steel caught a sudden glimpse of the screen. It was a map of the area with red flashing blips, which he took to mean the location of other teams in the sector. The man sat on a log next to the fire and searched through other images.

'You got a lock on them?' asked one of the men.

'No, the asset has stopped sending, but that is the least of the problems,' replied the man with a strong Scottish accent.

'What do you mean, boss?' asked another man.

'He means that someone is on to us, that someone led us here to throw off the scent,' said a smaller man.

'How can you be sure? Maybe you got us lost,' said another man with squinted eyes and a broad grin.

The blonde man shook his head. He had known the man long enough to know he was trying to get him worked up.

'Maybe I was lookin' for water, hoping you'd finally take a bath,' the blonde man shot back, making the others laugh. 'No, we were led here; I suggest you all sleep with one eye open tonight.'

'It's probably nothin', an old trail perhaps?' said another.

The blonde leader shook his head.

'No, these tracks are fresh, and don't forget the markers the asset left,' the leader said, tucking the device away.

Steel scowled. Someone in the group was working with these guys, and it got under his skin. He would deal with these guys and then head back for the survivors. He needed to know who these people were and what they were after.

CHAPTER TWENTY-FOUR

STEEL WATCHED THE MEN. A SMALL MAN HAD SWAPPED with the tall guy on the guard post. The man was stocky with broad shoulders. The thick jacket enhanced his frame. He had short black hair underneath a black baseball cap, which he kept removing to rub his forehead as though the cap was new and irritating his skin.

Steel lay there calmly, just watching while he formulated a plan. He knew something had to be done about the men; he didn't know what.

Killing them was an option, but then he wanted answers to questions like, What are you doing here? All he knew was that they were strangers in his part of the world, and they weren't a rescue team.

The already diminished light was fading. The sun was setting, and soon it would be pitch black. These were excellent conditions for the guard's night vision goggles but bad for Steel.

If he was going to do something, it had to be now while he still had the element of surprise. Things would be much easier if he could get the NVGs away from the guard.

Steel knew he had to move silently. A smile crossed his face at the prospect of taking out these highly trained men without making a noise—at last, something to amuse himself. To him, these were no longer men; they were prey. No. They were something worse; they were trouble.

Steel did a final check on the men in the camp. Two were sleeping, the guy who had just come off sentry was preparing his meal, three were playing cards, and the last three were still collecting firewood.

Steel had seen the men head off to the wooded area in front of the campsite, the direction in which the guide was transfixed. All eyes were elsewhere.

Steel snuck closer to the sentry, pulled out the hatchet, waited, found his mark, and threw it. The hatchet made no noise as it hurtled through the air. The only sound was a dull thud as the guard's body hit the undergrowth on the other side of the fallen tree.

As he moved silently towards the sentry's body, the others didn't stir or acknowledge that they had heard anything.

The guard lay flat on his front. Luckily, the force of the blade smashing into the back of his head had pushed him forward.

Steel jammed a knee into the corpse's back and levered the hatchet from the man's skull. Blood was already oozing from the mouth and seeping into the ground. He flipped the body over and checked the pockets and pouches for anything useful.

He took an electric storm lighter, a torch, a pack of gum, a cigar in a metal tube, a 9mm Glock 17, and several magazines for the pistol and rifle.

Steel slung the Steyr AUG assault rifle, then slipped the NVGs from the man's head before dragging the body away to conceal it. If anyone were to check, they'd think he'd gone to take a leak.

Steel moved around the fallen tree. There was one spot where the ground bowed under the tree's base—deep enough to crawl through but shallow enough to be hidden from view. He began to move through the gap.

The ground was moist and filled with rocks, which made it uncomfortable and sometimes painful as they hit the joints of his knees and elbows.

Steel remembered one training camp where they had to go through a crawl space, a maze of tunnels under a house. He had no idea how long it was or how long he had been down there. All he knew was that it was dark and confined. The permanent training staff had placed small stones in the shaft, making the soldiers take their time as they went.

Steel leopard-crawled through the undergrowth to the other side of the tree. Long grass, bushes, and the fading light made him invisible to the man's gaze. From here, he had a perfect vantage point of the mercenaries. He would have to take the leader last; if anyone had information, it was him.

The blond man was resting with his back against a tree trunk, which prevented attacks from behind. He would have to get in unseen and kill them all without any noise—in this case, no shots fired.

Steel knew they had more teams out there, and a shot would bring them running.

'Where you goin'?' asked Lockwood.

'Gonna take a leak. Why, you wanna hold it for me?' laughed the standing man.

'Nah, I forgot my tweezers,' laughed Lockwood.

The big man laughed as the merc headed into the bush, holding up a middle finger.

'Don't go too far,' yelled Lockwood.

The man raised a hand as if to say, *Yeah, yeah,* before blending into the forest.

Steel had already moved back from where he had crawled and was moving swiftly but silently towards the man.

CHAPTER TWENTY-FIVE

THE MERCENARY, A MAN CALLED MARCO BROWN, WAS AN average-sized man with not much in the way of mass, but he was a killer—one hundred per cent pure scum of the earth. The chances were that if he hadn't become a soldier for hire, he most probably would have become a serial killer.

The man had fought worldwide and enjoyed every minute of it. But for him, Bosnia had been the best playground. He had raped, murdered, mutilated, and a whole lot more—and got paid to do it. That was until the UN and then NATO turned up. Even then, he had carved himself some soldier wings.

Marco found a spot in front of a tree and unzipped. As he began to piss, he started to whistle to himself—a merry tune that he had just made up.

To him, all was right with the world. He was off to track some poor lost souls and had permission to do whatever he wanted to them until he got what he wanted, and even then, he could unleash himself upon them. A sick smile crossed his face as he imagined what he would do to them, especially the women.

He had never heard Steel's approach and didn't even notice that someone was standing right behind him.

Marco finished, shook off, zipped up, and turned. He felt a sudden pain in his stomach. His hands reached down and grasped at his middle. Blood flowed through his fingers, followed by his lower intestines. Marco dropped to his knees, a panicked look on his face. Then, he felt the presence of the other man crouched before him. He wore a pair of NVG goggles and held a lethal-looking tactical hatchet. Marco went to cry out, but Steel covered his mouth and stabbed him in the leg.

Steel wanted him alive. He had recognised Marco—a man whose face had come up on the army's wanted board more than once. A man who had raped and brutalised two female soldiers and civilians that Steel had known. A family who had made bread for the soldiers. A quiet family. Good people. The women, including two other soldiers, had gone to pick up their morning order for the camp.

Marco and his band of killers had attacked the small village, and the soldiers had been outgunned and outmanned. They had called for backup, but it had come too late. Steel and the QRF, a quick reaction force, got there in time to see the last woman die. They had all had their bellies slit open, their throats cut, and had been left there to die slowly.

'You're going to tell me about your friends and your camp.'

'Fuck you,' Marco said in a strained voice.

Steel covered the man's mouth, then squeezed his balls tightly.

Marco screamed and shook his head from the pain.

'Let's try that again, shall we? So, how many men, and how is your camp secured?'

'Fuck y...' Marco went to say, but Steel covered the man's mouth and twisted the knife that was still in his leg. Marco passed out, falling to the ground, but Steel didn't try to catch him. He grabbed the back of Marco's tactical vest and dragged him deep into the forest.

His men would find him eventually, but the animals would find him first.

After he had told Steel everything.

CHAPTER TWENTY-SIX

Marco had told Steel the camp was lightly guarded; this was Alaska, not Afghanistan. Despite this, some of the men had set up Claymore mines. This had been more for their protection against bears and wolves than against attacking soldiers.

Steel had thought it was a slight overkill, but it was nearly winter, and the last thing they wanted was to be attacked by a hungry grizzly.

Steel watched the mercenaries. They weren't like the other team he had left earlier; these were more like irritated ex-soldiers on exercise. The others were also ex-soldiers—there was no doubt about that—but the others were veterans, probably having been from one conflict to the next. They were battle-hungry. However, these guys looked more like ex-infantry who needed a job. Another sad case of what happens when the military has no more use for its personnel. Some were discharged with no pension, others hadn't been in long enough to get one, and for others, their pension didn't cover their debts.

Steel had seen it a lot, especially with the British Army; pension plans changed, so some guys didn't get anything until they were in their sixties, which was great—apart from when they got out in their forties. He had seen too many ex-military people end up homeless because they weren't eligible for a council house or help from the government, regardless of serving twenty-two years.

These guys before him were just men looking for simple cash doing what they had been trained to do without the bullshit.

These were men who were just there for a payday, nothing more. It was nothing personal—just men trying to get by. He almost felt sorry for them. Almost. At the end of the day, they were soldiers for hire who were there to do whatever the guy paying the wages said. He had no idea what these men had done in the past or, indeed, what they would do when they found the survivors. He had no illusion that it involved giving them a ride back to Washington or New York.

The three men who went collecting wood cursed under their breath as they foraged for pieces of branch or anything small enough and dry enough to burn.

Pete, Karl, and Jacob weren't actually wicked men—or at least, they hadn't started out that way. They had left the French Army together after three years of being bored of being told what to do. Each man was looking for a quick payday with minimal effort. They had been recruited in a bar in Algiers. A man in the bar had told them of cash—and lots of it.

The three had met with another man some days later—a tall blonde guy with a thousand-yard stare and a personality to match. To say it was the scariest job interview they had encountered would have been putting it mildly. A meeting that lasted four hours and ended with them shooting a hooded guy.

Pete had thought the people had watched too many movies,

but the intention was the same. *How far are you willing to go?* Of course, they had all done it without question.

Karl had done it without hesitation, which had impressed the blonde guy.

Three guys on the job. On the hunt for survivors and whatever the boss was after. The three men had been sent to collect the wood because they were the new guys. They could see that and didn't question it—or dare to—because if it got back to Sven, they would be in deep shit.

Sven was a big man with a temper—something they never wanted to be on the wrong side of—and they were glad when they had been picked to go with Lockwood, who wasn't as much of a psychopath as the others.

Pete was the largest of the three—six-two with a bulky frame. That meant he got to carry while the others loaded his long arms. He didn't mind. In fact, he was used to it. His brothers used to do the same back home on the farm. Karl stacked a load of short branches onto the already growing pile and smiled at Pete.

'Have you told them you are leaving the group yet?' Karl asked.

'No, not yet. Thought I would wait until this job is done,' Pete replied with a reluctant shake of his head.

'They'll never let you leave; you know that, right?' Jacob added.

'This life isn't for me, man,' Pete said with a slight shrug. 'You saw what they did with those two guys we found wandering in the woods. Poor bastards thought that we were there to help them.'

'Yeah, wasn't right. I thought Sven was gonna shoot them after he was done, but he strung them up so the bears could get at them. That's sick, man.'

'And that's what I'm talkin' about. We didn't sign up for

this shit. We're soldiers, not... well, whatever this sick outfit is,' Pete said, his words deflated—a man caught in the middle of a nightmare.

'Doesn't matter; you've seen too much, know too much,' Jacob explained.

But Pete already knew this. Either way, he was done.

As Karl turned and bent down to pick up another armful of wood, Steel came up behind Pete, kicked his legs from under him, and held the hatchet to his throat.

'I'd stay still unless you want a close shave,' Steel growled.

Karl heard Pete yell, and the sound of the wood hitting the ground caused him to turn. His hand reached for his weapon, but he froze at the sight of a huge bearded man dressed in a long, worn leather coat, holding a military hatchet in one hand and their friend in the other.

Steel loomed over Pete, who was on his knees. Steel was behind him, one hand pulling Pete's head back by his hair, revealing his large throat, and the other holding the sharp blade of the hatchet at his carotid artery.

Karl went for his pistol on his hip, but Steel shook his head and nicked the flesh on Pete's neck just enough for a trickle of blood to appear.

Karl raised his hands, his eyes burning with fear and anger. Who was this guy, and what did he want?

'What do you want, man?' Karl screamed.

'I want to know what you and your friends want with the survivors,' Steel asked calmly.

'We were sent to pick something up... a package... it should have been on the plane,' Pete struggled to say.

'What package?'

Karl shook his head. 'We don't know. Our boss, Mr Jones, knows what we are looking for; we are just backup.'

'What the hell do you need backup for? They're just civilians.'

'Hey, we just get told what to do. We don't ask questions.' Karl sounded bitter, but his anger was with someone else.

'Why did you kill the other survivors, the ones you found?' Steel asked, trying to calm himself, stopping himself from slitting Pete's throat and throwing the hatchet into Karl's head.

'That was Sven. He is Mr Jones's second-in-command, Bravo team leader, and a guy with serious issues,' Karl explained. 'We started by asking the two guys about what had happened to the passengers.

'Then Sven got bored, shot one of them in the leg, and started interrogating them. It was apparent they had no idea what we were talking about, so he told us to string them up, and then he shot the other guy in the leg.' He continued, shaking his head at the memory. 'He made us watch as the bears came. Big fucking brown bears. They just ripped those poor bastards apart. Sven just laughed. Sick fuck.'

Steel thought for a moment. He almost felt pity for these men... almost. However, he needed to do something to distract the others in their team.

'Well, gents, it seems this could be your lucky day.'

'What do you mean?' Karl asked, confused.

'I heard you guys talking just now, so if you're going, I suggest you go now, both of you. You want to live, then leave. Just turn around and leave,' Steel said, his gaze locked onto Pete.

'I can't. The others, they'll track me down... you don't know them,' Pete said, his voice ringing with fear.

'Don't worry, kid. The others won't come after you,' Steel replied gravelly as emotion kicked in. 'They won't be coming after anyone.'

With that, Steel turned and disappeared back into the dark forest.

The three men looked at one another and ran in the opposite direction.

CHAPTER TWENTY-SEVEN

THE MERCENARY CAMP HAD GROWN QUIET. THERE HAD been a seven-man squad, but after making three of them run off and killing the sentry and Marco, two were left: the big man who had come off the sentry and Lockwood.

Lockwood was still leaning against the tree, and the big man was filling his face.

Steel was unsure how to handle the situation; it had been easy so far. However, according to the law of averages, one of these would be difficult. He weighed his options and decided on the direct approach, so he moved out of his hiding place and started walking.

The big man was the first to notice Steel's approach and went to shout. As he did so, whatever he was eating fell from his mouth.

Lockwood looked up, confused at first, until he saw a man in a long leather coat with a beard, glacier sunglasses, a hatchet, and a hunting knife.

The big man scrambled for his weapon, which he had foolishly left against a tree several feet from where he was sitting.

As he lunged for it, Steel hurled his knife, which found its mark in the man's hand, pinning him to the tree. Steel hurled the hatchet, which severed the man's arm at the elbow. The big man screamed, holding his bloody stump. The arterial spray spurted from the wound with every beat of his heart.

Lockwood's hand froze over his weapon as Steel drew the assault rifle from his back and aimed it at Lockwood's crotch.

'Who are you?' he said, panicked. 'What the fuck do you want?' Lockwood's eyes searched the area, hoping that, any minute, the three idiots would be back from gathering the wood.

'If you are looking for the others, they're gone. It's just you and me,' Steel sneered.

Lockwood moved his arm and placed his hand on his leg, his eyes burning with venom. 'Why did ye kill me boys?' he asked, his accent thick.

'What do you want with the survivors?' Steel countered.

Lockwood looked surprised for a second, then nodded with a satisfied grin as though a question had been answered. 'So, it was ye that was helpin' them lot. We coulda figured that one oot. How a bunch of snivellin' civis could get this far?'

Steel sauntered up to Lockwood, pausing only to retrieve his knife from the tree and the hatchet from the ground; then he wiped the blood off using the man's shirt before placing them back in their sheaths.

He left the man screaming, knowing it wouldn't be long before he passed out from either the pain or blood loss, and stood before Lockwood, the rifle still aimed at the man's balls. 'What do you want with the survivors?' Steel asked again in a calm voice.

'Fuck you, and fuck them. The big man will find yous and all youse little pals, nae fear of that, and when he dae...'

Before he could finish, Steel had shot the man in the knee.

The leg exploded, and Lockwood screamed, grabbing his leg. Steel thought he should be worried about the two men screaming—the thought of the other team hearing and running over—but just as he was contemplating shutting the big man up, the big man fell silent. Steel turned and found the man lying on the ground, the blood still spurting from the wound, but it was less of a gush and more of a squirt. Soon, it would be a trickle.

Steel smiled and turned back to Lockwood. 'I'll ask one more time again.'

'Fuck you, pal,' Lockwood spat.

Steel nodded, then looked around the camp for something.

Lockwood stared in confusion. What was he looking for? Then his expression soured as he saw Steel pick up some paracord.

Steel took the thin, strong army rope, which was a little bit thicker than regular string but very strong. It was used by most of the world's armed forces for lashing things together, holding up bashers, or tying assholes to trees.

Lockwood could see what was coming and tried to get up, so Steel shot him in his other knee.

Lockwood fell, screaming, unable to move or stop what was about to happen.

'I hear you people like to shoot innocent people, then watch animals rip them to pieces?' Steel whispered in Lockwood's ear before dragging the man over to the tree and tying him to it—first with his arms behind it and securing them, then his waist. Steel knew this man had possibly been special forces of some kind, so just binding his hands might not be enough. To ensure there was no movement, he broke his arms at the elbows.

It was possibly over the top, but then, these people had tortured two innocent men and fed them to the bears while they were still alive, which, to Steel, denied them any sympathy.

Happy that Lockwood was secure, he began to walk back to their camp, hoping to find anything the survivors could use, such as sleeping bags, ponchos, ready-to-eat meals, or MREs. He gathered what he could.

All the while, Lockwood stared on, confused. Why had the man stopped asking questions? He had only asked him twice. Had he expected more of an interrogation?

Then it dawned on him. The three idiots gathering wood, the sentry, Marco! He had already interrogated them; he was just a loose end, someone to confirm what they had said.

He knew then that, because he was the only one alive, this was not going to end well.

'Hey, pal, look, we had nothin' tae do with them poor bastards. It was all Sven—it was him.' Lockwood's voice was filled with fear. Not so much fear of dying—he had been close to death so many times he didn't feel it anymore—but how he was about to die was what terrified him: being torn apart, eaten alive.

Steel gathered what he could, stuffing it into one of the men's backpacks, and walked over to Lockwood. He gazed around and saw the tablet on the ground. He had seen Sven holding the same sort of device. He placed down the pack and picked up the device. He turned it on. There was a flicker, and then a map appeared with several red dots. Then he understood what it was—this showed all the locations of the other teams.

Lockwood smiled. 'Ta very much.'

Steel's gaze switched between the tablet and Lockwood. The tablet wasn't just a locator; it was also a beacon. Once it was opened, it showed the location of that team, and Steel figured the men were only meant to open it at certain times.

That way, if it was switched on, it was as good as a cry for assistance.

Steel looked around for a radio. If he were correct, there would be a call from this Sven. He needed to answer it—if not, the cavalry wouldn't be far behind. No matter—either way, he would be long gone.

A noise from a distance made Steel smile, and Lockwood pissed himself. 'I guess the dinner guests are here,' Steel said before grabbing the pack and running.

As Steel put as much distance as possible between himself and Lockwood, he knew he had to keep going. He had to put more of a gap between himself and the bears. He wasn't bleeding, but he had left a scent; he just hoped the two men would be more than enough to satisfy them.

When he reached a small river, he heard a scream. He shivered. Had he gone too far? Then he thought about the survivors. Would these men be merciful?

They had already shown what they could do, and there were women in the group. Who was to say these bastards wouldn't have fun first? They weren't soldiers anymore. There was no code of conduct, and there was no Geneva Convention.

Steel pulled the pack's shoulder straps tight on his shoulders and ran. He needed to get to Sherman and the group. These men were not rescue teams; they were hired killers, and they wanted something—or someone.

The question was—who and what?

CHAPTER TWENTY-EIGHT

STEEL HAD PICKED UP THE TRAIL AND WAS AT THE forest's edge. The bright full moon had forced him to remove the night-vision goggles. The air was fresh and carried a slight easterly wind. Above, a trillion stars hung in a cloudless sky. He looked up, took in the view, and sighed. The wind broke the silence in the trees behind him, and the sound of the high grass being brushed by the breeze filled the air.

He thought back to the mercenaries' camp, the men he had killed to prevent them from getting to the survivors. They hadn't died honourably, not like soldiers. But then, they gave up that right when they decided to hunt down innocent people for cash.

Steel checked his compass to get the bearing he had taken before he said farewell to Sherman. He picked up the point, looked up at the stars, and searched for a constellation he could follow. He saw the almost W shape of Cassiopeia; the stars making up the constellation seemed to stand out more than the others, almost as if they were calling out to him. The moon was bright, like a nighttime sun.

Steel could see the landscape as if it were midday, not midnight. This forced him to stick to the tree line rather than march straight to the other forest. If he could see well enough, then so could someone else.

Steel didn't know where the other teams were, only that they were close.

He hoped the big guy would contact the other teams and inform them that the Delta team was in trouble. He would make them aware of the situation and tell them to carry on while he checked it out. That was what Steel would do—no need to compromise the mission.

Steel knew he had to cause a little more damage. He smiled at the thought of messing with these assholes and making them take each other out. As he neared the corner of the wood line, Steel stopped and crouched. Across a clearing was the second area of the forest, which had curved around, making it appear as two separate wood lines. This was where the survivors would be camped out.

On either side of him was an extensive tree line, and to his front were roaming meadows of knee-high grass beneath the enormous, bright moon. It was one of those moments when people wished they had a camera, but Steel was happy with the 9mm Glock 17 he'd taken from the guard.

Steel knew he had to follow the wood line as much as possible. The moon's brightness would make him stand out as if being struck by a searchlight.

He moved as quickly as he could without causing too much noise. The other team would be close by, possibly on the other side of the wooded area. He had to get to the survivors and lead them away from their campsite.

He needed to thin the mercenaries' numbers. From what he had seen, there had been five teams—now four—but that was still too many for him to take on at once.

Steel had quickly rechecked the tablet while he was near Lockwood's location. If the red blip signalled on the other tablets, they would see it hadn't moved. He made note of the locations; luckily, above the blip was a letter: A, B, C, D, E. Now he knew where everyone was. Steel planned to move through the forest and take the Echo team out. He also needed to take all the teams out while they were a good distance from the survivors.

If things went wrong and there was shooting, any stray rounds would be a problem, especially with hysterical people around. He had seen people run into gunfire because they had been frightened to death. When fear takes control, all rational thought goes to hell. No. Getting them to a safe area and then going back for the mercenaries was the best option.

The safer they were, the better. No one to get in the way, no one to make a noise when they shouldn't, and more critically, nobody that could be used as a bargaining chip.

Steel followed the darkened cover as he made his way around, the hatchet gripped loosely in his right hand. He knew that seizing it too tight for too long would give him cramps and reduce his grip strength.

He'd had it before when he was in the army; holding the pistol grip of his rifle too tightly had made his hand hurt at the joints, and he spent most of the patrol shaking his hand off to get the blood flowing. He smiled at the memory of those days when things were simple, back when his family was still alive.

CHAPTER TWENTY-NINE

Somewhere in New York State, a blacked-out Rolls-Royce Silver Spirit cruised at eighty miles an hour down the country lanes. The headlamps cut through the darkness, revealing the avenue of trees and a lonely country road. It was a good hour's drive to the airfield where the private jet was waiting.

The Chairman sat comfortably in the back of the grand vehicle, sipping his glass of champagne. Although not everything was going according to plan, he was confident that Mr Jones would make it come together—he always did.

The Chairman was on his way to Washington to ensure progress. The plan would have to be scrapped if they could not retrieve the package. That would mean a lot of planning and money had been wasted for nothing, and that was not an option.

As far as he could see, they had considered every eventuality. Every variable had been planned for. As far as he was concerned, nothing could get in their way.

However, he felt uneasy. Something had gone wrong; the plane had crashed and had not landed at Ridgeway Creek. He knew the pilot they had paid off to make the detour was not a young man, but he had never envisaged him having a heart attack or something.

Regardless, it had happened, and they were dealing with it —or rather, Mr Jones was. He had every confidence in Mr Jones, despite the fuck-up at Lord Steel's estate. He had read the report, and it had been down to one overzealous individual, who had been dealt with.

In truth, the entire incident had put a face on SANTINI that they didn't need. It should have been just a lot of men with guns scaring the crap out of Steel and his guests; the plan was to make it look like the Albanian or Russian mobs that were striving to take control in Europe. Unfortunately, that had not gone to plan, and when the shooting started, there was only one other course of action: kill them all, then frame the mob.

However, John Steel had come home early. He had taken out a number of the mercenaries, but he had been cornered in an attic and then shot six times.

For all intents and purposes, he was dead. Then he heard the news that John Steel had survived and was under police protection somewhere while he recovered. The reports made him out to be in bad shape but alive.

Good news for the Steel family's company shareholders: while at least one of them survived, the company didn't have to be sold off or broken up. Also, with the young soldier in such bad condition, there was no fear of him going after them. That was, of course, if he could find out who they were. For most of the world's governments and investigation bureaus, SANTINI didn't exist.

The Chairman gazed out of the window. The world

blurred past them as they travelled. He took another sip from the champagne and smiled. Soon, it would all come together, and they would have the arms deal in the bag.

CHAPTER THIRTY

JOHN STEEL STOPPED AT THE POINT STRAIGHT ACROSS from where he had broken cover before. He figured that the survivors would have gone direct. Why shouldn't they? As far as they were concerned, the only people looking for them were a rescue team, not a group of mercenaries. He moved into the dark forest and put on the NVGs. The image was bright and clear, good enough to manoeuvre the terrain and also pick up the trail the group had made.

He was looking for a campfire, which the night-vision goggles would pick up as a bright, glaring light. He knew they would have one, possibly more, to ward off any beast more than anything.

Sherman wouldn't stop them; what would his reasons be? Telling them Steel's theory would cause a panic—something they didn't need right now.

Steel made his way through the knee-high bracken and over several fallen trees. The ground was uneven and had thick moss patches that covered the fallen trees and underfoot. The smell of deadwood, wet vegetation, and animal scent filled his nostrils.

He felt alive and invigorated, like a dead man who had risen from the ashes. Steel remembered the old gardener from his family's estate. After the shooting, the man had found Steel and cared for him, nursing him back to health.

He smiled as he made his way through the forest at the thought of the old man. He had known him for years growing up, and yet, in the end, he had never truly known him. Steel found out later that the old man had worked with his father during the Cold War. His father had been MI6, and the old man had been in the Japanese secret service.

Both men had fought for the same cause but on different sides that didn't trust each other. The old man had been captured and held in an interrogation prison in Poland in '74. In '76, he was saved by agents of British intelligence who were there to extract a defecting Russian scientist who had been captured, and they were breaking him out. They could have left the Japanese agent behind, but Steel's father had known it was the right thing to do.

The old man had been certified MIA by his government, so Steel's father had employed him as his gardener. He had changed his name, and Steel's father had got his family out of Japan. And so it was for eighteen years until that day—the day everything changed—the day the old John Steel died and the new one was born.

Steel touched the area on his left shoulder where the exit wound lay under a layer of clothing. He shook off his feelings and moved on. He had a job to do and questions to ask. Something was going on, and he wanted to know what.

'I can't believe he left us,' Natalie said as she sat on an old tree stump, nursing her sore ankles.

'I was surprised he stuck around after all the shit you were giving him,' Karen said with a bitter tone.

Sherman smiled to himself. He knew that the stranger hadn't left them. If anything, he was watching over them from a distance. He knew men like that—the overwatch teams. You couldn't see them, but you knew they were there.

'So what's the plan now?' Bob asked before taking a small bite from the wolf jerky.

'We stay here for the night; at first light, we head for the other side of this lake. The map shows there are some houses or something. We can seek shelter there, see if there are provisions, maybe a radio to call for help,' Sherman said, stoking the fire with a long stick.

'What if the map is wrong? What if there aren't any cabins or a radio?' Natalie barked.

'You know something, Natalie?' Karen asked.

'No, what?'

'I'm thrilled you're here to lift our spirits with your positive way of thinking,' Karen said with a bitter tone, causing everyone to snigger.

Natalie just sat in silence and sipped her water.

'What if Nat is right? What if there isn't anything there?' Bob asked, a panic suddenly coming over him.

'This map belonged to the pilot. The cabins and a red tick are marked on the spot where the lake is. Do you think he would do this if there were nothing there?' Sherman explained, hoping to calm everyone.

All the while, he was hoping that what he was telling them was correct. There was an unpleasant silence as everyone sat and stared at the fire's orange glow.

'God, I wish we had some beer and marshmallows right now,' laughed Karen.

'Twenty-ounce steak and a bottle of Jack,' Bob said, joining in; he began drooling at the thought of it.

'Fish and chips from Whitby and a pint of local ale,' a voice from the shadows said.

They all turned around to see the stranger who had appeared from the darkness.

'You came back,' Claire said with a broad smile.

'I had things to take care of,' he said sombrely. 'Here, sort through these, but it has to last us,' Steel said, tossing down the backpack he had taken from Lockwood's camp.

The group tore open the packs like children at Christmas, excited at what they might find.

Steel walked over to Karen and carefully lifted her leg.

'How's the ankle?' he asked, producing a bandage from his jacket pocket.

'Still sore, but manageable,' she replied, wincing slightly as he took her boot off.

Steel began to wrap the bandage around her slender ankle, tight enough to support the injured limb. He took out a cold pack and pressed the middle of the white packet. There was a crunching sound as he activated the chemicals inside.

'Put this on it for a while; it should take down the swelling,' he said, passing the small package over.

She smiled and nodded a thank you.

He returned the gesture, turned and headed over to Sherman, who was still sitting on a rock tending the fire.

'Did you find them?' Sherman asked, not looking up as Steel sat down beside him.

'Yes.'

'Take it they weren't a rescue team, then?' Sherman said, glancing over at the backpacks and scattered contents on the floor.

'Not really.' Steel smiled at Sherman's apparent small talk.

'Did you get them all?'

'Let three rabbits go; the boss man is chasing them down now,' Steel said before taking a sip from his water bottle.

'Made it look like they did it, nice touch; he's gonna be pissed when he finds out otherwise,' Sherman said with a slight laugh.

'We have other problems,' Steel said in a low voice so the others couldn't hear.

'More than one team?'

'Possibly four; the boss had an electronic tablet showing location markers,' Steel explained.

Sherman read something in Steel's cold expression—an evil smirk, as if he was enjoying the chase.

'There's another group nearby; I'm going to see if I can... persuade them to leave,' Steel said coldly.

'What the hell happened to you, son? Why are you out here?' Sherman asked, not knowing whether to worry about the group or the people chasing them.

'I died,' Steel said, standing up and moving towards the shadows.

'Where the hell is he going now?' Natalie said, ripping open a packet containing a giant cookie from the MRE meals.

'Hunting,' Sherman replied with a shiver.

CHAPTER THIRTY-ONE

THE ECHO TEAM WAS TO THE EAST OF WHERE HE HAD taken out Lockwood's men. From what Steel could gather from looking at the tablet, Alpha was the central command group and was staying at Ridgeway Creek; he had taken out Delta, and Bravo was still on the move and heading east. He figured Sven was Charlie Team, which left Echo.

Steel knew he had to take out as many of these teams as possible; there was no point in risking them all coming together at some point, especially when he and the survivors were cornered somewhere.

He hoped Echo was of the same standard as Lockwood's team, but something told him he would be disappointed. There was no way that the organisation that had sent them would dispatch five teams of mercenaries that wouldn't get the job done. He could live with the thought that Lockwood's team were just cannon fodder—the people you sent forward to test the water without any regard for what might happen to them. Better seven idiots than seven good men.

Steel found the Echo Team five miles to the east. They

were set up in good positions, and the sentry was in a tree with a full view of the area. Their bashers were set out in a circle, so they had all-around defence if something happened without the need to leave their bashers.

This was a good team, definitely more competent than Lockwood's team—meaning it was a possible problem. There would be no sneaking up on the sentry or taking out the first guy to go for a piss.

It was going to be difficult but not impossible; he just needed the right plan and a bit of luck.

Luck came in the form of a porcupine. The small, spiky animal had found its way into one of the men's sleeping bags, so as he eased himself into the bag, he yelped in surprise and shot the sleeping bag several times. The others rushed to see what the commotion was and found the man aiming his Glock at the sleeping bag. The men looked at him with puzzlement, then at the bag.

'What the hell are you doin', Dicks?' asked Finch.

Dicks, who was a tall, broad-shouldered man with no hair on his head but the rest of his body covered, pointed at the smouldering sleeping bag. 'There was something in there, a bear, I think,' he explained. His voice was high-pitched, with a Bronx accent.

As the others watched, the bag began to move. They all raised their weapons and aimed, ready to take on the ferocious beast.

The head appeared first, its nose sniffing at the air, then the rest of it waddled out, unnerved by what had happened. The others laughed loudly at Dicks, who was not amused, least of all because he had no sleeping bag for the rest of the mission.

'Hey, Dicks, looks like your date just left,' laughed one man.

'Yeah, it saw how tiny his dick was and went to find somethin' bigger,' laughed another.

'OK, boys, fun's over. Get back to what you were doin'—but not you, Dicks; I need my sleeping bag,' mocked Finch as he reholstered his pistol.

'Yeah, yeah, fuck all of you,' Dicks groaned, kicking what was left of his sleeping bag.

As Finch turned, blood splattered across his face. Stunned at first, he gazed around. He watched as the two men who had walked in front of him were cut down; another to his far right was suddenly hurled backwards, a large knife sticking out of his right eye. Then his army lizard brain kicked in, and everything cleared. He reached for his pistol but was pushed backwards; something had hit him in the chest. He half expected to see a large gaping hole but found a muddy boot print.

As he lay on the ground, he watched as a wild man in a long brown coat cut down his men with little more than a knife and a hatchet. Finch drew his pistol and heaved himself up, only to have something slammed against his head. The world began spinning, and he fired indiscriminately. Then—blackness.

When Finch opened his eyes again, he stared at the carnage—bodies strewn everywhere, and the sentry hung limply from the tree. He gazed around; his head was still hurting, and he had trouble focusing correctly. Then he stopped and stared in horror. The man in the brown coat sat there—a big man with dark hair, a beard, and glacier sunglasses.

'Who the fuck are you?' Finch asked, his voice full of anger and fear.

'Just a man who wants to be left alone, but you people are messing with that,' Steel said softly.

Finch looked at him, puzzled. 'You're British? What the hell are you doing out here?'

'Like I said, a man who wants to be left alone. Now, the question is, what are you doing here?' Steel was sitting on one of the packs he had taken from Finch's camp. He had already gone through the camp and gathered four more, each holding enough provisions for the survivors. They were going to need them more than the mercenaries now.

'Fuck you!' Finch yelled defiantly.

Steel remained seated, not saying anything, just staring over at Finch, the bloody hatchet and knife still in his hands.

Finch began to squirm; Steel's actions were beginning to unnerve him. 'I'm saying nothing,' he exclaimed.

Steel remained still and silent.

'Look, dickhead, I was in the SAS for five years, so you don't scare me.'

Steel frowned, his first action in what seemed like hours. 'What were you in—22, 23, or 21?' Steel asked coldly.

'What?'

'It's a simple question: what were you in? 21, 22, or 23? And when were you there?'

'22, and I was there up until two years ago. Why?' Finch asked nervously.

Steel leaned forward, his nose almost touching Finch's. 'Because, dickhead, up until last year, I was there for five years, and I've never seen your ugly bastard face ever.'

Steel never waited for a reply; he just forced the blade upward through the bottom of Finch's skull and, with an upward thrust, drove the blade into the man's brain, twisted it once, and then ripped the blade out.

As blood gushed down Finch's vest and jacket, Steel became enraged at himself for killing him before he had any information, but after Finch had lied and insulted Steel's regiment, he lost it.

Steel looked down at the remains of Finch and the others and began to wonder what he was becoming. He hadn't just killed these men but butchered them. Had being in this wilderness actually made him feral? He slumped down onto the ground and looked at his bloodied hands. Whatever he had been—a soldier, a husband, the son of an earl—all of these things seemed lost to him now. He was tracking men down and killing them—for what?

He started to wonder if it was too late. Had he become some kind of wild man, a wilderness animal? Before, in the army, he had a cause, a mission—but what was his here? Saving a bunch of ungrateful survivors from a bunch of mercenaries?

However, one thought did click. This Alpha Team was still in Ridgeway Creek; would there be a bloodbath if the survivors ever made it there? The sheriff was a good soul but no match for a bunch of highly trained soldiers. And let's face it—if you are the leader of a platoon of mercenaries, you are going to keep the best with you.

Perhaps he was overthinking this. These men were here for someone and something. Maybe when this person identified themselves, the rest of the group and the town would be out of harm's way.

Maybe. But he doubted it.

Steel picked up the packs and made his way into the forest; he needed to get back to the group of survivors. He had started on this path and had to see it through. Besides, there were a few people in the group he could tolerate.

Steel made his way away from the camp, hoping to find a small stream. He needed to wash up before returning to the group—not just because it looked bad, but because there were hungry beasts out there that could smell blood from great distances. At the moment, he was as good as a marinated steak.

CHAPTER THIRTY-TWO

THE FOLLOWING DAY SAW AN EARLY SUNRISE AND A strange mist that clung to the ground, covering the forest floor in what looked like a blanket of cotton wool.

Karen was the first to wake. Sherman was awake but hadn't really slept. He'd stayed up to tend to the fires and wait for the strangers to return, but Steel never returned.

Sherman had feared the worst at first, but then there was something about the man. Something was not right, as though the man had faced death and laughed it off. It was almost as if Heaven and Hell didn't want the guy.

Karen didn't speak; she just waved hello, not wanting to disturb the others.

Sherman waved back and gave a quick smile. The treetops masked the sun's brightness, allowing only shards of light through the gaps in the canopy. Inside the forest, it was like an early morning in winter, with a grey-blue haze everywhere.

Karen was sick of the forest, sick of the outdoors. She looked over at the sleeping group before her and then at Sherman. She hadn't had time to think before or for anything to set in. Then it dawned on her. Something was very wrong. Karen looked around again, this time feeling fear and helplessness.

Sherman looked over and spotted her. Her expression told him that she had figured something out. He stood up and walked over to her, carrying a cup of coffee he had made from the ration packs and the metal mug he had found in one of the backpacks.

'Here, drink this,' he said, handing over the brew. 'Careful, the cup is hot,' he warned.

Karen looked up and smiled as she took the cup from him. 'So, how you holding up?' he asked in a low but concerned voice.

'I'm OK, I guess,' she lied.

'But?'

'How did this happen?' she asked.

Sherman shot her a puzzled look. 'The plane crashed,' he replied, almost sounding like he had no idea what she was talking about.

'No, I mean, how did all this happen? Yes, the plane crashed, but I saw the map; we were going in the wrong direction to the airport. And who the hell is this stranger who keeps tipping up to rescue us?' she said, trying not to raise her voice. 'Something is going on; I can feel it.' She took another sip from the coffee and looked around at the group who were still sleeping.

'Sounds like this place is getting to you,' Sherman said, trying not to sound unsympathetic.

'Don't you think it's odd that the pilot, who has made this trip for years, gets lost and crashes?'

'So, what's your theory?' Sherman asked, trying to humour her.

'I think the pilot went off course on purpose. Sure, the crash was an accident, but he was trying to take us somewhere,' she explained.

'To what end?' Sherman asked curiously.

'That's odd, I was thinking the same thing,' came a familiar voice behind them.

They turned to see Steel standing there with more back-packs, but he looked like hell this time. His clothes were dirtier than usual; he had slash marks on his thick coat. He had scratches and dried blood on his face and hands.

'Dear God,' Karen spoke, her hands cupping her mouth.

'Not quite,' Steel laughed, tossing down the packs, which contained some handguns and ammunition, along with more rations and medical supplies. In one of the bags was a multi-fuel camping stove with a lock-together pan and pot set.

'Where do you keep getting this stuff?' Karen asked, almost afraid to actually know the truth.

Sherman shot Steel a look and said they had *to talk*.

'Everyone up, now,' Steel yelled loudly.

Sherman looked at him with surprise. 'What's up? What's wrong?' he asked, suddenly feeling this stranger had had enough of the games he had been drawn into.

'What's going on?' asked Karen.

'What time is it?' Bob said, struggling to find his watch.

'What's for breakfast?' moaned Natalie.

'We need to move. Now,' boomed Steel. His voice was angry and tired.

'What happened last night?' Sherman asked in a low voice, hoping to keep the truth from the group.

'Another team. I got something from them this time,' Steel said, pulling out a small tablet and tucking it back away in his jacket.

'What's going on?' Bob asked, standing up straight in an authoritative stance. 'We demand to know.'

Steel turned to Bob, and his stony expression made Bob nervous, causing him to fidget.

'Well, Bob, people are looking for you,' Steel said, making everyone let out a chorus of *Woohoo*. 'However, these are not good people or rescue teams; they are here to abduct you or kill you. Why? I do not know,' Steel explained.

'And how do you know all this?' Natalie barked with distrust. 'They could be rescue teams, and you could be the abductor.' Her words made everyone nod and jeer.

'Because rescue teams don't bring automatic weapons and explosives. They don't wear tactical gear, and most of all, they don't bring handcuffs and bags for the heads,' Steel said, tossing the items down onto the ground. The stainless steel of the cuffs glinted in what little sun there was. 'However, if you think I'm the bad guy, you can go on your way; you have the map and a compass. I wish you luck,' Steel said before turning and walking away.

Sherman grabbed Steel's arm to stop him.

Steel looked down at Sherman's hand and the tight grip he had on him.

'You can't go; we need you,' Sherman said, hoping to use some guilt or appeal to his ego.

But as far as Steel was concerned, he had gotten them to safety.

'Not my fight,' Steel said, his voice hollow.

Sherman looked at Steel and saw no emotion. There was nothing to appeal to. This man was either running from something or was dead inside—possibly a little of both.

'Will you help us, please?' Claire asked, her large blue eyes sparkling with emotion.

Steel paused for a moment, then reached out to touch her face.

'Ah, let the loser leave; he's been no help so far,' barked Natalie as she searched one of the ready-to-eat packs for a breakfast menu.

Steel snatched his hand back, and the cold expression crossed his face again. He said nothing as he turned and left, disappearing back into the wild.

CHAPTER THIRTY-THREE

SHERMAN GATHERED A GROUP AND GAVE THEM EACH A backpack. They had split everything, so there was an equal amount of rations, water, medical supplies, and ammunition in each of the six packs. The group was quiet, and tension hung in the air. Everyone was pissed at Natalie, most of all Sherman, who had an idea of what the stranger had been through to get them this far. But he also knew the man wouldn't be far behind. He would keep to the shadows and do what was necessary until the group was safe. This alone gave Sherman some comfort.

'OK, so we need to head north,' Sherman said, pointing in the direction the compass hand was leading them. 'When we get to the lake, we need to follow it round by the easterly route or take the right-hand path,' Sherman explained as blank faces stared back at him. 'Now, it is apparent there are people after us, so do as I say. If I say stop, you stop; if I say hide, you'd better damned well hide. We have supplies and a place to go. Any questions?' he said, looking around.

'Yeah, just one,' asked Natalie.

'What is it?'

'Who put you in charge?' she said, putting her hands on her hips and standing tall.

'I'm the eldest, have more experience, and know when to keep my mouth shut,' Sherman growled. He hated himself for wishing she hadn't survived the crash. Of all the people who had survived, it had to be her.

'Nat, are you here just to cause problems, or what?' Claire said with a scowl.

'No, I'm just wondering whom to blame when this goes tits-up. This whole trip has been one cluster after another.'

'Yeah, I'm sure the pilot meant to crash, kill himself, and leave us all stranded,' Bob said, shaking his head at her selfish stupidity.

Sherman pulled on the backpack Steel had given him and fastened the straps.

'Right, if that is all out of the way, let's go,' he instructed the group as he led the way. Natalie and Bob hung back, keeping a safe distance from the rest of the group.

CHAPTER THIRTY-FOUR

SVEN WALKED AND STOPPED BEFORE THE SECOND GROUP'S campsite. The fires were still smouldering. Beasts had ripped apart the bashers after the fresh meat. All of the second team were dead. Some had been slashed, and others attacked by animals.

As he looked around, he couldn't help but notice the similarities to what had taken place at Lockwood's site.

Then he noticed the missing backpacks—three of them— and also the lack of ammunition for the pistols and assault rifles. Enough for three people; the rest had been left.

Sven could feel his blood beginning to boil. Someone was killing his brothers. He looked around, checking bodies and the shredded tents. He stood up straight and roared in contempt.

'Search the camp; I want to know how many attacked this camp. I want to know what we are dealing with,' Sven ordered.

George nodded. The Indian was a damned good tracker; if anyone could find anything, he could. Sven had always been fascinated by how the man could see some footprints and create a story of what had occurred—even to the point of what the person who had created the prints looked like. It was almost scary but very useful. Especially now. They needed to know if they were up against five or ten men.

As the rest of Sven's team searched the camp, George got to work. He moved about, twisting and spinning, his arms swaying as though performing a dance.

The rest of the men stopped and watched. Sven couldn't blame them; it was strangely hypnotic. Finally, George knelt where Steel had sat. He touched the ground, took some dirt, and sniffed it. His eyes narrowed.

'OK, George,' asked a tall, dark-haired mercenary. 'How many are we up against?'

George closed his eyes for a second as if he was working something out. 'One man did this, a big man, an angry man. But he isn't native; he is an outsider.'

'Bullshit, there is more than one guy. You've seen what they did to Lockwood, and now here. I'm tellin' you, *it's* more than one guy, a squad at least,' said the tall mercenary.

Sven dismissed the man and turned to George. 'An outsider? What do you mean? How can you tell?'

George remained where he was. 'Because this man, despite how it seems, cut these men with precision. He didn't hack; these knife wounds are precise. I've only known British special forces to use these killing strokes, especially the Marine Commandos or the SAS.'

'What the hell are the SAS doin' out here?' yelled the tall mercenary.

George shook his head. 'No, just one of them. He is angry and well-trained. A very bad combination.'

'Do you think he was part of the group that went down?' Sven asked.

George thought for a moment, then shook his head. 'No, he

doesn't smell like the rest of them—less, dare I say, *perfumy.* The others smell of hotel room soap, but this one doesn't. This man is something different.'

'So, a man who has left the British Army to live in this godforsaken country?' said the tall mercenary.

George scowled at the man, forcing him to swallow hard.

'I mean, the wilderness, not....' The man stopped, feeling he was going to make it worse.

'Options?' Sven asked nobody in particular.

'We track the bastard and kill him,' answered the tall mercenary.

Two others nodded in agreement; three others said he was nuts, and George didn't answer at first. He continued to check the spot where Steel had sat.

'Well, George?' asked Sven.

George looked up at Sven and shook his head. 'This man has questions. He is looking for something—answers to many questions.'

'What questions?' asked one of the mercenaries.

'Simple. What are we doing here, and why are we tracking the survivors?'

Sven stared at his friend. He had learned to trust his judgement, but it didn't stop him from asking questions. 'How do you know?'

George pointed towards Finch's body. 'Finch is sitting against a tree; he hasn't been killed like the others. I think our new friend questioned him, just like I think Lockwood was questioned.'

'Shit, that means he knows about the package,' said another one of the mercenaries.

'Who is to say he didn't already? Perhaps he got that from the three we never found. Doesn't he know about the package, but does he know about the asset? I think that is more important,' George replied, heaving his bulk off the ground. 'As to what should we do? Nothing. We continue as normal. At some point, we will meet up with our friend; there is no point rushing into the arms of death. But I suggest we change course and head for the lake. Leave these people to wear themselves out. The best time to corner them is when hope is lost.'

Sven nodded in agreement. It seemed like a good plan. If they were lucky, they would be at the lake where the Bravo team should already be waiting. At least the group would have two teams to contend with, not one. However, changing course would add a couple of days to the journey, meaning they would get there after the survivors. It wasn't ideal, but it would catch them off guard.

Sven got on the radio and informed Mr Jones of the situation and what they were about to do. Reluctantly, he agreed. There was no point losing another team to this wild man. These men didn't know the land; the stranger did, and he had the advantage. All they could hope to do was outflank the group.

After Sven had finished talking, he put the radio back into his pack and told everyone to get ready to move out. George was busy studying the map and plotting the best route. They would come in from the west. That way, they would be pushing the group east, where the nearest town or settlement was nearly a hundred miles away, whereas to the west was Ridgeway Creek. The last thing they wanted was for the survivors to make it to the town, regardless of whether Mr Jones was there or not.

The town had a sheriff, a railway station, even a small airfield. There were plenty of ways the group could make it back to Talkeetna and then back to Washington or New York.

They needed the group tired and hungry; otherwise, it

might start breeding animosity, fear, and even rebellion. Scared people were easier to manipulate and catch off guard.

George showed the team the route they would take. They would have to cross a few streams, which meant freezing water. The team readied themselves and started walking west—it was time to go hunting.

CHAPTER THIRTY-FIVE

STEEL SAT HIGH IN ONE OF THE TREES. HE HAD A
fantastic view of the ground below, and shards of sunlight
warmed his skin. He had watched the group. Sherman had
taken control quite nicely; shooting down Natalie was particu-
larly delicious to watch. She was trouble, that was for sure, but
he wasn't sure why. Was it some rebellious streak? But she was
in her twenties, not some spoilt teenager. Possibly just a spoilt
brat who had no idea what was going on or just some bitch who
liked to cause bother. Either way, she could create a lot of
unwanted problems.

Steel checked the tablet and the location of the others. He
knew he would have to keep turning it off just in case Sven
used it to track him like he was tracking the others. There was
another group north of the cabins at Twentymile Lake.

It was a possible threat, but Steel knew he had to cause
problems elsewhere, hoping to lead the others away.

It was early morning, and the others wouldn't be making
camp until the last light. What he needed was another disrup-
tion. Steel checked the location of the closest team in the south.

There was one just east of another lake. They would be there to ensure the survivors didn't go there. *Cover your bases*, Steel thought. He needed to make a diversion, but it wouldn't be quiet this time.

The survivors were in good hands. Sherman would see them to the next step; all Steel had to do was ensure they made it back to civilisation in one piece. To do that, he had to minimise the threat. He knew he couldn't take any more of the teams out. The big man would call for reinforcements, making things a thousand times more difficult. No, all he had to do was a spot of misdirection.

He had checked the tablet he had discovered at Finch's location and found that there had been two teams to the west and three to the south. Now, there was one north and two south.

He then turned off Finch's tablet, smashed it, and tossed it into the forest. He had no use for two tablets; besides, once they found Finch's camp, they would know it hadn't been Finch who had turned it on, and they already knew that Steel had the tablet from Lockwood.

Steel needed answers, and he also needed to make the other teams change tactics. An obvious one would be for the big man's team to make a course change; the question was, in which direction? It did not matter for now; the point was to put some distance between the survivors and the mercenaries.

CHAPTER THIRTY-SIX

Steel returned the way he came, heading north to Twentymile Lake. He had caused enough trouble for the time being. The other two teams would either sit and wait for the next attack or figure the three were moving south towards the nearest town to hitch a ride out of there. He hoped the big man wasn't thinking straight and just wanted revenge, that he would forget about the survivors for a while—long enough for Steel to find them a ride. Steel had left the team to the north alone. The boss would have to call in reserves if they weren't there. Leaving them there gave the big man a false sense of security.

Steel returned to the survivors at the same pace he had gotten there—swift but steady. He had been surprised to see the bears at the lake but used them to his advantage. It was nearly winter, and the beasts would be stocking up on that winter fat, eating what they could. It seemed reasonable to figure that once they smelt blood, that would be the signal to feed. Steel had to be honest; his original plan sucked—it may not have worked without the bears. But he knew that was the last time. The last thing he needed was to bring more of the beasts to their location. That would make his and the survivors' situation worse.

Steel wanted to check the tablet but fought the urge. The chances were high that the big guy was checking to see if his men were still alive and in position. Steel knew that if he went online, he would give up his location and endanger the group. No, he had to leave it alone for the meantime, to be sure. His only concern was finding a means to get the people back to the town.

CHAPTER THIRTY-SEVEN

THE PRIVATE JET CARRYING THE CHAIRMAN HAD LANDED earlier that morning. Now, he was sitting in a blacked-out Mercedes limousine heading for the capital. The flight had given him time to review paperwork and enjoy a fine brandy. His business meeting wasn't until later, so he had time to get to the hotel and possibly rest for a while. Even though he was in his early sixties, he was a picture of health, but a quiet twenty minutes of shut-eye never hurt anyone.

As he travelled in the luxury vehicle, he flicked through *The London Times*; the front page was still full of the shooting at the mansion of Lord Steel.

The chairman's face contorted as he read about the massacre. He had given orders for the family not to be harmed or taken alive. How did it go so wrong? He had read Mr Jones's report, and only one man was to blame. He had been sent out of the country long before they could figure out what to do with him. Besides being a complete psychopath, he was good at his job, and talent like that should be used in the correct locations. It was a bad judgement call to have sent him to the

Steel residence. One mistake the chairman would never make again.

And the fact that an essential piece of the game had been taken off the board still made him snarl—the daughter of an American senator.

The one person who could have made this operation move more smoothly, but now they had to improvise. The shooting of John Steel made another plan fall through. But then, he wasn't meant to be there for another week. *Greater laid plans of mice and men*, he thought. However, this new plan was seeing setbacks as well. He couldn't help but feel that someone from the inside was sabotaging their operations.

The only thing that mattered was to get that package from the survivors; then, they would have control of the Staff Secretary. They needed that vote to go through. They required FOUNDATION TECH to win the bid. They had millions riding on it. The only problem was that they had no idea what the package was. The computer analyst who had discovered the information, which was damning to the Staff Secretary, had been aboard the aircraft that had crashed.

The chairman had to admit it was a great leap of faith on their part, but the window of opportunity had been small.

For some time, there had been rumours that the Staff Secretary was hiding something. The organisation assumed this was the very thing they were after. The new guy, Mr Williams, had been unconvinced. In fact, he said it was like trying to catch a unicorn to find the truth about Area 51—one didn't exist, and the other was possibly a lie to hide something else. The chairman read on through the article.

His eyes widened at the onc sentence explaining how a secret third party would manage the estate and the family business for the time being. The board would run it, but the mysterious third person would have the final say.

He found it interesting but paid it no heed. Thomas Steel and his band of do-gooders were gone. But John Steel had survived and was now in hiding. The rest of the Steel family was gone, meaning the organisation could work without hindrance.

The man turned to the financial page and studied the information. He smiled at the prediction of how well one of the stocks was doing. Soon, that would change.

CHAPTER THIRTY-EIGHT

It was around two in the afternoon by the time Steel had reached the outskirts of the woods. Before him lay a clear line of sight to the cabins at Twentymile Lake. He knew Sherman wouldn't go straight in. He would stay in the woodline and try to circle the area to see if anything was amiss.

There wasn't much there, just a large cabin the size of a small bungalow, a barn, a boathouse, and a runway. The runway was really a field that the old man mowed to keep the grass short enough. Steel figured the old man usually kept his plane in the large barn in the winter.

He was a jolly old man called Jet Parker and lived there with his wife, Molly. Both were in their sixties and, by all accounts, fit. They put it down to healthy eating and fresh air. Jet put it down to the moonshine he was brewing in a small shed. He had met the couple several times, mostly back in Ridgeway Creek when they were getting provisions and sharing a few cups of coffee together at the local café.

Steel looked up at the afternoon sun and smiled as he felt the warm rays against his skin. He had spent too long in the shadows, possibly in more ways than one. He took the electronic tablet from his pocket and tapped the device on the side with his index finger. His gut told him it was too soon to check. Steel nodded to himself and tucked the equipment away. *Always go with your gut, and you can't go wrong,* his father used to tell him. This advice had saved his arse more than once. He dug into a rucksack he had quickly grabbed from the guy in the foxhole, hoping to find anything useful.

He smiled as he pulled out a pair of laser rangefinder binoculars—a decent pair at that, not some cheap wannabe set. He laid down the binos and began to empty the backpack—a silver hip flask with a carved emblem on the front and a twenty-year-old Scotch.

Steel noted the distinctive eagle on the world with the anchor tucked behind it. The guy had been a Marine. Given his young age and the fact he was with these psychos, Steel figured the guy hadn't left of his own accord. A full plastic canteen of water and a packet of gum were always useful, as was a torch with a green filter and a couple of spare mags for the rifle he had to leave behind.

Steel groaned at the misfortune but shrugged it off as the rounds were the same calibre as the rifle he had left with Sherman. There were some other items that Steel promised himself he would look over later, but for the time being, he knew he had to get to the survivors.

He moved on a little further before spotting the perfect spot to use the binoculars. The spot was just on the edge of the woodline, behind a fallen tree that he could use as cover. He took out the binoculars and removed the protective end caps. The glass at the objective lens was covered in a mesh to prevent sun flash.

When he was in Bosnia, Steel remembered using a pair of

women's stockings to do the same on the scope of his sniper rifle.

Steel scouted the area by looking through the precision devices. Everything appeared normal—quiet, but normal. Then he saw Sherman. The man was walking towards the house with his pistol drawn. Steel looked around, but the edge of the house blocked his view. He figured Sherman had seen someone and was going to make contact. He cursed his lousy positioning and decided to head further around.

Steel stopped again and took another look. There was definitely someone there, but he couldn't get a clear look. Grabbing the binos in one hand, he made his way around, using the woods as cover. He had that bad feeling again. *Always trust your gut,* he heard the words in his head, and his gut was telling him something was very wrong.

CHAPTER THIRTY-NINE

SHERMAN HAD SEEN THE MAN FROM THE WOODLINE USING the scope of the Mk14 rifle. He was a well-built man with grey hair and a beard. Sherman had only seen parts of his face, and the man had his back to the group most of the time.

Sherman watched for around ten minutes before deciding it was safe enough to say *hi*, but just in case, he had left Clarke with the rifle with clear instructions. *If the shit hits the fan, fire, kill as many as you can and get the fuck outta there.* In truth, Sherman thought the briefing was informative and to the point, with no grey areas to ponder over. He hated *What if?* questions. He was a *There you go, now just do it* kind of guy.

Sherman sauntered, his hand behind his back with the magnum revolver tight in his grip. Usually, he'd have it tucked between his trousers and the small of his back, but the cold weather suit made that impossible.

Any sign of trouble, and he was going out shooting. However, if the man turned out to be friendly, Sherman would have to distract the man and tuck the weapon away in an inside pocket.

He held a steady pace, his gaze switching from left to right to ensure no sun flashes from rifle scopes from the woodline or the nearby buildings. Sherman could feel his heart thumping in his ears, but his breathing was steady. He was ready for anything.

The man stood in the open doorway of the house as though he was going inside.

'Hi there,' Sherman finally shouted. The man turned around, his expression shocked.

'Howdy, you must be lost or somethin',' the man said, scratching his head with bewilderment.

'Yeah, me and the missus were off to Safri Lake, and I must have taken a wrong turn somewhere,' Sherman lied, hoping to get the correct response.

'Yeah, I'd say that lake is way south from here. What, did you come in a helicopter or something?' laughed the man.

Sherman laughed as he held the weapon high at his back, waiting for the opportune moment to hide it. A sudden noise behind the man made him turn, giving Sherman a split second to tuck the gun away.

'Something like that. Let's just say my wife had the map.' Both men laughed as Sherman stepped forward to shake the man's hand.

'My name is Walter, Walter Monroe,' Sherman lied.

'Jeff, Jeff Parker, and my wife Milly are around somewhere,' said the old guy. 'So, you say you're here with your wife; is anyone else with you?' asked Jeff as he looked around.

'Nah, just me and the missus; she's back at the campsite we made,' Sherman said, his hand going for his side pocket.

'Tell you what, you go and get the others, and we can have supper together,' said the man with a big smile.

'You mean my wife? There are no others, just us,' Sherman said, feeling the man was trying to trip him up.

'Yeah, you know what I mean,' said the man, the smile sliding off his face suddenly as he reached for a gun stashed in his belt.

There was a noise like the crack of thunder, and the man was thrown backwards through the cabin's open door. The bullet hit him square in the chest.

Then there was another shot. This time, a window shattered in the top section of the barn, followed by a hollow thud as something hit the ground inside. Another shot rang out, followed by another. There was a burst of fire from one of the windows, but the shooter was firing wildly, as if hoping to keep the sniper's head down. Then there was another burst from a lower window—then it stopped. Perhaps the shooter was trying to make out that there were more people than the sniper first thought? It wouldn't be the first time that trick had been used.

There were several shots, this time from the survivors, and windows disintegrated as bodies fell.

One man ran from the rear of the house, hoping to flank the shooter, only to be blown sideways with a body shot, his weapon firing blindly as he fell.

Five shots created five fatalities.

'Jesus, this guy is a photographer?' Sherman yelled to himself as he saw body after body drop.

He had run for cover behind the main house, the pistol held up, ready to fire. He had no idea why Clarke had taken the shot or what had tipped him off. However, in the back of his mind, he was sure it hadn't been the reporter who had made those shots. It was more likely that John was back and had saved his arse once again.

Earlier, before the shooting had started, John Steel had returned and pushed Clarke to the side but got him to use the binoculars to spot for him. Where Steel concentrated on one or two targets, Clarke could pick out ones he had not seen. Steel figured it was easier to have a spotter than to try it alone; after all, Sherman's life was at risk if it went wrong.

It would have been possible if it had been a larger area—woodland or a field—but a small, confined space, such as the cabin, barn, or other buildings, meant there was too much cover to try and watch. He needed someone to spot for barrel flashes so he had a point of aim.

Back in the SAS, Steel had been a sniper, but he hadn't been the best; that had been a man known as WHISKEY.

The man had been scarily good. He had held the record for the longest kill shot; unfortunately, it wasn't recorded because it had been a covert mission, but he was happy that a Royal Marine had snatched the record.

Steel and Clarke had made a good team. Clarke's background in war correspondence had given him some insight into what to look for, like the best places for a sniper's nest and where other shooters might try to outflank the group once the shooting had started.

Once it was all finished, Steel turned to Clarke and nodded. 'Good job. Looks like you're in the wrong shooting business.'

'Thanks, but I prefer my telephoto to an assault rifle.'

Steel smiled, then lay down the weapon and took the binoculars from Clarke.

'Is there a problem?' Karen asked, just as she was about to stand and run to the house, thinking it was safe.

'There should be seven, not five; that means there are two still waiting for us to do exactly what you were thinking of doing,' Steel said without looking back towards her. He wasn't some great detective—it had been more intuition. He had heard someone getting up, and it was just a guess that it was Karen because she had asked the question so nervously.

'And you know this how?' Natalie's words hung with suspicion and a touch of hate.

'Because the other teams I encountered had seven men, not five.'

'Encountered?' she asked suspiciously.

'There may have been some interaction, but yes. Look, I've no idea who you think these people are, but they are not here to help or bring you to safety,' Steel argued.

'And you know this how?' she pressed.

'I don't know—automatic weapons and claymore mines might have given something away. Look, if you want to bugger off and see if you have a better chance with these people, be my guest; otherwise, shut the hell up,' he barked and turned back to searching the area with the binoculars.

'Then who are they? What do they want?' Natalie asked sheepishly.

'We could ask them if he would leave someone alive,' Bob shrugged.

'Everyone's a bloody critic,' Steel moaned. These people were twitching his last nerve.

As he looked, something caught his eye—the boatshed. The small structure was optimal for a 360-degree observation post. If the men were anywhere, they would be there.

Steel reloaded the Mk 14 with the bullets he had taken from the backpack. He said nothing as he clicked on the magazine and cocked the weapon.

'I knew you would come back,' Laura said, her voice soft and soothing.

Steel turned towards the group and met their mixed stares.

'Stay here and keep low,' Steel said, pulling on the backpack and leaping over the fallen tree.

They all watched the stranger move in a zigzag formation before joining Sherman at the house.

'Guy's watched too many war movies,' Bob laughed.

'Or been in too many wars,' Clarke noted the stranger's fluid movement and how he handled himself. He had been shocked when the stranger had turned up and grabbed the rifle from his grasp. Clarke hadn't heard Steel approach—almost like he moved like the wind in the trees.

They looked over at Sherman and Steel. These two men seemed alike somehow, knowing each other's movements without a word of command. Their only communication was through hand signals.

Steel and Sherman knew that for perfect cover fire, there would be at least a forty-five-degree arc of a clear line of sight.

The men in the barn and the house had been taken care of; this left either the tree line or the boathouse.

Steel took out the binoculars and crawled as low as he could, using the piles of freshly chopped wood as cover. He searched the tree line first but quickly dismissed it as too far away. The merc would get a shot off for sure, but it would take him fifteen minutes to run over if necessary. Then he turned his attention to the boathouse. He zoomed in and saw what appeared to be a scope and barrel peering out of cover from a tarp covering a boat.

Steel crawled back and gave the signal that he had seen the target. Sherman nodded and gripped the rifle. He was about to move into the same position Steel had taken when Steel stopped him.

Sherman saw a grin appear on Steel's face. He had a plan—possibly a dangerous and devious one.

CHAPTER FORTY

Steel's plan was to crawl to the water's edge, using the reeds and high grass as cover. All Sherman had to do was keep the mercenaries' attention on him.

Sherman didn't like the idea. Not because it was a waste of time but because it could get one of them killed. He had no idea how he would distract the merc, unless he shot at them or stuck his head around the corner. Both ideas were as dumb as they sounded. He could find something to distract the guy if he could get inside the cabin.

Sherman charged through the open door with the revolver held in both hands, pulled close to his chest, ready to extend his arms and fire—a classic tactical position. Only in the movies do cops and soldiers race into a room with their arms extended.

The inside was larger than he had expected. There was a separate kitchen, sitting room, bathroom, and one bedroom.

Sherman imagined this had started as a one-room cabin but, over the years, had grown into a comfortable home. It was still made of logs and stone, but it had a solid, homely feel. The sitting room and kitchen sat back to back, enabling them to share the same chimney. The furniture was old but functional, possibly bought from the second-hand store in Ridgeway Creek.

It wasn't cluttered inside, with only a few necessary pieces of furniture. There was no TV, but a radio and two bookshelves stacked with various novels.

The sitting room was a large square room, the central part of the house, with three doors. The door directly in front led to the kitchen, a door to the right led to a long master bedroom, and a door to the left led to the bathroom.

He found the bodies of the previous owners in the bedroom. Both had taken a single shot to the back of the head.

He liked to think they hadn't seen it coming, but then he guessed a bullet was much quicker than a blade.

He found the corpse of one of the mercenaries. The guy had taken a shot to the chest, leaving a nasty exit wound. He smiled at the image—a small payback for the couple.

Sherman picked up the body of the mercenary, placed him in a chair, and then pushed it towards the window. All he needed was for the mercenaries to see the silhouette; all Sherman had to do was be quick enough to get out of the way.

Steel had made good progress, considering he was moving, stopping, moving, stopping. He knew constant movement would cause the reeds to wave about suspiciously. He waited for every stiff breeze, making the overgrown plants sway. Soon, he would be in the shooter's blind spot, and if Sherman had done his job well enough, that would be sooner rather than later.

He knew that the sniper wouldn't be alone. After all, two men were missing from the calculation, given the count. This time, Steel planned to take at least one alive. He wanted to know who they were, whom they worked for, and what they wanted. It would be a bonus if he could take both alive; using one against the other often worked well.

The boathouse was small—twenty feet by fifteen, if that. It was single-storey, so there was no second level to worry about. The shooter was under a thick tarpaulin, so any sound in the building would be muffled. Steel looked at the wooden construction—one way in and out through the front on foot; however, the back opened out for a boat to enter or exit. There was a small skylight, but climbing up would make too much noise.

Steel looked at the water, which was cold and uninviting. He wasn't happy about the simple option. He hated being cold and wet.

CHAPTER FORTY-ONE

Two men lay in wait inside the unlit wooden structure of the boathouse. The sniper was a man called Louise. He was in his thirties, an ex-Foreign Legion combatant who had been thrown out for being too aggressive. Gone were *Beau Geste's* days, when the only people to join were those who wanted to forget or disappear.

The other was a man named Finn. Apart from camp, he had no real training but was a good hunter and tracker. Finn was in his late twenties with enough gambling debt to ensure his allegiance to the organisation. They kept him in steady employment and managed to smooth things over with the gambling house—unbeknown to him, they owned the establishment.

Finn didn't want to be there; he wanted to be in the woods with nature, not stuck in a barn for boats with a nut job like Louise. The guy was a complete nutbar but also a complete coward when it came down to it. Finn figured that's why he chose to be a sniper—he didn't have to be close to danger. Most snipers had a natural talent and could get up close if necessary; they were trained in camouflage and concealment. A good sniper could be in a field, and the enemy could march past without noticing them.

However, Louise wasn't like that; he hated confrontation and people being too close to him. Finn knew deep down that was why Louise was kicked out and not because of the bullshit he had been spinning.

The organisation tolerated him because he was a good sniper and expendable. Finn listened as Louise's muffled voice commented on what was happening at the house. Finn rolled his eyes and clenched his fists as the sniper's voice began to chip at his last nerve.

Louise laughed at how stupid the others had been to have gotten taken out like that. Finn's blood began to boil. Those had been as close to friends as he had ever had, and now they were dead, and Louise was laughing about it. Finn held his hands over his ears to block out the incessant crap coming from Louise's mouth.

Finn was too angry and preoccupied to see the figure slowly rise from the water or Steel climb onto the boathouse's wooden deck, and he definitely didn't see Steel creep up behind him.

A swift punch to the back of the head rendered Finn unconscious in seconds. Steel laid the boy down onto the deck and slowly moved towards the sniper, who was still babbling on.

'I see movement in the house; I think it's one of them. I'm going to take the shot,' Louise said, almost as if he wanted the boy to watch. 'Hey, you heard what I said?'

'Anyone ever tell you that you talk too much?' Steel said, ripping back the covers.

As Louise shrieked at Steel's sudden appearance, he fired

off a shot, but Steel managed to kick the rifle sideways just in time. There was a distant *thwack* as the high-calibre bullet impacted a tree in the distance. Louise raised his hands over his face as if to beg not to be hit with the rifle, but Steel did it anyway.

CHAPTER FORTY-TWO

THE SHOT FROM LOUISE'S RIFLE HAD EVERYONE DIVING for cover.

Sherman stayed hidden, expecting the window next to him to explode and the head of the dead man to disappear. But none of those things happened, only the sound of Steel's voice asking for something to tie up the two men.

Sherman searched the house first. He found nothing suitable, so he went to an old tool shed out the back. Inside, it looked like a hardware store, with tools, saws, chainsaws, and enough nails, bolts, screws, and tacks to repair the cabin. There were about five large toolboxes; inside one, he found what he needed: some plastic ties. They were thick industrial ties, not the small things found for home electrics. He grabbed them all and made his way to Steel, who was still standing over the two unconscious men.

The rest of the group assembled at the house but waited outside per Sherman's instructions. Natalie complained about how a nettle had stung her while Steel stood in wet clothes.

'The old man and his wife?' Steel asked.

Sherman said nothing; he just closed his eyes and shook his head.

'They were good people, didn't deserve this,' Steel said, feeling anger and guilt.

'Can you check the old couple's plane? It might be in that barn,' Steel nodded over to the large structure just behind the cabin. 'I'm not sure how much fuel is in it or if the bloody thing works, for that matter,' Steel said, pulling Finn onto his shoulder and looking down at Louise with disdain. 'We'll take these two back to the house; at least the others can make coffee for us all. I need to have a chat with these two.'

They carried the two men back to the cabin and tied them to a pair of kitchen chairs. These were sturdy, robust things. Like everything else in that part of the world, they had to be. Unlike in the big cities or small towns, if something broke, you couldn't just go to the local store and get a new one.

The old couple's place was at least sixty miles from the nearest small town; in between, there were a couple of cabins here and there and, of course, the railway line, which brought their post.

Getting mail in the outback of Alaska was something else entirely. You would have to set out days before to reach the allocated spot, and the train would stop at a designated time. If you weren't there, you didn't get your mail. For some people, that meant no supply replenishment. The rail was an absolute necessity out there.

Steel had considered the rail line and getting the survivors on the train. It was safe, covered from the elements, and they could relax, but the track was at least two days' travel, and even then, he had no idea of the timings or schedule. They might get there only to find it had already left hours or minutes before; the next one could be the next day.

He cursed himself for not considering the train sooner

when he had started to make his exit strategy for when, or if, SANTINI came for him. However, now it was a backup plan in case the plane didn't work.

Steel waited until the others were busy in the kitchen before asking the two men questions.

But he also knew he had to play a little mind game. There was no way he could interrogate them together—safety in numbers and all that. But get them alone, maybe make it look like the other guy wasn't coming back—nothing like a bit of psychological warfare. The cops always did it: separate the suspects so the other had no idea if he had rolled over. The military did it as well, but with different scenarios.

He needed the men to be scared and on edge. That way, he had a good chance of discovering what was happening, who they worked for, and precisely what they wanted.

CHAPTER FORTY-THREE

THE MEN SAT WITH LOOKS OF DEFIANCE ON THEIR BRUISED faces.

These were soldiers, probably not the best of the best, but nonetheless, soldiers or ex-soldiers. This meant that they were trained in interrogation techniques. However, Steel knew that just because you were trained in something didn't mean you were good at it.

Training a person for the worst-case scenario was a double-edged sword. Sure, it prepared a person for an eventual or likely outcome so they could best prepare, but it also gave a person of not-so-sterner stuff the knowledge of exactly what would be coming.

Steel was hoping that one of these two was that person—the one who would sing like a canary at the thought of pain. Not death, but pain, and lots of it. These men had seen what Steel could do. He had moved like a ghost, taking them out before they knew he was there. He was the one who had taken out the other teams. This was a man capable of anything.

The men sat, while Steel and Sherman stood and leaned against the wall. Nobody spoke.

Louise stared at Steel. She took in this strange-looking man of the wild: his long hair and beard, this long brown leather coat, the cargo trousers and combat boots, but most of all, the sunglasses. Why the hell was he wearing sunglasses?

On the other hand, Sherman was shorter than Steel by about a head. He was a stocky man with broad shoulders. He wore the wrong clothing for hiking, but that was to be expected, considering their disposition. He looked like a soldier or even ex-military, but not a man to mess with. Louise figured the man was ex-SEALs, Ranger, even DELTA. He had that special forces vibe about him. The question going through Louise's mind was whether the soldier could control the animal—or if he would even try.

'OK, assholes, let's stop fucking around and get this over with,' Louise said, breaking the silence.

Steel and Sherman remained silent.

'Look, you're not getting anything out of us, so you may as well kill us already,' Louise continued while Finn remained quiet and still wore his angry glare.

Steel and Sherman said nothing, didn't move, just stared.

Louise began to sweat. He was getting nervous; the silence was getting to him. Good.

Steel actually thought it was Finn who would snap first. He owed Sherman ten dollars.

'Hey!' Louise screamed more out of fear than impatience. 'You idiots gonna...'

'How many?' Steel asked, cutting Louise off.

Louise and Finn stared at him with puzzlement. 'How many what? Men, do we have? More than you...' Louise braked.

'Ways to cook a steak?' Steel asked calmly.

Louise and Finn stared at Steel with confusion. 'What?' Finn asked.

'Well, there's grill, barbecue, fried, smoker,' Steel said, counting each one on a finger.

'What the hell are you talking about?' Louise barked.

'Seen one guy use a clothes iron,' Sherman interjected.

Steel thought about it with a bob of his head, then counted it on a finger.

'Have you guys lost the plot?' Finn asked. Now he was getting agitated.

'My grandmother used to stew them and made an excellent pie,' Steel smiled, thinking back, then reminded himself to try it when this was all over.

'What the fuck...?' Louise barked.

Steel shot the chair between his legs, causing Louise to lean back, toppling the chair.

'Didn't anyone tell you it was rude to interrupt?' Steel asked before pushing off the wall and sauntering over to Louise. Sherman followed, still calling out recipes for steak.

Steel and Sherman picked the trembling man up and returned to their places on the wall.

'Okay, I guess we started with a hard one, I know. Let's try something simple, like, I don't know?' Steel said, waving his hand in the air as though he was looking for a question.

'Who are you working for, and what do you want with us?' Sherman barked.

'Fuck you,' laughed Louise.

Steel smiled at Louise and kicked him in the chest, knocking him to the ground once more. Then, he grabbed Finn and carried him to the boathouse.

Louise just watched as his colleague was hauled away.

'You gonna answer the question?' Sherman asked, pointing the barrel of the rifle at Louise's knees.

'Go ahead, old man. The only people out here are my people,' Louise smiled, unaware of Steel's damage to the mercenaries' numbers.

'What?' Sherman laughed. 'You think you have backup?' causing Louise to ponder. 'See that guy over there? He's been taking your teams apart while you've been slumming it in that boathouse,' he finished.

'Yeah, nice one, gramps, like I'm gonna fall for that,' Louise laughed in disbelief.

'Yes, it's true; look, see for yourself,' Debbra said, pulling the tablet from Steel's backpack and switching it on. There was a flicker, and the map showed only three red dots on the screen.

Louise smiled and looked up at Debbra, who had a puzzled look on her face.

'Why is he smiling?' she asked.

CHAPTER FORTY-FOUR

Sven and Jones looked at their screens. Miles apart, but they had the same image. The missing tablet's signal flickered on.

'There you are,' Sven said with a hungry growl.

Mr Jones sat up and marked the location in case the signal faded again. For all he knew, his men were in trouble, and that could be one of the teams signalling for assistance. He took a map and plotted a route to the lake. He turned to his men and grabbed his modified M4 assault rifle.

'Let's go,' he said with no further orders, only a look in his eyes.

The men picked up their packs and weapons, preparing for the next march through the forest. Each of them was hungry for blood. This hadn't gone as planned. None of them were supposed to get hurt, let alone killed. However, something had gone wrong. There was someone in the group who wasn't a dumbass civilian.

The plan had been simple: they would meet the agent in Ridgeway Creek, confirm they had the package, and then bring the asset home. What they still didn't know was why the plane had crashed. The pilot had been paid off to land in Ridgeway Creek instead of heading back to Talkeetna. However, they had crashed for some reason.

Sven had checked the wreckage and couldn't find any reason for the accident unless someone had taken out the pilot. But then, what kind of person would purposely kill the person flying the plane in the hope that it would crash? Also, why didn't anyone stop them?

Unless, of course, they hadn't been on the flight? Poison would do it, but even that had to be controlled if you wanted it to do what was required at a certain time. Some poisons are quick; others slow; either way, the killer must have had a plan if they needed that plane to crash before it reached a town.

As they went through the forest in single file, Sven thought about the crash and the attacks on his men. What had gone so wrong?

Sven knew that Mr Jones was under some pressure from the boss ever since the shooting at the Steel estate. It was meant to be a small gathering of friends and family, not a gathering with over a hundred witnesses. Even the intel on when the son, John, was coming back from Bosnia was incorrect. However, from what they had learned of John, he was unpredictable. They were meant to go into the estate and show Lord Steel that he wasn't safe, even in his home. To make him understand, it was best if his interest in certain organisations was ignored.

He smiled at the thought of his army instructor telling them all, 'The best-laid plans go to shit after the first encounter with the enemy.' Unfortunately, he was correct.

CHAPTER FORTY-FIVE

STEEL HAD GOTTEN HALFWAY TO THE BOATHOUSE WHEN HE saw what she had done through the window. He felt like running over and smashing the device over her head. But he knew the damage was already done. Whatever information these two had was going to die with them.

Steel knew he couldn't take them with him; they would use every opportunity to slow down the group or escape. No, the men had to die. A decision he didn't have a problem with, not after what he had seen they had done to the old couple. He dragged Finn back to the group and threw him to the ground.

They had just lost the edge, and Louise knew it.

Louise was still smiling, and Debbra had no idea what was happening.

'Next time you want to help, make sure you're alone and far away from the group,' Steel said, snatching the device from Debbra and switching it off.

'I don't get it; what did I do wrong?' she said, still oblivious to the situation.

'You just sent for the cavalry, darlin'. Thank you kindly,' Louise laughed again.

Steel hit the man once in the jaw, not as hard as he would have wanted, but enough to knock him out cold.

'How long do we have?' Sherman asked.

Steel looked around and shrugged. 'Not long, but long enough,' he replied with a smile that sent a shiver down Sherman's spine. 'Pick them up and carry them to the house. Make sure they are tied up nice and tight on some chairs. Place them near some windows. Oh, and make sure laughing boy is wearing some of the old lady's clothes for effect,' Steel said, heading off to the barn to check on the aircraft.

'Dress one of them up? What has he got planned?' asked Bob as they helped carry the two men over to the house.

Steel hoped there would be enough time to execute his plan and get the plane off the ground. As he moved past the bodies of the dead mercs on the ground, he picked up as much ammunition as he could carry. His plan was crazy and had a massive risk factor, but it would be spectacular if it worked.

By Steel's calculations, they had fifteen minutes to get things rigged up and in the air. Not much time, especially as he had no idea if the plane would start or had fuel; he hoped the old boy had kept her shipshape and ready to go.

Louise and Finn were bound, gagged, and placed in front of the windows. Rifles had been strapped to them, and the barrels poked out of the open windows.

'Are we set?' Steel asked.

Everyone nodded.

'Can you fly a plane, Sherman?' Steel asked, hoping for the correct response.

'Sure, what kind?'

'The one with wings and our ticket out of here,' Bob said, rushing for the door.

As Steel went to leave, Louise began to mumble loudly as if he had something desperate to say.

Sherman had already headed for the barn, where a hysterical Natalie sat on the ground.

'What is it?' Steel said, taking the gag from the man's mouth.

'The others will be here soon, and they'll get the package...' Louise started to say.

'Package? What are you talking about? What package?'

Louise laughed. 'You have no idea, do you? Poor dumb bastard.'

'So, what package?' Steel asked calmly.

Louise went to answer, but a movement from the corner of Steel's eye made him turn and look over to Sherman, who was pointing to the front of the plane.

Steel stuffed the gag back over Louise's mouth and ran to Sherman. He found Natalie on the ground, holding her knees and rocking while muttering to herself. The last few days had taken their toll, and now, with the threat of being murdered by a gang of mercenaries, she was tearing at her nerves.

He stopped and looked over to where Sherman was pointing. There were several large bullet holes in the front of the plane where the engine sat.

Lifting the collapsible cover, they saw the damage. At least two of the bullets had destroyed cables and parts of the engine and radiator.

Steel let the cover fall. The direction of the bullets made no sense. They were from the side rather than the front.

'There were a lot of stray bullets flying around,' Steel noted, but even he didn't seem convinced by something.

'Shit, shit, shit,' Natalie mumbled. 'We're all going to die, and it's all his fault. Why did he have to come and ruin everything?'

Steel looked at Sherman, who shrugged confusedly. 'I think she means you?'

'Nah, couldn't be.'

'Why's that?' Sherman asked curiously.

'She'd be angrier.'

Sherman nodded. 'I can see that; you have proven to be a bit of a pain in the arse.'

'Plane broken, all his fault, all his fault,' Natalie continued to mumble, but she wasn't looking at Steel or Sherman; she was staring at the cabin.

Sherman nodded to the side as if to usher Steel to follow him, leaving Natalie on the ground, babbling about how it was all someone's fault.

Steel looked back at her. He knew she was a little crazy, but he had figured she was just obnoxious, not that the last train had left the station. He felt sorry for her for a brief moment, and then he saw the expression on Sherman's face. He was worried about something other than Natalie.

The two men stood out of earshot of Natalie, and then Sherman turned to Steel. 'Is it me, or...?'

'Are the bullet holes in the wrong place?' Steel finished the sentence.

'One of us did this? But why? I mean, why sabotage our way outta here?'

Steel thought for a moment. Ever since he had picked up the survivors, he'd felt something was off. He had never understood why the mercenaries had been tracking a bunch of tourists.

At first, he'd thought SANTINI had discovered his location and it was him they were after. But now, he was convinced it was one of the group. But not to kidnap them—to bring them to safety. One of the group was working with the mercenaries. This led to the question: what were they doing on the trip in the first place? A cover? A secret rendezvous? But the plane had crashed. Was that also an accident? Steel couldn't see the logic in someone purposely crashing the plane.

None of it made sense. However, one thing was clear. There was a traitor amongst them, and they had to find him or her before they reached the town's safety.

'Who knows? All I do know is we need to go, and quickly.'

Sherman nodded, then looked back at the group of survivors. 'And what about the traitor?'

'One thing at a time. First, let's get moving. I suspect we'll have company soon, and we've had the advantage—I don't want to push it.'

CHAPTER FORTY-SIX

STEEL LED THE SURVIVORS FAR INTO THE NEXT FOREST. HE knew they needed to get into cover and out of the open. The mercenaries were closing in, and he feared they wouldn't be asking questions once they caught up with the group.

As they walked through the forest, Steel's thoughts returned to one recurring question: what was this package? Clearly, the mercenaries had no idea who had it or what it was.

He stopped and looked around at the small open space before them. It was on a slightly elevated slope. Usually, that would be good for having a perfect vantage point of the surrounding area, but this was in a dense forest, making their site almost invisible until you got near.

'We are stopping here?' they asked, dropping to the ground from exhaustion.

'It's getting late; we need to stop for the night. That means we need a fire and something to eat,' Steel said, throwing off his pack.

'What about the mercenaries?' the group asked.

Sherman shook his head. 'It will be too dark soon, and it

will be even darker in this forest. They're smart; they won't risk coming in here until morning when they can pick up a trail.'

Steel remained silent, but a smile cracked from the corner of his mouth. He was glad Sherman was there—a voice of reason. In fact, he was sure that if it hadn't been for Sherman, he would have abandoned the group ages ago.

'Sherman, can you organise a fire? There should be some MRE rations in the backpack; dish them out,' Steel ordered as he took off his pack and tossed it on the ground.

'Where are you going?' Sherman asked, almost afraid of the answer.

'Like you said, first light, they will be looking for tracks, so I thought I'd give them some.' He smiled, took out his compass, and made a bearing on the camp. Then, placing the compass and his notebook back in his jacket pocket, he disappeared into the forest.

The group watched as Steel seemed to merge with the forest.

Natalie shivered as an uncomfortable feeling swept over her while she watched him disappear.

Sherman noticed their expressions and coughed. 'Right then, Laura, Mike, you get some firewood together. The rest of us will make some camp for the night.'

They all stared at Sherman in wonderment, as if what had just happened hadn't affected the man. They were tired, being chased, not trying to be chased. They were exhausted from the forced march they were having to endure.

He looked at their faces and sighed. He could motivate troops; that was easy, and they did as they were told. But trying to get unwilling civilians to do something—now that was nearly impossible. 'Look, I know it's been a hard few days, and it has. Hell, it's been hard for me too.'

The group looked at him in surprise. But nobody spoke.

'But we must keep going, or we won't survive this. We need to stick together and help one another. We have to dig deep and give that little bit more.' As Sherman finished, he gazed upon the group; their expressions had changed slightly. The look of despair had gone at least and had been replaced with a little spark of hope—all except Natalie, who still looked scared and confused.

'Horse shit,' Natalie barked. 'We don't have to do anything. I don't know why we have been listening to you or that freak of a stranger. Ever since he showed up, we've been running here and there. We have only his word that these others are mercenaries and are the bad guys. How do we know **he's** not some asshole trying to kill us, and they are trying to rescue us?'

'But they have been shooting at us, Nat,' Debbra said.

'Yeah, I'd be a bit pissed off too if some asshole went around killing all my friends,' Natalie barked back.

'OK, Nat, so why are they here in the first place? They sure as hell aren't a search party, not with that sort of firepower,' Sherman interjected.

'What they started out for is irrelevant now; the stranger has seen to that and made us all enemies of the people tracking us. But we do know they are looking for a package. So why don't we use that as some peace offering? They can get us off this damned mountain a lot quicker than the stranger could.'

Sherman shook his head. He knew if these mercenaries had been shooting to kill before, they wouldn't stop now. Also, if the group gave up this package, what was to say that the mercs wouldn't just kill them all there and then? He knew this group would march on to the mercs altogether, thinking that the whole "safety in numbers" or even a show of solidarity would keep them safe. But that would make it easier for the mercenaries. The whole group would be together—one nice target.

He watched as Natalie stood up and started walking towards Sherman. As he bent to stand up, something struck him in the head. As he looked up to see what was happening, the last thing he saw was Natalie and the thick piece of wood coming towards his head. Then everything went dark.

CHAPTER FORTY-SEVEN

JOHN STEEL INCHED HIS WAY THROUGH THE THICK FOREST. The wind was picking up and carried with it a biting cold. He knew the weather would change soon, and it would snow. When that happened, it would be impossible to cover their tracks.

But then, it would be the same for the mercenaries.

He had picked up a trail of something—a deer, possibly, or so he hoped. The tracks weren't large enough for a moose or bear. He was good at tracking, but nothing like his father had been. He smiled at a memory. They used to take holidays at the cabin when he was younger. He would go off with his father, and they would go hunting and tracking. He learned what he could eat and what was poisonous, how to navigate using the sun and stars, and how nature had a natural compass—how trees would bend, and moss would grow in certain directions.

Steel stopped and crouched. Fifteen feet in front of him, a deer was grazing. It was a young buck. He smiled at the sight. He could sit for hours just staring at wildlife; it was calming. His smile faded. Unfortunately, he had to hunt this beautiful beast. The group were hungry and needed fresh food. As he drew the hatchet from his belt, Steel felt the wind against his face. He was upwind from the buck, so all he had to do was creep up as close as possible and find his mark.

Steel hated killing animals, whether necessary or not. However, he also knew that sometimes survival came first.

He came from a rich background. His father had been an Earl—Lord Steel—a title John Steel had inherited after the brutal slaughter of his family.

Steel's father was a minister and part of the British Security Service, a service that had once had eyes on John. Lord Steel was also head of a family business that John's grandfather had created. The company focused on technical and scientific advancements for both military and civilian purposes. A company that John had also inherited.

However, John Steel was a soldier, not a businessman or politician—something that, at some point, he would have to accept, pick up the reins for, and learn. The business—both of them.

The murder of Steel's family had a massive negative effect on the company; shareholders were ready to sell. The news that John was still alive but was taking time to recover gave them some resolve. In fact, it had the opposite effect—people started investing more.

Steel had left the company in the hands of a good friend, Arthur Hendricks, who was also one of the company's senior partners.

Hendricks had been told of Steel's hiding grounds, and they used the cover story that Steel would take time to recover rather than hide, as the latter would cause panic.

It had been eight months since the massacre at his family home. Eight months that had seemed like a lifetime since he lost everyone he cared about. The day, in his eyes, he had died along with everyone else.

Now, he was fighting not just for his life but for the lives of strangers—which made him feel alive again. He wasn't the same man, the same soldier. No, he was something more. Something more feral. Someone more deadly.

He finished gutting the deer and washed out the carcass. Then, heaving it up, he slung it over his shoulder, causing him to wince in pain. His wounds had healed from the shooting, but the damage to his muscles was taking a little longer. Taking a breath, he turned and started walking back to the camp. He needed to get back to the group. He felt that their last encounter with the mercenaries had broken the group's little spirit. If there were to be a voice of contention, it would be Natalie. From the first meeting, she had gone against everything.

Steel stopped and began to think. That was right. She was the one who wanted to stay and wait for what they thought was the search party; she had also lagged behind on more than one occasion. Was she working with the mercenaries? Had she got this package?

He thought back to the markers he had left behind that he had discovered. Were those from her?

CHAPTER FORTY-EIGHT

The Chairman was not amused. He had just finished talking with Mr Jones. The mercenary had explained that they had run into a problem—that someone in the group of survivors was taking his team apart.

After he had finished with Mr Jones, the Chairman called another asset. This person's job was to find out everything they could about the people on that plane.

Normally, they would have checked, but unfortunately, it was impossible because nobody on the flight had pre-booked. However, now there was a flight manifest.

The Chairman didn't think there would be a team of special forces personnel looking for some downtime on the flight, but someone was causing problems, and he didn't like problems. He knew it would take some time to check; in the meantime, he would spend his time at the local Social Gentlemen's Club. He needed a good whiskey to get the bad taste out of his mouth.

His driver took him to one of the oldest clubs in Washington, which was his favourite. It was a grand old building with a history that went back two hundred years. It was a place where men sat in silence, with only a cursory nod of greeting to one another. It was a place to think.

The car stopped, and the driver got out and opened the car door for the Chairman.

The driver was a huge bulk of a man—six foot three, with broad shoulders. His suit bulged at his size. He was Fijian but had a European name because his own name was too long and unpronounceable.

'I'll be fine here, Talbot; get yourself something to eat, relax for a bit. I'll phone you when I need you.'

The driver nodded his thanks. Then, as the Chairman made it to the front door of the club, Talbot closed the car door, made his way to the driver's side, opened the door, and got in. He started the engine, checked his mirrors, then drove away.

CHAPTER FORTY-NINE

JOHN STEEL RETURNED TO THE SURVIVORS' CAMPSITE AND found the mood sombre. Something was wrong. He heaved the fresh carcass off his shoulder and knelt next to it, drawing his knife as he did so.

The others watched him carve up the meat and place it on the wooden scores they had used so often. No one spoke.

Steel could feel a tension in the air. It wasn't from the battle they had just encountered; he would have expected that. No, this was more—anger. He didn't look up as he prepared the food. There was no reason to see what was written on their faces; their silence said it all.

As he finished the last scene, Steel wiped off his knife and placed it back in the sheath. Finally, he looked up and saw Natalie holding one of the guns they had retrieved from the mercenaries, aiming it at him.

He went to speak, but something hit him on the back of the head, and everything went dark.

'Tie him up. We'll take his stuff; we might need them,' Natalie ordered.

The others looked at her blankly.

'We can't just leave them—not without anything to defend themselves,' Clarke barked.

Natalie smirked. 'They're big boys; they can take care of themselves.'

Clarke shook his head. 'This ain't right, Natalie.'

'Well, if you aren't with us, you'll just have to join the stranger and Mr Sherman,' she said, nodding over to the unconscious Steel and Sherman, the rifle held tightly in her hands, pointing towards him.

Sherman was propped up against a tree and facing outwards. When Steel had seen him, he would have thought Sherman was taking five minutes or was on watch.

Clarke shook his head and stood up, taking one of the cable ties they had brought with them. The rest of the group unstrapped Steel's belt, carrying his hatchet and the knife on his leg. They placed them down on the ground before carrying Steel to another tree once his hands had been secured. Then, they leaned him against it.

Natalie picked up the hatchet and said, 'This will come in handy.'

'Let's just get out of here,' Clarke's words gritted with venom.

'OK, Clarke, you get to read the map; Debra, you can carry the stranger**'s** pack; Karen, you and Bob can take the rest of the equipment,' Natalie ordered.

She said with a maddening smile, 'OK, let's get out of here and try and find the rescue team. Hopefully, they won't blame us for what this asshole has done,' she said, kicking Steel in the chest.

'Right, let's go, chop chop,' she ordered. The group moved off silently, looking back at the two men they had abandoned. A feeling of guilt flowed over them—all except Natalie.

ICE COLD STEEL

Clarke took the map and compass from Steel and oriented the map to head back the way they had come.

Bob looked nervously over at Natalie, who held Steel's rifle as though she knew what she was doing. 'So, what's the plan, Natalie?'

'We go and see those men and make a deal; we give them the package, and they get us out of here, simple,' she said confidently.

'Yeah, one slight problem with that, Natalie—we don't have this fucking package,' Karen yelled in frustration.

'Not...' Clarke stopped and turned to face the group. 'Unless you have the package, Natalie?'

Everyone stared at Natalie with suspicion.

'No...' Natalie replied, somewhat nervous at the accusation. 'Of course I don't.'

'Then what the hell are we doing?' Debra screamed into Natalie's face.

Natalie shot backwards out of fright and butt-stroked Debra in the head, felling her with one blow. The others looked on in horror. Natalie had come unhinged. The whole experience had broken her.

Natalie stumbled backwards, shocked at what had just happened. The rifle waved in front of her defensively. 'It was an accident, you saw—she went to attack me, you all saw, didn't you... DIDN'T YOU?' she screamed, hoping for a response.

The others just stared in disbelief, unable to move. They just stared at Natalie and the gun she was holding.

Natalie kept moving backwards, the weapon moving in a sweeping motion, and then they watched as she disappeared into the forest. But no one went after her; they all rushed towards Debra, hoping she wasn't dead.

203

CHAPTER FIFTY

SHERMAN WOKE FIRST. HIS HEAD HURT LIKE HELL. He had to admit that he didn't expect everyone to side with Natalie, but then, the way things had been going lately, they were all strung out. These were civilians, not military personnel. They weren't used to getting shot at or hunted by mercenaries.

As he went to turn, he found his hands were bound by something; he figured they had used the plastic ties they had found at the old couple's place. He shuffled around the tree, not expecting the others to be there, and was even more surprised to find the unconscious stranger.

Sherman's blood began to boil. Why hadn't he noticed that Natalie had snapped? Why hadn't any of the others tried to stop her? Fear, quite possibly—especially after she had gotten the gun.

As he looked over at Steel, he noticed him beginning to stir.

Slowly, Steel began to move, and then he stopped. He had discovered his hands bound behind his back and let out a low growl of disapproval.

Sherman watched Steel use the tree to help himself stand. Steel strained as though he was pulling the plastic cuffs apart, and then, with a final effort, he was free.

'Neat trick,' Sherman called over.

Steel looked over at Sherman, who was still sitting on the ground.

'Quite surprised you aren't free by now,' he replied, walking over to Sherman.

'Too much leave,' Sherman admitted as he looked down at his stomach.

Steel smiled and helped him to his feet, then went over to the fire and stirred the embers until a flame rose.

Steel placed a small piece of wood into the fire until it was alight. Then, he carefully blew it out and placed the smouldering wood onto the plastic. There was a pungent smell of melting plastic before Sherman eventually became free.

'So, what happened?' Steel asked calmly.

'Natalie—she's snapped. I should have seen that this whole damned mess had affected her. She knocked me out when I wasn't looking.'

Steel nodded but said nothing.

'What we gonna do about the kids?' Sherman asked, rubbing his wrists.

Steel waited for a moment as he looked in the direction of the old couple's place and the bullet-ridden plane. 'I'm tempted to say fuck 'em, but I get the feeling Natalie has them under duress. I feel that not all of them are too eager to go along with her.'

'What makes you say that?'

'Because the person who tied me up left enough slack so I could pull my hands through the loops. Someone isn't playing Natalie's game.'

'They'll be at the mercenaries by now, probably carting them off to the nearest town,' Sherman shrugged.

'Or just killed them where they stood,' Steel replied.

Sherman gave him a curious look, as if he was unsure whether the man was joking.

'You always this glass-half-empty kinda guy?' Sherman mocked.

'After what they pulled, they better hope the mercs got to them first. But yes, I guess we should go after them.'

Sherman nodded. 'Yeah, the others might need our help if you're correct.'

Steel shrugged. 'What? Oh, right. I was just thinking that I wanted my stuff back,' he replied, then headed back into the forest towards the old couple's cabin and possibly the rest of the mercenaries.

Sherman followed behind. He knew it was too early to formulate a rescue plan. That was, of course, if they weren't too late.

CHAPTER FIFTY-ONE

SVEN AND THE OTHERS HAD MADE THEMSELVES comfortable in the old couple's cabin. He didn't need to follow; it would be dark soon. The survivors would have to make camp and possibly find shelter and food for the night, whereas his team of men had food and shelter. They could get a good night's sleep without worrying about being attacked by nature, and guards would ensure no more attacks from the survivors.

One of the mercenaries had gone to get firewood from the woodshed, while another oriented himself in the kitchen after being named the cook for the evening.

The others got to work, taking out the bodies of the old couple and fallen comrades and then building a bonfire to burn them all. The last thing they needed was the smell attracting the wildlife.

Sven reluctantly untied Finn and Louise, thinking it was suspicious that they had been kept alive. However, they explained that the sudden arrival of the other team had forced them to run; they had even left the plane in the barn.

He called Mr Jones to give him the situation report, or SITREP.

Mr Jones had been less than happy that they still didn't have the package but knew that, at first light, things would be different. The survivors would be tired from both the long trek over the mountains and the fear of being hunted. The last encounter at the old couple's cabin would have used up their last sense of fight. They would have been living off whatever they could find to eat. He doubted they had the knowledge to live off the land.

But that idea didn't quite fit with the attacks. Sure, some of them had been bear attacks, but from what he had seen of the campsites, it appeared almost orchestrated, as if someone had lured the beasts there to feed.

He was still waiting to hear back from the Chairman about the background check on the passengers. At least two of them were not who they appeared to be. They knew about one, but the other was proving to be a problem.

Back at the cabin, Sven and his men settled down for the night; a sentry plan had been organised so each man got enough rest. The cook had found lots of tinned food and made an all-in supper. Another had made plenty of coffee and placed it into three thermos flasks he had found in the small pantry.

While some men, including Sven, slept, others took the time to clean their weapons and check their equipment. These men would be next on the rotation. The sentry points were in the house; one looked through the kitchen window, which had a rear view of the cabin. This covered the forest and the boathouse; the other was in the old couple's bedroom, which covered the front of the cabin.

Sven preferred the men to be close. Firstly, they were within reach, so if one did fall asleep, the rest would know about it. Secondly, and more importantly, they would avoid accidents, such as someone sneaking up on them without the others knowing until it was too late.

What had happened to the other teams had made Sven cautious. He wasn't about to let anything happen to his team, that was for damned sure.

CHAPTER FIFTY-TWO

Steel and Sherman had backtracked, following the trail the others had made when they had hurried back towards the old couple's cabin.

With each step, they had an uneasy feeling. Had the others made it to the cabin? Had the mercenaries killed them, or were they tied up, ready to be interrogated? After all, someone in the group had the package. However, Steel figured that whoever had the package worked for the mercenaries, so why all the cloak-and-dagger stuff? This person could have left the group on the first night and snuck off to meet with the mercenaries, and all this cat-and-mouse crap wouldn't have been necessary. People would not have died needlessly, like the old couple. The mercenaries—Steel wasn't too bothered about them.

The point was that the person with the package was scared. A deal gone wrong, perhaps? More likely, they were holding onto the package until they were safely out of the country, afraid that once the mercenaries had their prize, the carrier would no longer be useful. Expendable even?

This made Steel wonder what this package was. Information, most certainly. But information on what, or even who? Then, he began to consider the events, starting with the crash. Why had the plane gone down? After talking with Sherman and some of the others, it appeared the pilot had just died— they figured it was a heart attack. Luckily, the pilot hadn't been flying at normal altitude, or they would all have been killed.

He remembered seeing the men in Ridgeway Creek, whom he had a bad feeling about; these men were most certainly part of the mercenary team, but they were hanging around town. Perhaps they were doing forward reconnaissance, but more likely, the plane was meant to land there in Ridgeway and not Talkeetna. Had the pilot been paid off? If that was the case, what had gone so very wrong?

Steel stopped momentarily, causing Sherman to walk over to him.

'What's up?'

Steel wasn't sure, and he said so.

'You thinking about whether the kids made it to the cabin?'

'Not just that, how did all this start?'

Sherman thought for a moment before shrugging. 'It depends on which point we are talking about, the crash or before the crash; I mean, this mysterious person with this damned package, whatever the hell it is?'

Steel cracked a smile. Great minds and all that shit, he thought. 'You've been thinking about it too?'

'Yeah, it's been bothering me ever since we got to the old couple's place and we interrogated that asshole. If this package was so important, they had to get it to the mercs. Why didn't they do it sooner?'

Steel told him his thoughts about the pilot, a possible course change, the possible strong-arming of the mercenaries to get them out, and how he had more questions than answers. And what was the package?

'I figure it is leverage to get them out of the country. I think the person is no longer useful once the mercenaries have it. I also think that whatever it is, it's on something small, like a stick drive, because, unless I've missed it, nobody is lumbering around with anything heavy.'

'Information on someone, perhaps?'

Steel shrugged. 'Could be anything, but it is certainly worth something to someone.'

'Certainly enough to get four mercenary teams out here,' Sherman replied.

Steel thought for a moment. 'Yeah, good point.'

'See, told ya... wait. What is a good point?'

'Why so many people? Why were there so many mercenaries if it was a simply arranged meeting at the airport after a short detour? One team would have been enough. It's a small town in Alaska, not New York or LA.'

'Maybe they were expecting problems?' Sherman said, too many scenarios whirling in his head.

Steel looked towards the direction they were heading. He started to wonder about the others and also about Natalie. Why had she suddenly had a breakdown? Then he remembered what she had said when he found her near the barn containing the plane. *Is it all his fault?* Who? Whose fault was it? More to the point, what was his fault?

'What did Natalie mean? *It's all his fault?*' Steel asked.

Sherman stared at him, confused. 'What?'

'At the barn, she said, *It's all his fault.* Who? And what was his fault?'

Sherman stared at Steel blankly. He had no answer; the last thing he needed was more questions. 'I have no idea. You, perhaps; she always blamed you.'

Steel shook his head. 'No, when she said it, she looked at

the cabin. She was talking about someone who was in the cabin.'

'Yeah, but who? After all, you said she mentioned a *he*, not a *she*. So, it could only be Bob or Clarke.'

Steel kept his gaze on the downtrodden undergrowth, a path that had been forged under duress. He could imagine Natalie pushing the group onward, the rifle aimed at them, her finger ready on the trigger. She was scared and paranoid, not the sort of place you want to be while people are hunting you.

Sherman agreed with a slow nod.

'There is another option, of course,' Steel said.

Sherman watched as Steel turned to face him. 'That she's the courier, and she was talking about the person she had made a deal with.'

'At the moment, it's the most feasible explanation. She has the package, and she has realised it's all gone to rat shit.'

'So, what do we do?' Sherman asked.

'Same plan, I guess. Rescue the survivors and make sure everyone goes home. First, we need to take care of the rest of the mercenaries; we don't need them on our arses,' Steel shrugged.

Sherman nodded in agreement. 'Sounds like a plan. What are we gonna do about Natalie?'

'See what state she is in when we find her, but I'm more worried about the courier,' Steel admitted.

'What do you mean?'

'They had a plan that has gone to rat shit; the question is, do they have a plan B, and does it involve us or throwing us to the wolves?'

Sherman said nothing as he pondered what Steel had said.

'Either way, we continue as normal until the time arises.'

'And then what?'

'And then I'll gut the courier for causing all this shit.'

CHAPTER FIFTY-THREE

THE GROUP OF SURVIVORS KNELT BY DEBBRA'S BODY. SHE was breathing but unconscious. There was a cut just behind her right eye, leaving a bloody smudge on the side of her face.

Tears of fear and anger cascaded down Bob's face. He had no idea what to do, afraid that if he moved his wife, he might cause more damage.

Natalie had gone into the forest, taking everything with her: weapons, food, and medical supplies. She had snapped; the gun battle at the old couple's place, then finding out that the plane had been shot up, making it useless, had been the final breaking point. Where others had taken their misfortunes in their stride, Natalie had snapped. This had left her paranoid and frightened. Everyone was the enemy. This made her dangerous, but they had to find her before the mercenaries did.

As they gathered around Debbra, they never saw or heard two men approach. They never noticed the men who stood behind them. Anger suddenly turned into sympathy.

'What happened?' John Steel asked, looking down at Debbra.

'Jesus!' yelped Karen, suddenly noticing Steel was beside her. 'I'm going to buy you a bell when we leave here.'

Steel shrugged and said, 'Bah.'

'It was Natalie; she just snapped and hit Debbra with the gun,' Bob explained.

'Which way did she go?' Sherman asked, looking around for any tell-tale signs or tracks.

Clarke pointed in the direction they had seen her head for. 'That way, but she won't get far; I've got the map,' he said, patting his pocket.

'In this instance, I don't think she is rational enough to use a map. Most people have a fight-or-flight response to danger, but hers is bouncing around. I should have noticed something was wrong, but I chose to ignore her, mostly because she was doing my bloody head in. That incident at the old couple's place, I think, was the final marble dropping,' Steel said, his eyes still on Debbra.

'Will she live?' Bob asked.

'No way of telling yet. But we will have to get her somewhere warm and dry,' Sherman said, kneeling beside her still body and checking her pulse using two fingers on her right carotid artery. 'There is a pulse, but it's weak.'

'We can take her back to the old couple's place,' Bob said excitedly.

Steel shook his head. 'The mercenaries will be there, remember?'

'I don't care; they have to help us!' Bob yelled.

Steel shook his head. 'No, all they have to do is get this package, whatever the bloody hell it is, and then leave. That is their only concern; we are inconsequential to them.'

'OK, so what's the plan?' Laura asked.

'The way I figure it, they will stay in the house; they won't risk any patrols or using any outer buildings, such as the barn where the plane is. So, I think we will be fine until early the next morning.'

Everyone looked at Steel with amazement.

'Are you utterly insane?' Karen asked.

'It's the last place they would look for us. I figure they have already checked out the barn to see if there is anything useful; after that, it would not interest them. Luckily, it is behind the house, so we head in from the rear of the barn, one side facing away from the house, so we would be safe there. Two windows at the rear are locked from the inside, so if I can get inside, I can open the windows and let you all in.'

'Like she said, you're nuts, but it's our only plan. And as you said, they wouldn't think to look for us there,' Sherman said with a grin.

'Look, these men, like us, are tired, so at the first sign of creature comforts, such as a bed or a warm meal, they will be a little lax in their attitude. Sure, there might be one or two that are on the ball, but I've seen hardened troops on exercise, and once they get a little comfort, they relax a little. It's just the body's way of recharging the batteries. They know it's not always healthy to run on 100 per cent.'

Sherman looked at Steel with curiosity. When had this man seen battle-hardened troops?

'The team leader has probably got the six men on an hourly rotation—two sentry posts, one facing the rear and the other the front of the cabin. He himself will get some shut-eye but be on alert if needed. So, I figure the best time would be just before shift change; that means the mercenary will be tired and more concerned about whether his relief is awake.'

Sherman nodded; it sounded like a decent plan.

'How are you going to get in? You can't use the front doors; they squeak like hell,' Sherman noted.

Steel nodded. 'The skylight on the roof is possibly the only way. I noticed it left ajar, possibly to let fumes out. The old guy had some right crap stored in there—quite surprised it hasn't combusted by itself by now.'

'You sure we will be safe there?' Laura asked.

Steel shrugged. 'Who knows, really? All I know is we need shelter—the only place for miles. With Debbra in this condition, they will probably find us eventually anyway. If we are lucky, they will leave without checking the barn and head into the forest at first light, then we go in the opposite direction.'

'Doesn't sound like we have much choice,' Clarke said, sounding and looking tired.

'There is always a choice; it is just a question of which will give you a better chance of survival,' Steel answered.

'OK, what do you want us to do?' Laura sighed.

Steel stood. 'Clarke, I need you to use the compass and get us back to the old couple's place, or at least the woodline. We will make a plan from there.'

CHAPTER FIFTY-FOUR

SCARED, TIRED, AND CONFUSED, NATALIE RUSHED through the forest. The sound of nature being alerted to her presence made her all the more panicky. Low twigs from branches scratched at her face; she stumbled on loose undergrowth and tripped on moss-covered fallen branches.

Beads of sweat collected on her brow and ran down her spine.

She was lost and losing light. A fine mist was starting to form. Natalie stopped and looked around. Which way? Where was the old couple's place? She had been positive it was this way. But then... it was their fault. The others had tricked her. They had made Debbra shout at her to confuse her. She bet they were all having a good laugh right now.

She could tell they had never liked her, especially that stranger. He was the worst, always picking on her. But Clarke and Karen had always been good to her; they had waited for her when she fell behind, especially Clarke. He would go back and make sure she hadn't left anything behind. He was nice.

She had known Karen for a long time, but they had gone to

different universities. In all honesty, she still wasn't sure what Karen did, but she went away a lot, which was odd considering she was doing computer work most of the time.

Natalie stopped to catch her breath; the light was fading, almost as if everything was closing in on her. Soon, it would be pitch black, but she didn't worry. Soon, she would be out of the forest and talking with the rescue team that had been following them. She still couldn't understand why everyone thought they were dangerous—some mercenary group. That made no sense. Why would so many people come after them?

Then she thought about this package everyone was talking about. She hadn't seen anyone with big parcels or boxes, so perhaps this was another of the stranger's tricks. It made sense. After all, everyone was OK until he arrived.

She began to sway. She felt lightheaded. The forest was spinning. What was this? Then everything went black, and she collapsed.

CHAPTER FIFTY-FIVE

The group followed Steel to the edge of the forest. The twilight coloured everything grey-blue. Mist started to rise from the lake; the silver-white cloud crept over the open land like a creature.

Steel looked at the old couple's place, which sat in darkness. He knew that the men would either be on watch or sleeping. He waited momentarily, hoping to see movement from the windows, but everything remained still.

Steel knew that if it were him or one of his old team, they would be sitting back from the window, letting the room's darkness shroud them. It was easier to see out of a dark room than to see in—the perfect cover.

He checked the open ground between himself and the cabin. It was at least over five hundred yards. The mist was starting to cover the surrounding ground; he just hoped it wouldn't be a full moon, or they would all be lit up for everyone to see.

His plan was simple: he would keep low and make his way to the barn, hoping to stay in the blind spot that the barn created. He was counting on the mercenaries being comfortable, which meant there was a chance they wouldn't be as alert as they should be. They were in a warm building, possibly well-fed. All he hoped for now was for nature to take its course.

He had experienced it when he was in the army. After a long exercise, mostly doing a point-to-point drill in the Brecon Beacons, as soon as you got into cover and had a warm meal inside you, you relaxed, became comfortable, and became lax.

Steel thought about the mercenaries' team leader in the cabin. Had he made the guys on watch wait until they came off guard before they ate? It would have been the smart move; nothing kept you awake like hunger.

Steel needed to get the group inside the barn and out of the weather. He made his way along the edge of the forest until he had the barn directly in front of him, but he could no longer see the cabin. He looked over at the group, who were observing him. He had told them to wait where he had left them, feeling it was safer, just in case he was seen.

Taking a long stick from the forest floor, he marked his spot, looked over to the group, and gave a thumbs-up to say he was ready. Then, he ran.

It took him fifteen minutes to get there because he was constantly swerving, trying to keep the barn between him and the house, staying in the blind spot.

Steel hoped that the sentries were just there to stop them from being attacked. That suited him fine. Perhaps his surprise attacks on the others had been more counterproductive than he first thought.

Eventually, he reached the barn and leaned against the back to catch his breath. He was shocked at first. Despite all the training he had done, he was almost out of breath. But then, that had been training under controlled circumstances. Maybe after this, he would work on a programme that was less of a gentle jog and more of a combat training situation. He thought back to the assault courses the army had made him nearly kill himself on.

He held his middle; the pain from one of the places he had been shot was unbearable. He bit through the pain and waited. Nobody came.

After five minutes, Steel made his way to a stack of old crates that he had seen previously and started to stack them in a triangular shape. This would be more stable, and each box would serve as a climbing point.

Eventually, he was high enough to climb onto the roof. Slowly, he slid across the roof towards the skylight. It was partially open, held up by a flat piece of metal with holes that could be placed onto a pin fixed to the window frame. This meant he wouldn't have to force it open, unlatch it, and then replace it on the pin.

He opened it fully, laid the window onto the roof, and climbed inside. Once inside, he drew back the window and placed it back on its latch.

Inside was almost pitch black. The only light was through the three skylight windows. The skylight was just above a walkway cluttered with more boxes and tools. Steel had to walk steadily as he moved towards the ladder. Due to the stillness of the evening, if he knocked anything over or anything fell to the barn floor, it would be heard for miles. He might as well open the barn doors and shout, 'Here I am, ya bastards.'

His visibility was limited, so he had to use touch. Steel felt his back ache as he moved in a crouched position. As his hand touched a pile of machine parts that were close to the edge, he moved his hand to the other side, and his fingers knocked against a bottle that fell against another.

He gasped, hoping there wasn't a whole row of bottles. He could imagine the noise as twenty bottles rolled around, some of them falling from the walkway. The noise of shattering glass filled his imagination. He could see it; it was almost like a comedy film from the eighties, where you think that was the last one, and then another came, then another, and another.

He closed his eyes and waited. Silence.

Steel exhaled heavily with relief, then continued, hoping the ladder wasn't too far away and that there weren't any more hidden surprises.

He couldn't see the ladder; he was working mostly from memory. When he had gone to check the plane earlier, he had glanced around the barn to see if there was anything useful; that was when he had noticed the windows, skylights, and ladder. So, he knew the ladder was between the two skylights; what he hadn't seen was what lay on the walkway above.

Slowly, and after a few more close calls, Steel made it to the ladder. He ventured down, using his toes to feel where the rungs were. Then, with a sigh of relief, he was down.

Steel made his way past the plane to the rear of the barn and the window. It wasn't completely dark outside yet, so the light from outside illuminated the window, giving him a focal point.

The inside of the barn was thick with dust and fumes, but it was warm and, for the moment, a lot safer than being outside.

He reached the window. The three-foot -square frame was fitted with a four-pane glass window that opened outwards on a hinge. Steel had noted this earlier because it had been the only one where the outside shutters weren't closed. He had no idea why this one had been left open; he was just thankful for it.

Steel had to admit the plan was completely nuts. He hid out right under the noses of the people hunting them, but he had to do something. This wasn't London or New York or even a small town; this was one of the most inhospitable places in the world. Sure, it was beautiful, but there was more nature than there were people—thousands of miles of rugged mountains and bear-infested forests. Winter was approaching, and animals needed to feed. Even what some people would consider cute, raccoons would eat your face off if you were given a chance.

He checked the window for locks but found it to be an old leaver handle and a bar-and-pin securing mechanism, just like the skylight. Carefully, heHe carefully levered the handle upwards; it was old and full of crime grime and took a little more force than he had first figured. Eventually, the window was open, and he inched it slowly open, waiting for the inevitable squeak. But none came, and soon, the window was open and ready to receive the survivors.

CHAPTER FIFTY-SIX

THE CHAIRMAN WAS SEATED IN THE HOTEL'S RESTAURANT. He had just finished his glazed Chilean sea bass and was sipping a glass of Sauvignon Blanc from the Napa Valley.

He checked his watch, then his phone. It was late, and there was still no word from Mr Jones.

Time was ticking. Everything was off if they didn't have the package by four in the afternoon the next day. There was no contingency plan. Usually, there would be, but the asshole asset had made sure that they held all the cards.

The Chairman held admiration for the asset; they had done what he was sure he would have done in the same circumstances. After all, being stuck in the middle of nowhere for years would do that to a person.

However, the asset did not consider two things. First, they were working for a criminal organisation that would be more inclined to kill them once they had the goods. Secondly, they had made this time-sensitive, which meant that they and the information were no longer needed once that time was up. Either way, they were screwed.

Of course, unless the asset had a countermeasure. It was a bit like a 'Do something to me, and this goes to the cops' sort of thing.

Something the Chairman had just considered. After all, if this analyst was smart enough to find the information they needed and bold enough to ask for the deal, they were definitely intelligent enough to have insurance in case something went wrong.

The Chairman cracked a smile at the thought. It was a shame that this asset would have to be dealt with; if they got away with it, it would undoubtedly make others think they could do the same. No, this would have to be stamped out; an example would have to be made of this person.

It was a shame but necessary.

He placed his glass down on the white linen tablecloth and looked around, studying the people in the restaurant. Couples and a few people were sitting alone. Everyone there was above forty, he figured. This was a top hotel for good reason. The clientele was mostly business people on business trips, politicians, and movie and music stars—in other words, people who would appreciate fine dining and fine wine—his kind of people.

A woman next to the bar caught his eye. She was tall with short, styled hair and high cheekbones. Scarlet lipstick made the fullness of her lips stand out. She wore a red sequined backless dress and red high heels. He figured she was in her early forties. She could have been a model, but he suspected she was of a different profession.

She looked over at him and raised her martini glass. An invitation? Perhaps. Unfortunately, he wasn't interested. He didn't need that kind of distraction.

He shook his head and then returned to looking at his phone, considering phoning Mr Jones for an update.

The Chairman felt someone standing next to the table. He

looked up; it was the woman. He remained silent, hoping she would get the hint and move on. Instead, she sat.

'I saw you sitting alone, and I thought you looked kind of lonely,' she said. Her voice was soft and alluring. Her accent was Eastern American, possibly New York or Boston.

'Appearances can be deceptive,' he replied. 'For instance, I took you for a....' He paused, choosing the more diplomatic of descriptions. 'A person who specialises in relieving someone of their loneliness.'

She smiled, her large brown eyes sparkling in the candle-light from the table decoration. 'You could have said hooker, but then, you would have been wrong,' she replied.

'So, Miss...?' he said, his curiosity now piqued.

'You can call me Maeve,' she replied, offering her hand for him to shake.

'A curious name—"she who intoxicates."'

She gave him an approving smile. 'Very good.'

'So, tell me, Miss Maeve, what do you want? Now we have established what you are not,' he asked, more curious than before.

'I believe we have a common interest, Mr Chairman. Unfortunately, my employer doesn't like sharing and is intent on pursuing our common interest. I, however, see that we could both benefit from... a partnership, of sorts.'

The Chairman stroked his chin as he listened, as if consid-ering the proposal. 'An interesting invitation; however, I must speak to my boss. You understand I'm unable to give the go-ahead to such a... curious proposal.'

She slid a business card onto the table. It was white and had her name, mobile phone number, and a picture of a horse's head on it.

He took the card and looked at it for a moment before slip-ping it into his jacket pocket. As he went to speak, he found the chair where she had sat empty, and she was walking across the room. The Chairman smiled. He knew this was too good to be true, but if they could double-cross the other organisation before they had time to double-cross him, all the better.

The organisation was known as Trojan. Unlike Santini, Trojan was only interested in power; they didn't run guns unless they had alternative means. Santini's goals were blackmail, corruption, murder, assassinations, gunrunning, and anything else to make money and gain power through fear.

As the Chairman picked up his glass and took another sip of his wine, he couldn't help but wonder how they had found out about the package. Only a few people knew of its existence. All Mr Jones and his men knew was that there was an asset and a package; they had no idea what it was or who the asset was. So, who leaked the information? The asset, perhaps? Maybe they thought they could get a better price; perhaps that was their insurance? If it was, then the Chairman had misjudged the intelligence of the asset and was glad to be rid of them. He had not figured the asset was that stupid. After all, Trojan wouldn't hesitate to kill them once they had the package.

He put down his drink, picked up his mobile phone, and then searched for Mr Jones's number. After finding it, he pressed the call.

Mr Jones picked up on the third ring. 'Yes, sir?'

'I was hoping for an update,' the Chairman said calmly.

'Team Bravo has tracked the group to an old couple's place; we were en route but had to make camp. It gets fucking dark quickly around here. However, I'm assured Bravo has everything under control.'

'Wrong, Major, everything isn't under control. I've just had a surprise meeting with the opposition. They are after the goods as well, so fuck the camp and get moving. You'll be having company shortly,' the Chairman scowled.

'But how, sir? Nobody else knew about any of this... unless!'

'Yes, precisely. We have a leak.'

The Chairman ended the call and returned to his wine. Things were getting out of hand. However, he knew, regardless of whether they had the package in time or not, they couldn't let Trojan have it or the asset. Everything had to be destroyed.

CHAPTER FIFTY-SEVEN

THE GROUP OF SURVIVORS HAD MOVED SLOWLY, ONE AT A time, leaving a five-minute gap between them. The mist was now becoming thick, and they only had a few moments before the barn would be lost from view.

Sherman was the last to leave, carrying Debbra in a fireman's lift. It was not ideal, but he could move better with her on his shoulder than in his arms.

The others had gathered at the open window and then waited for Steel to help them in. Finally, Sherman had reached the safety of the barn, and as he got to the window, Steel grabbed Debbra under the arms and heaved her inside. Bob and Clarke carried Debbra's limp body over to the rear of the plane and laid her onto a pile of old folded tarpaulin Karen and Laura had found.

Steel reached down and grabbed Sherman's outstretched hand, helping him inside. Once they were all in, Steel secured the window. He wished he could have closed the shutters, but that would have meant either going through the front or risking the skylight again. Either option was too risky; better leave it as it was. Plus, closing off their only exit was not the best idea if they had to get out quickly.

Steel looked out into the forest as the group found a place to settle down for the night. Natalie was out there somewhere. She was armed, but she was also not thinking straight. He figured the pressure of everything that had happened had made her snap.

He thought back to the tablets she kept taking. She had said they were magnesium for cramps, but now he wasn't so sure. He turned to Laura.

'Laura, had Natalie any problems that you know of?'

She stared at Steel in confusion. 'No, why?'

'Those tablets she kept taking—I was wondering what they were,' he replied.

'She said they were for her legs that kept cramping; that might also explain why she kept falling behind,' Clarke said.

Steel shook his head. 'I think they were something else. I think she was taking them for a psychological problem. That's why she had this breakdown—I think she had run out of them because the last one I saw her take was yesterday morning. I think that seeing the plane shot to pieces was the breaking point. Before the engine took a hit, we had hope of getting out of here.'

They all thought for a moment, and then Karen shook her head. 'No, not possible. Laura and I would know; we've been friends for a long time. She would have said something.'

Laura nodded in agreement.

'Are you sure? You did say that you hadn't seen each other for a while; perhaps something happened while you were apart?' Steel asked.

Karen shook her head; she was adamant. 'No, we would know if she had changed.'

'Then how do you explain her behaviour?' Sherman asked

curiously. 'I know people with PTSD who seemed fine at first until the smallest thing made them explode. You can't dismiss the fact she is....'

'Fuckin' nuts,' Bob said angrily.

'I was going to say strange, but what you said just about sums it up,' Sherman added.

'I'm no expert,' Steel began, 'but I think your friend has at some point had a breakdown or something that has made her paranoid. Those tablets were to help her stay—dare I say—normal. But things started to chip away when they ran out, and I suspect they have. She needs help before she does something.'

'What, like smashing someone's head in with a rifle? Sorry to disappoint you, but she's already done that,' barked Bob, pointing down at his wife.

Steel and Sherman glared at Bob and placed a finger over their lips to signal that he should shut up.

'Keep your fucking voice down, man,' Sherman hissed.

Bob went to speak, but the look that Sherman and Steel were giving him gave him the impression that it might be the last time he did.

'Look, it's too dark now, but come first light, I'm going after her. Hopefully, by then, she has come to her senses. Everyone will stay here, but the first sign that the mercenaries are moving out, you all head in the opposite direction. There is a town called Ridgeway Creek; it is quite a walk from here, but you have come this far, so I can't see any problems. Clarke will keep the compass; all you have to do is head west. With luck, you might find one of the logger settlements. They are all over the place,' Steel continued.

'How will you find us?' Laura asked, concerned.

'Our rendezvous will be Ridgeway Creek, and if you can get a plane back home, do it. Don't wait. I'll make sure Natalie is on the next one.'

'But wouldn't it be best if we stuck together? I mean, what if something happens?' Karen asked.

'What? To me? Ah, bless,' Steel smiled.

'No, jackass, us!' she replied.

Steel's smile fell away. 'I guess sarcasm is wasted on you lot. Yes, I figured that's what you meant, and thank you for your concern,' Steel scowled. 'Sherman is with you; he'll take care of any... eventualities, I'm sure.'

'And in the meantime?' asked Clarke.

'Find a place to sleep; you'll need your rest. I'll keep watch, make sure those assholes don't decide to get nosey and come over here.'

Steel moved carefully over to the door and one of the shuttered windows. He found one on the right side of the door where the wood split, giving him a view of the outside and the side of the house.

The cabin was still dark and lifeless, but he could feel the eyes of the sentry keeping watch. As he sat, he rubbed his shoulders as his healed bullet wounds were beginning to ache. He wanted to leave and find Natalie, but he knew that there would be no chance of following her trail as soon as darkness fell. Besides, he had to be there just in case one of the mercenaries had the need to check out the barn; it wouldn't be fair to leave Sherman to take on all those mercenaries by himself if the shit hit the fan.

Deep down, he wished one of them would; then they would have weapons and one less mercenary. He had considered attacking the mercenaries, but something stayed his hand. He needed them alive and to start moving in the morning; that way, whoever was in charge of the operation would also think they were heading east. The boss would probably call for reserves if they took out these guys.

No, the best thing would be to leave them alone. Then, as

soon as the mercenaries moved out, they would head back the way they came, hopefully putting some distance between them before they realised what had happened.

The group had organised a shift rotation: Steel would go first, then Laura, followed by Bob, then Karen. Clarke would be next, and Sherman last. Steel had made Sherman last because he knew you would stay awake if Sherman woke you.

Steel glanced over into the barn. He couldn't see past the plane or the back of the barn, so he smiled. If someone did peer inside, they would see an empty barn, save for a plane and tools. The smile fell away from his face, and he hoped that nobody would decide to snore.

CHAPTER FIFTY-EIGHT

THE NEXT MORNING, JOHN STEEL WAS AWOKEN BY A SHAKE of his leg. As he opened his eyes, he saw that it was Sherman.

'What's up?' Steel asked sleepily.

'Time to go, dawn is almost breaking.'

Steel leaned to the side and looked out of the window they had entered through. The sky had a grey-blue tint. Twilight was here.

Steel stood, using one of the plane's wheels as support. His body ached. He hadn't done this much physical work for a long time.

'You okay?' Sherman asked, concern ringing in his voice.

'An old injury. Don't worry, it only hurts when I'm awake.'

The two men walked gently to the window and then carefully opened it.

'Remember, once they have gone, head west and make your way to Ridgeway Creek; it shouldn't be that far from where I found you.'

Sherman shot him a puzzled look. 'So, why didn't you take us there in the first place?'

Steel nodded and cracked a smile. 'Because a couple of days before, I saw our bald-headed friend there with a couple of his mates. I thought there was something off about them—you know, that feeling when someone is an asshole. So, when your plane crashed, I put two and two together and got four. I thought they might be up to something and figured it was best not to lead you into the arms of what I considered bad people. As it turns out, they had left the town, and we would have been better off going there after all.' He shrugged.

Sherman thought for a moment and then shrugged. 'Hey, at least we know where they are now, right?'

Steel shook his head. 'There is still one more team we haven't met yet. According to the tablet, they must be the command team. I think these assholes here have contacted their boss to stay. They are close. So, expect company and keep to the forest—there is no open ground if it can be helped. There is a road nearby, so you might be able to follow that, but I wouldn't suggest hitching a ride unless you are sure they are locals.'

Sherman shot him a confused look. 'And how are we supposed to know who is local?'

Steel gestured around. 'Look where we are. They won't be driving anything new and shiny; most of these people work in the hills or in the stores. You know—mercenaries, big cash, so big vehicles, probably rentals. They are going to stick out like a turd in a swimming pool.'

Sherman nodded. 'Roger that.'

Steel opened the window and climbed out. As he dropped down, Sherman grabbed the handle, ready to close it again.

'Remember, don't wait for Natalie or me. Get the group out, and also, try and sniff out who might have this package. There must be a reason they haven't given themselves up to them. I think whatever they have is either no longer of use, or they have figured they are no longer of use. Whoever it is, they are running scared.'

Sherman nodded once. 'Godspeed, and don't get yourself killed.'

Steel gave a quick flick salute, then headed towards the forest, ensuring the barn was between him and the house.

As Sherman watched, Steel disappeared from view. Then he closed the window and returned to his post.

As he sat, he heard a whispered voice and turned. It was Laura.

'Do you think he will find Natalie?' she asked. She was lying on the ground, wrapped in an old tarpaulin.

Sherman thought for a second and then nodded. 'Yeah, I think he'll find her. The question is, what will he do after he has?'

Laura smiled softly. 'I just hope he brings her home. Despite what she did, she wasn't herself. John said that himself —she was on medication.' Her thoughts drifted, and sadness covered her face. 'Strange—we thought we were best friends, but we knew nothing of her illness.'

'Me too, kid, me too. But for now, we have to look after ourselves. That means keeping quiet until these assholes have left.'

Laura nodded before turning and going back to sleep.

Sherman returned to gazing out of the gap in the wood, hoping it wouldn't be long before the mercenaries moved on. He knew they would want to get an early start and grab as much daylight as they could.

As he watched, the sky was turning a salmon colour. Dawn was here. It looked like it was going to be a nice day. He hoped that was the same for all of them. He hoped that the next dawn sky he saw was back home in Little Creek, Virginia.

CHAPTER FIFTY-NINE

As soon as John Steel reached the forest, he started to run, stopping only to search the area for something familiar, such as a tree or a pile of rocks—anything to give him an indication that he was at the place where he had found the group.

He sprinted in short bursts, avoiding creating a trail. The last thing he needed was to give his pursuers a way to track him.

The air was thick with the smell of the forest—pine needles, ferns, bark, and decaying wood from fallen trees. Steel loved that smell, especially in the early morning after a mist had disappeared; it had a damp crispness to it, one you didn't get in the city.

After a short while, Steel came across the spot where he had discovered the others the night before. He looked down at the disturbed ground where Debbra had lain and grimaced at the thought of what might have been.

Steel turned his attention to the direction Bob had pointed to when Steel had asked where Natalie had gone. He walked over and soon found a small trail of disturbed grass and pine needles; some ferns had been crushed, as though she had been dragging her feet rather than walking—no, not dragging—she had been walking backwards. He could see the distinct pattern of where there was nothing, followed by the same disturbed foliage. She was turning and walking backwards every ten steps as though she was making sure she hadn't been followed.

Was this from her illness? Or was she... A thought occurred to him. Was she the one they were looking for? Did she have this package, and she wasn't ill after all—just scared for her life? That would make more sense than an illness even her best friends didn't know about. Also, hadn't Laura told him that Natalie had been working in Alaska on some kind of project?

As he manoeuvred his way through the forest, he ensured he picked up her trail and, when he did, attempted to cover it.

Soon, he came upon his backpack and knelt beside it. It was still fastened up. He checked inside; surprisingly, everything was there except his water bottle.

Heaving it onto his back, he continued on. Something wasn't right. Why would she discard her only means of food and all the extra ammunition? It made no sense unless he had been wrong and she had indeed had a breakdown of some kind.

Steel stopped and looked up. The sky breaking through the trees was no longer dark blue; the stars had gone, and he was out of time. He had to find Natalie, and he had to do it fast. Soon, the mercenaries would be coming his way, and he was outgunned and outmanned.

He glared at the path before him and said, 'Oh, fuck it.' And ran.

Tracking Natalie started to become difficult. As the forest thickened, there was less foliage, and sunlight was diminishing. Where before, the forest had let grass, ferns, and bushes grow— foliage that could be trampled or broken—this part of the forest yielded nothing but dry dirt, rocks, and tree roots.

As he ran, Steel began to think of the forest in one of

Tolkien's books; he imagined tree elves looking down on him in disdain. *A mortal in our forest?* Or the tree ents, getting ready to swipe him away. He froze for a moment as he thought about the giant spiders and shivered.

He shook off the thought and pressed on, forgetting about any tracks, just heading in a straight line and hoping she hadn't wandered off in a different direction.

Steel vaulted over fallen trees and tree roots the size of rolled carpets from trees that had possibly been saplings when the dinosaurs were roaming.

Animals scattered here and there; a family of raccoons watched him while they sat chewing on something. He vaulted over another fallen tree, but as he landed, he slipped backwards, and the floor seemed to move.

Steel breathed out as the wind had been knocked out of him. Heaving himself up, he investigated the floor and found it was his belt and hatchet. He wondered why she had taken it off, but when he checked out the tree, he saw why. Somehow, the belt had snagged on a broken branch, so in a panic, she had undone the belt and let it fall. Any lucid person would have picked it back up, but now, Steel saw more evidence that she was not thinking straight.

Picking up the belt, he strapped it on, arranging the hatchet in its rightful place next to his right leg. Now he had a weapon; things had just improved.

Steel readjusted his pack and began to run again. He hoped he was getting closer and that his rifle would be the next thing he found.

He did. But Natalie had it, and she was pointing directly at him.

CHAPTER SIXTY

LAURA WOKE WITH A START. SHE LOOKED AROUND, confused and disoriented. The dream, or rather nightmare, was so real that she believed she was somewhere else.

She had dreamed that she was in a forest and wolves had chased her, but they weren't wolves—more like men wearing wolf skins.

Laura looked at the door and saw Sherman sitting. He had been keeping watch, always the good shepherd. Now, he was looking over at her, a smile cracking on one side of his mouth.

'Bad dream?' he whispered.

She nodded and pulled the tarpaulin tightly around her. As she looked around, she had a better view of the barn, as daylight was breaking through one window and the skylights. It was larger than she had imagined; from the outside, it looked smaller. Perhaps it was the plane that made it seem longer and wider. Luckily, the plane took up most of the room, so if someone did peer inside, all they would see was the plane.

Laura gazed at the group. They were still sleeping, and the past couple of days had passed, and this was the first time they had proper shelter. Then she noticed Steel wasn't there. She knew he had planned on leaving early to try and find Natalie; she couldn't think why. However, if he had been correct and she was on medication, she did need help despite the trouble she had caused.

She was still shocked that Karen and she had never noticed after all those years, but then, perhaps it was something new; maybe something traumatic had happened while she was away. Was she now making excuses so she didn't feel as bad?

Laura stood, dropping the tarpaulin, and walked carefully over to Sherman.

'When did he go?' she asked, her voice shivering from the morning air's chill.

'Twilight. Hopefully, he has found her by now, but that depends on if she kept moving or if she found a place to sleep,' Sherman replied, his gaze fixed on the cabin.

There had been no movement all morning; he had expected at least one of the mercenaries to venture out to stretch or take in the morning air, but it was silent and still, and that was beginning to unnerve him—even one of the sentries lighting up a cigarette, something.

'All quiet over there?' she asked.

He nodded slowly. 'Too damned quiet for my liking.'

'Maybe they are still sleeping?'

Sherman shook his head. 'These are ex-soldiers, special forces, the elite; no way are they still sleeping. If anything, they should have left an hour ago at dusk.'

A noise from behind them made them turn. It was Bob. He was still curled up with Debbra but was starting to wake up.

Sherman turned his attention back to the cabin, hoping for movement. None came.

'Look, you must be tired; why don't you get some sleep?' Laura suggested, laying a hand on Sherman's shoulder.

He turned slightly and thought for a moment before nodding. 'You'll wake me at the first sign of movement?'

'Count on it. Now, get some rest.'

Sherman stood, and she took his post, then watched as he went to the tarpaulin she had used as a blanket.

She smiled softly as he got settled, and then she turned her attention to the cabin. As she watched, one of the mercenaries walked out and started pissing while he lit up a cigarette. She watched intently as lights were switched on and the men sprang to life.

Laura smiled, then looked back at the sleeping group of survivors and back towards the cabin. Soon, the men would be leaving, going on the hunt for them all—except they were here. Once the mercenaries had left to hunt them down, the survivors would be long gone by the time the mercenaries figured out they had gone in the opposite direction.

The only tracks they had to follow were those of Steel and Natalie; she just hoped they had put a good distance between them and the mercenaries.

Laura stared intently through the gap, not out of fear but fascination. She knew she should say something, warn Sherman, but she was frozen. It was almost surreal; they were feet away from their hunters, and one single noise or movement could put them in jeopardy. It was like a deer in headlights, not that she understood the terminology.

Suddenly, as her head turned to warn Sherman, Bob rose to his feet and stretched. Her eyes widened with horror because she knew what was coming next. Every time he stretched, he would roar as if to announce to the world that he was awake.

She raised her hand in a stop sign and was about to say something, but Bob was already in mid-stretch, his head tilted back, ready to give a loud roar.

As Bob took a breath and was just about to let out his usual wail, a hand cupped his mouth.

'Don't even think about it,' Sherman growled.

Laura exhaled deeply with relief; she hadn't noticed Sherman was awake or that he had moved with such speed.

Bob swallowed and nodded, then released the breath slowly through his lips.

Sherman removed his hand and let Bob go, then turned his attention to Laura, who looked away sheepishly. He sauntered over to her and then knelt by her side.

'I thought you said you were going to wake me?' His voice was soft, not angry, almost playful. He could understand what she had done. The exhilaration of being so near to the enemy you could smell them, watching them. Knowing you were no longer the prey, that somehow, in a split second, it could turn to shit, but also, in that moment, it had a strange fascination.

He'd had that feeling many times over his career, but he had learnt to control it because it was dangerous. It didn't take much for it all to go horribly wrong.

He knew yelling or scolding her would not make her feel any better. She had made a mistake, and it had been averted. Learn from it.

'I was going to, but...' She nodded over to the cabin. The mercenaries were now all outside, weapons on their shoulders, packs on their backs. They were getting ready to move out.

They smiled; Steel's plan was working. But then their smiles faded as the men turned and watched three black SUVs turn up. They stopped, and a huge blonde man got out and walked up to Sven. The men shook hands, and then they talked.

Sven's arm moved about in the direction of the forest, then the cabin and barn.

Sherman started to have a bad feeling. Who was this new guy, and were there more reinforcements waiting?

The big man spoke, and Sven nodded, saluted, and hurried his men to him. There was a briefing, after which all the men nodded to confirm they understood their orders.

Sven and his men gathered their equipment and then moved into the forest, with the Indian taking the lead.

The big man returned to his vehicle, and the convoy headed south.

Sherman stared, unsure what was going on, but he had an idea.

'Good, they've gone,' Laura smiled.

Sherman shook his head. 'No, not good. If I've figured this correctly, they are going to drive south, then east. They're going to head our people off; they'll be caught in a crossfire.'

'So, what do we do?' Bob asked, looking down at his sleeping wife.

'As we were instructed, head west and make our way to that town,' Sherman said with a heavy heart.

'But we can't leave them!' Laura shouted, forgetting the mercenaries might hear.

'And we can't help them. John will be okay because he doesn't have to worry about us. If he thinks we are sticking to the plan and heading for the nearest town, he can concentrate on getting out of there alive, maybe even take a few of the assholes out along the way. This guy is a fighter; he'll make it out of there,' Sherman said confidently.

'And Natalie?' asked Bob.

'Strange. I thought you'd relish the idea of something happening to her,' Clarke said, waking from the commotion.

Bob reddened with embarrassment. After hearing that Natalie was ill and could no longer comprehend what was going on, he felt bad. Before, he thought she was just a spoilt, self-absorbed woman; now he knew she had run out of medication, which had resulted in her becoming scared and paranoid. He had no idea what it would be like to suddenly feel as if the world was against you, that everyone was your enemy, to feel trapped and alone.

'I guess I did, but after hearing how ill she is, I guess I feel kind of different,' Bob shrugged.

'This is all very heartwarming,' Karen interrupted, 'but what do we do? I mean, if we are leaving, shouldn't we have already left before they come back?'

The barn fell silent as everyone stared at Sherman as if for guidance.

Sherman nodded slowly, as if the decision was painful despite being the correct one. 'Karen is right; we need to leave now.'

Bob looked down at Debbra, who was still lying under one of the tarpaulins, her eyes shut. 'What about Debbra?'

'Have you tried to wake her?' Clarke asked.

Bob shot him an angry look. 'Of course I have; she is still out cold.'

'Okay, okay, keep your shirt on, I was just asking, Jesus,' Clarke grunted. 'I just thought she might be at least conscious by now, that's all.'

Sherman scowled as he coughed loudly, getting everyone's attention. 'We don't have time for this shit,' he nodded towards the tarpaulin that covered Debbra. 'We make a makeshift stretcher from that and some of those long poles,' he gestured to a pile of long, thin wooden poles that looked like broom handles. He had no idea what the old man had used them for, but the six-foot poles were just what they needed to complete the stretcher. 'There are more than enough of us, so four people will carry while the other navigates. We'll take turns with the navigation so everyone gets a rest,' he added.

Without another word, they got to work. Clarke grabbed four of the poles while Laura and Karen stretched out the other tarpaulin. Sherman searched the tool chests and lockers for rope or heavy-duty string to secure the material to the poles; all the while, Bob kept watch through the back window, just in case any of the mercenaries returned.

As Bob stared out of the window, his breath began to fog the glass. He backed away quickly, fearing he was too close. Then, using his sleeve, he wiped the condensation from the glass, and as he did so, his mood soured. It was beginning to rain... and hard.

CHAPTER SIXTY-ONE

JOHN STEEL FROZE. HIS EYES LOCKED ONTO THE BARREL of his rifle, which pointed directly at him. He saw Natalie lying behind a small fallen tree. The rifle was perched on top of the tree like a sniper would use a sandbag to keep the weapon steady. She was behind the weapon, but from where he stood, he could only make out the top of her head, so he could only assume her finger was on the trigger.

Steel did not move, thinking any sudden movement would cause her to panic and fire. But as he stood there, staring past the barrel and onto her face, he saw something in her eyes. They were cold and unblinking, but there was something else. Lifeless.

He began to edge closer, expecting any minute for her to scream and start shooting, but she remained still. He could see no rise or fall from her back as he grew closer. Her skin was ashen. Natalie was dead.

He knelt beside her and checked her carotid artery for a pulse. Nothing. Her skin was ice cold. He figured she must have died during the night. He carefully pulled the weapon from her hands and took out the magazine before sliding back the bolt. A round ejected onto the ground. He stared down at the shiny brass bullet. Had that been the one with his name on it, he thought? He replaced the bullet back into the magazine and then placed it back on the weapon until it clicked into place.

He checked her pockets for anything she might have taken from either himself, the others, or the mercenaries. He found his knife, the hatchet, and a few other items, including a small hip flask, which, upon examination, contained rum, some chewing gum, and her pill bottle. Steel stared at the orange container; it was still half full. He checked the label, which told him the medication was called Clonazepam. He had no idea what it was or what it was for until he read the side label, which gave instructions on how to use it and what it was for.

Clonazepam was an antipsychotic, and from the list of side effects, he wondered why she was taking it. As he read, one thing caught his attention. DO NOT USE WITH ALCOHOL. He thought back to the hip flask and wondered if she had taken one of her pills and washed it down with the rum.

He sat for a moment and stared down at her lifeless body. He found it curious that he felt nothing. No pity, remorse, nothing. No anger at what she had done or even sadness that she had died while being ill; it was that he did indeed feel nothing. Was this a by-product of losing his family and almost dying? He wasn't sure. However, the more he thought about it, one thing became clear: the less feeling got in the way, the clearer his mind worked.

He thought about burying her but then thought, *What was the point?* Any animals hungry enough would dig her up again; besides, he had no tools. He stood, picked up the rifle and slung the pack on his back. The most he could do was cover her with branches, making it harder for the beasts to get to her.

Steel was just about to start when the first raindrop hit the ground. He grunted, knowing what was coming next. He looked down at Natalie's corpse, shrugged an apology, and started to run in the opposite direction from where he had come. A storm was coming, and he needed to find shelter. There was nothing he could do for her; he could only save himself.

Steel knew the mercenaries would be awake and possibly on the move, so he couldn't risk heading back to the survivors. He just hoped Sherman and the others had stuck to the plan and were heading for Ridgeway Creek. Steel would lead the mercenaries in the opposite direction until he got to the Susitna River, then double back and head for the town. Hopefully, he would get a chance to thin their numbers further.

Obviously, his plan wasn't to swim the river, not in those temperatures, but he knew if he followed it, eventually, he would get to Ridgeway Creek or, worst case, Talkeetna.

The rain came down in torrents; raindrops the size of peas felt like he had been stung by a thousand wasps, but he had to keep going. Steel hoped that the thickness of the forest would take the brunt of most of the weather, but the rain came through the gaps in the canopy, making the once-dry ground thick with mud and turning the moss-covered surface into something as slick as glass.

The only consolation was that if the mercenaries were now following his trail, they too would be caught in the downpour. He just hoped that the man called Sven hadn't seen the weather and ordered his men to stay put, meaning the survivors would be stuck in the barn for another night. He was always on edge, hoping one of the mercenaries didn't go to the barn because they were bored or wanted to check if the plane could be repaired.

If this did happen, he would never know, not until it was

too late anyway. By that time, the survivors would most certainly have been killed, and the package recovered.

John Steel began to consider this package. It was obviously something small and valuable, possibly information, not monetary value but more leverage. That said, who was the person carrying it? If it was information on a disc or drive, that meant the person was a computer expert, not a spy or someone that went undercover. This was someone who was using the information to bargain their way out of a situation, hence the reason they hadn't given themselves up the first time they knew the mercenaries were following.

He thought back to his previous theory that whatever they had was time-sensitive. This meant that whoever the carrier was might well be out of time, meaning they and what they had were now obsolete.

Steel found that by thinking about something else, such as who the asshole was who had started this mess and disturbed his peace and quiet, he wasn't thinking about how shit it was to be cold, wet, and muddy again. He had flashbacks from all those exercises in the Brecon Beacons or Sennybridge in the UK.

As his mind wandered, he found he was actually starting to enjoy himself, despite falling over twice on moss-covered rocks —so much so that he had almost forgotten about his situation. That was until he stopped to check that his water bottle was in his pack. Something caught his eye as he slung off the backpack and let it fall. He remained crouched, frozen to the spot, fearful that if he moved, the beast not twenty feet away from him would react.

Steel marvelled at the majesty of the huge white stag grazing in front of him. The animal was enormous, at least the size of a horse. He stared at the stag for a while, taking in the moment, hoping it wouldn't end, hypnotised by this wonder of nature.

Steel eased himself down so he was sitting, careful not to make any sudden movements. The rain had subsided slightly and had eased into a shower; the sunlight broke through the canopy, illuminating the beast in a natural spotlight. The scene was almost angelic.

Steel gasped at the beauty of the scene, causing the animal to look up. Their eyes met, but the stag remained, as if sensing Steel was no threat to him. The two wild creatures of the forest, man and beast, gazed at one another until the stag broke the bond and returned to its feast. Suddenly, the stag looked up and over, alert, wary of someone or something else. Someone or something was heading in their direction from where Steel had come.

The stag bolted, and Steel lay down in the long ferns. The rifle lay next to his pack, ready for him to use it as cover and a shooting aid if necessary.

The forest was quiet. The birds had taken flight; the other animals had scattered. Steel's eyes darted all over, but he saw and heard nothing that could have spooked the forest animals. He hoped it was the mercenaries, but surely they couldn't have caught up to him that quickly? Rather men than a bear or a pack of hungry wolves.

Then he heard it—the roar of a grizzly. Steel shivered at the sound. This was not good; on a scale of one to ten things he didn't need right now, this was a fifteen.

Steel moved the weapon into position, using the backpack to steady it; if he was lucky, he could get a shot off, hopefully hitting the animal in the head. Anywhere else would piss the beast off, meaning he would have a really big problem—one that stood about twelve feet high and was full of claws and teeth.

As he lay there, waiting for a possible unpleasant death, he gazed down a long avenue of trees and saw something in the distance. It was around fifty feet away, sauntering along. It was just a speck, but he could make out the form of something approaching. It was a man.

Steel remained still, hoping that whoever it was would make their way in the other direction. As he watched, the man knelt, checked something on the ground, and made a hand signal. Then Steel saw two other figures, each of them spaced out in formation.

Steel watched in wonder. These men had come from a different direction, so they weren't mercenaries, which made him wonder who they were. Could they be an actual rescue team? He doubted it because these were soldiers. He continued to observe, remaining still and silent.

There were six men in total. The man Steel had seen first was still kneeling as he checked something on the ground. A tracker, perhaps?

The tracker stood up and pointed in the direction that Steel had come from, and the men left a five-metre gap between them.

Steel waited for a moment, making sure they didn't double back. Then, grabbing his pack and weapon, he began to run. If these weren't the same mercenaries, who the hell were they, and what did they want? And more to the point, whose day had just gotten worse—the mercenaries' or his and the survivors'?

CHAPTER SIXTY-TWO

THE CHAIRMAN SAT IN THE HOTEL'S RESTAURANT IN Washington, DC. He had ordered black coffee, an omelette, and a grapefruit for breakfast. He read *The Washington Post* while he waited, paying little attention to most of what had been placed in the columns; most of it was foreign news from Britain, Africa, or Germany.

He was curious about an uprising in one of the African townships. He wondered who had started it—SANTINI or their rivals, TROJAN.

A waiter carrying the Chairman's order placed the omelette before him. The grapefruit was to the left of the plate, and a pot of fresh coffee, along with a cup and saucer, was to the right.

The Chairman thanked the man, who bowed slightly before leaving. The Chairman filled the cup with dark liquid and took a long sip. It was hot, fresh, and strong. Just the way he liked his coffee. Placing down his cup, the Chairman took his cell phone from his grey suit jacket pocket. There were no messages. He frowned. There should have been word from Mr

Jones by now. He remembered his meeting with the TROJAN agent and thought about the warning. Were they really going to piss in his pool?

He found a number in his contacts list and pressed the call button. It was picked up on the third ring.

'Good morning, Chairman. How can I help?' asked a man.

'You can tell me what is going on with Operation Retrieve,' the Chairman growled.

There was a pause, and then the man replied nervously, 'Uhm, what do you mean, sir? We thought everything was going to plan. We were a little behind but on schedule.'

'Check again. I haven't heard anything from the teams all night. I fear someone else is playing in our backyard,' the Chairman ordered.

'You mean TROJAN? But I thought—'

'You are not paid to think. Just get it done. Find out what those bastards are doing and whether they've sent anyone to Alaska. Also, I need background on all those who knew about this operation.'

There was a pause before the man on the other end spoke. 'Why, sir? Do you think there was a leak?'

The Chairman didn't wait for a reply; he switched off his cell phone and placed it on the table beside his paper. He sighed deeply. Things were not going as planned. The courier had failed, but *why* was the question? Why had the courier not left the group of survivors and attempted to find the mercenaries? What had changed?

He could understand that the courier might have reservations about identifying themselves in case it was a double-cross, but a deal was a deal in his eyes. So what had made the courier so nervous?

The plane crash, perhaps? True, the timing was definitely suspicious. He was still waiting on the background checks on the passengers. Was one of them responsible? However, he couldn't see how—unless they wanted to commit suicide. Either way, the whole plan had gone to shit, and he was out of time. The vote in the Senate was tomorrow, meaning both the courier and the information were obsolete. Or were they? What was TROJAN's interest in it? That in itself made it worth getting—or at least destroying.

He pondered the problem while he sipped his coffee. Of course, he would have to speak with his boss. The Chairman's boss was an elusive figure—so much so that nobody had seen him. Or, if indeed the head of the organisation was a man. Nobody knew, and they preferred it that way.

Their only contact with the head of the organisation was through a specially created internet conference group, which was as secure as any government secure net. The signal bounced around several countries, making it impossible to trace the original source.

When they spoke to the head of the organisation, it was through a monitor, and even then, all they saw on the screen was a strange pattern, like looking through a kaleidoscope.

The Chairman cut up the omelette before taking a mouthful of the breakfast dish. It was **okay**—not the worst or, indeed, the best he had eaten, but it was good enough for his needs. This was no reflection on the chef because the Chairman **preferred** things the way he liked them; anything else was either good enough to achieve the task or completely wrong. Very few things were spot on.

He wondered if last night's meeting with TROJAN had upset his appetite. This was possible because every time he came to Washington, he stayed in the same hotel and had the same breakfast, and so far, the food had been excellent.

He took another bite, then chewed it for longer this time, with his eyes shut, hoping that his temper had soured the taste.

After chewing the omelette ten times, he swallowed, opened his eyes, and smiled. He was glad he had taken his time the second time; it was perfect. Then he realised what had nearly put him off his food: the thought that they had a mole—or worse, a leak, a double agent—the pains of working with high-class criminals.

He was surprised it hadn't happened sooner; after all, they were professional assassins, thieves, smugglers, mercenaries, blackmailers and, in most cases, much worse. However, there was always discipline; if someone had ever crossed the line, they had been dealt with, and when they had been picked, they had been vetted. SANTINI didn't take just anyone; they only wanted the most stable and professional in their field.

So, what went wrong? Or, more specifically, why now? Why this assignment?

The Chairman stared at his phone. He knew he had to make the call to inform his boss of the situation. Slowly, he reached down; his hand was shaking with fear. Picking up the mobile, he looked through the contacts list, found the number, and pressed call.

CHAPTER SIXTY-THREE

JOHN STEEL JOGGED RATHER THAN SPRINTED BECAUSE HE needed to put some distance between himself and whoever those men were—and the others who would be following—but he also needed to conserve energy. Besides, sprinting in a forest was pointless and dangerous; his previous falls had proved that.

He stopped for a moment to catch his breath. Evidently, he wasn't as fit as he thought he was, and his wounds were beginning to hurt where the backpack had rubbed on his back and shoulders.

Steel took off his pack and searched for a water bottle. His canteen was empty, but he found a second one, which must have been Natalie's. He shook it and was glad at the swishing noise. He opened it and took a mouthful but spat out the liquid. It was water, but there were strong traces of alcohol.

Steel went to tip away the liquid when he stopped. Why was there booze in Natalie's water? Then he thought back to the pill bottle and the instructions: Do not mix with alcohol. Had Natalie been poisoned? It would also explain her attitude and sudden irrational behaviour; it would also explain why she had died. However, it didn't explain who or why. Laura and Karen were the only ones who had known her, but they had told him they had no idea she had been sick, let alone taking medication. A lie? Possibly, but it didn't explain why.

Steel took a moment to look through the pack; he knew he didn't have long, but something was bugging him.

Natalie had made all the others throw away the weapons they had collected—mostly out of paranoia. However, she had kept Steel's rifle, hatchet, and knife, but what else had she kept? He wondered if she had made the others clear their pockets and kept their items just for safekeeping. It made no sense, but then she was on edge; everyone was an enemy, and she needed to be sure they didn't have knives or anything else that could be a weapon.

As he rummaged through the backpack, he found packets of cigarettes, lighters, dead mobiles, chewing gum, hairbands, lipstick, and wallets belonging to the survivors, along with some of the mercenaries' wallets, which had fake IDs and cash. There were several sets of keys; one had a toy Stormtrooper keychain, and another had a Snoopy.

Steel groaned at the useless items but put them back in his pack; after all, the survivors would need their stuff back when he got to them. He slung the pack back onto his back and began running again. He needed to put distance between himself and the mercenaries and get to the river.

As he jogged, ensuring he made as few tracks as possible, he wondered about the others. Had they actually managed to get out of the barn? Were they on their way? Steel knew Sherman would herd them towards the town if they had made it out. He had a way with these people—one that Steel didn't—but then Sherman was invested in getting to the town safely because he was one of them, and he also wanted to get home, whereas Steel was home.

He thought about the cabin, how he used to get up in the morning and watch the sunrise over the mountains. He missed being alone, with no responsibilities—just him and the wilderness. Then his mind wandered, thoughts of his old life back in Britain, his family, his mates in the regiment. The happy thought faded as he flashed back to the terrible event at his family estate—the men who had broken in and killed his family and friends—how he held his darling wife in the attic, thinking she was dead, staring down at her face as her eyes opened just as the bullets ripped through his body, the final one going through him and hitting her in the side of the head.

He heard a shot. At first, he thought it was a memory until there was a second explosion, and he was pushed forward. The bullet had hit his pack, which, luckily, was full and had cushioned the impact and stopped the bullet.

Steel groaned; even though the backpack had stopped the round, the impact still hurt like hell. He rolled over onto his side and aimed the rifle. One of the mercenaries from the old couple's cabin stood before him, his assault rifle moving, looking for a target.

Still, Steel was ready and took the shot. The bullet hit the man in the chest and threw him backwards. Steel didn't know if the man was wearing body armour, but he did know from that range that it didn't matter. The 7.62 bullet would have at least broken his ribs; if Steel was lucky, it might have broken the guy's sternum. Either way, he wasn't getting up to follow him.

Steel heard the others' cries, asking for a SITREP—a situation report. He smiled; the mercenaries' eagerness to fire had cost them and caused panic. This told Steel a lot; these were not the Alpha team but another bunch of expendable men, making him think: where was the Alpha team? They would have caught up by now. He wanted to check the tablet and his location against the others; unfortunately, they would have his location as soon as he did.

Steel heaved himself up; his old wounds were now hurting like hell, and his back felt like a horse had kicked him—something he had also experienced. He had been a boy, and luckily, it had been a pony, but the effect was the same.

The shot had knocked Steel off balance, and he was disoriented. Which way had he been heading? He looked over to where the mercenary had fallen. There were no moans or groans of pain; perhaps the guy was dead after all, or at least unconscious. Steel looked in that direction, then turned to face the opposite way. He had no idea if this was the correct direction, but he knew one thing: the bad guys were not coming from that way.

When he was sure he had put enough distance between himself and was safe, he would check with his compass, but for now, he would have to run and hope he could make it to the river in time.

CHAPTER SIXTY-FOUR

MIKE SHERMAN AND THE OTHER SURVIVORS HAD STOPPED for a rest. The way was rough; the ground had turned to mud after the downpour, but most of all, they were cold, wet, and hungry, carrying a makeshift stretcher with the still-unconscious Debbra.

Sherman was no medical expert; however, he was concerned that even after this long, she was still unconscious. He looked around at the others, who had collapsed where they had stood. They all looked exhausted, and it was no wonder—they had little water and rations with them. The last time they had eaten had been the night before. They were running on empty, and the extra burden of carrying Debbra was starting to show.

Even Laura looked at Debbra with contempt. Soon, if she didn't wake, he felt there might be a mutiny on his hands. The others might refuse to take her any further and decide to head off without Debbra and Bob, who would no doubt choose to stay with her.

He had seen soldiers on SEAL training give up after doing

ICE COLD STEEL

less, so maybe he was wrong. Perhaps the group could endure a little longer. However, he had no idea how long because there was no carrot to dangle at the end of the day. Sure, they were heading for this Ridgeway Creek, but what then? The nearest airport they needed was in Talkeetna, which, judging by the map, was an extra thirty to forty miles away from Ridgeway Creek. They also had no idea if the mercenaries were in the town waiting for them.

Sherman looked up at the sky. It was beginning to clear up, and patches of blue were straining to break through the grey clouds. Birds had started to take flight as if giving the all-clear. The rain shower had been a warning—*This was just a taste of things to come.*

He took out the map and studied it, trying to decipher where they were and how far they had to go. It didn't take him long, but he did this for a living. By his calculations, they still had a fair distance to travel. However, he noticed a train track about fifteen miles from their location. It seemed the best option—to get to the track and follow it, hoping that a train was going past and, more importantly, going in their desired direction. If they were lucky, it would take them all the way to Talkeetna.

Sherman told the others the plan, which brightened their mood as he had hoped. They had something to hope for. He explained that if they managed to get aboard the train, they would take it all the way to Talkeetna and not get off at Ridgeway Creek. At first, the group was unsure, but after he explained that it was best, just in case there were more mercenaries there, they all agreed.

Sherman knew that when Steel got to Ridgeway Creek and found them missing, he would assume they had gone straight to Talkeetna. He just hoped Steel had found Natalie and was bringing her back, but he worried—she had been alone in the

263

forest all night, the weather had been colder than usual, and where they had built fires to keep warm, he feared she wouldn't have been able to.

If that was the case, he just hoped at least Steel made it; after all, the man was an animal. He had no idea how long Steel had been living in the wilderness or what he had done before that, but Sherman knew a special forces asshole when he saw one. Sherman had done enough joint operations with the SAS to spot one of their men.

He folded the map and tucked it into his jacket pocket before standing. Sherman knew they had to keep moving; they needed to open the gap further between them and the mercenaries. Also, the longer they rested, the more likely cramps would occur. The group needed water and food. These were civilians, not soldiers. The hardest thing they had probably had to do was walk a flight of stairs because the elevator was broken.

'OK, people, we need to get going. I want to be at some shelter before dark,' Sherman explained. He hoped the thought of a warm, safe place to sleep might encourage them to put a little more effort into the next part of the march. He left out the *we need to get moving because we still have a bunch of mercenaries that want to kill us somewhere behind us* part. He didn't think that would boost morale much. The group was in a good place despite carrying Debbra on the makeshift stretcher.

Sherman looked down at Debbra; she was pale but appeared OK, though he wasn't a doctor. She could possibly have an internal head injury, swelling of the brain, or something. However, he still found it odd she had not moved, given a whimper, or anything. She just lay there.

'OK, folks, we need to get moving.' Sherman's voice was strong, but it wasn't an order—more encouragement. 'If the map is correct, we shouldn't be too far from the train tracks. We'll follow them; hopefully, the next train will go our way.'

Sore muscles and injuries from the crash made the group groan as they stood. After a quick shake-off, they picked up the stretcher and moved out.

Far behind, the new group of mercenaries from the TROGAN group had arrived at the old couple's cabin. They searched the area and found the bodies of the old couple and the mercenaries. The leader, a tall, pale-looking man, waited while their scout, an ex-Army Ranger, checked for tracks. The scout returned to the team leader, his face grim.

'And?' asked the leader; his voice was deep, and he spoke with an accent from the southern states.

'We got two sets of tracks. One set goes back into the woods, and seven men follow a single person. The other heads off that way,' he said, pointing towards the clearing and the woods in the distance. 'This is a single group, five people. The tracks show that they are carrying something or someone. I figure one of the group is injured, and they are using a stretcher.'

'Military?' the leader asked.

The scout shook his head. 'I figure civilians, and they are tired, judging by the tracks.'

The leader thought for a moment before speaking. 'OK, so who is the squad chasing? And why?'

Just then, a shot rang out from the forest, then another, followed by silence.

The mercenaries spun round to face the noise. The leader smiled. 'I guess whoever it is doesn't like company.' He nodded to his men, who formed up into a herringbone formation, and the mercenaries marched forward. The hunt was on.

CHAPTER SIXTY-FIVE

THE NEXT SHOWER CAME AS SUDDENLY AS THE LAST, bringing a stiff wind from the east. The sky became dark as thick grey clouds clustered above. Inside the forest, it became as black as night, making it hard for Steel to make his way.

However, he didn't mind because if it was difficult for him, it was difficult for his pursuers. All he needed to do was get to the river. If he was lucky and had timed it correctly, Old Man Burt would be taking the logs from the felling station downriver to Talkeetna via Ridgeway Creek.

Old Man Burt wasn't just a local. His family had been in the region since colonial days, and now he was the last of his family. He had married years ago, but unfortunately, no matter how many times they tried, they could not have a child. His wife had fallen ill years back and had died; now, Old Man Burt was alone, save for his Rottweiler, Jake.

He would use his old tugboat to transport the logs—he was sure it was called timber rafting. This was an ancient way of getting thousands of logs down or upstream to the mills, a method even the Romans had used thousands of years ago to transport timber from Corsica.

If he were unlucky, he would either be too early or too late, which meant following the river until he reached the train tracks and then following them to Ridgeway Creek. If that were the case, he would be in trouble—there would be no cover, and he couldn't afford to end up in the river. The water would be freezing, and he wouldn't have time to build a fire to dry off afterwards. He had learnt in the Army that in a river crossing, the best way was to strip off, put his clothes into his waterproof backpack, and then swim over. Once on the other side, he would put on his dry clothes and let his body dry off naturally. However, falling in by accident or getting forced in with little time to put his clothes into a dry backpack would be the only reason to go into the freezing swell.

All his hopes now rested on Bob not having already gone past or still being upstream, waiting for the logs to be loaded into the river.

His only plan B was to keep going downriver and hope to avoid the mercenaries. He knew the road wasn't too far away, but he needed to draw whoever was following him away from there, giving Sherman and the others a chance.

The rain came down hard, and the wind was picking up, causing the trees to creak with disapproval, but he put his head down and tried to keep the same pace. He no longer cared whether he made tracks or not, knowing that he didn't have time to be careful—he needed to get to the river.

He needed to get out of the forest; the last thing he needed was for one of the trees to topple in front of him, worse still, on top of him. He had seen it before—when one goes, there is a risk of a domino effect, meaning there was no way of knowing where they would fall or how many would until the motion stopped.

Steel picked up the pace but took care with his footing; at this point, the last thing he needed was to twist an ankle. The rain and wind were getting worse; the trees moaned as they swayed, and the rain was now the size of peas, stinging his face. He forced himself onwards, hoping his pursuers hadn't turned back.

He was thankful for his glasses as they shielded his eyes, but the cold, biting wind had numbed his hands and extremities. His ears and nose felt as though they were on fire, and several times, he had lost his grip on his rifle—so much so that he had to sling it onto his shoulder so he didn't lose it.

Steel was just about to give up hope of escaping the forest; he was disoriented. After all, all he had seen, for what had seemed like hours, were trees—some of which he could have sworn he'd seen before.

Steel hadn't had time to check his compass because he needed to keep moving, open up the gap between him and the mercenaries, but also force them to open the gap between them and the survivors.

John Steel wiped his face using his sleeve, but the rain-sodden coat only added to the water on his face. He was cold, hungry, thirsty, and lost. It reminded him of the selection with the SAS and the Brecon Beacons. He shuddered at the thought. He had been pushed to his limits there; only his pigheadedness not to give up had pushed him on. Unlike now, this time, lives were at stake—his included.

A flash of light lit up the forest as if someone had just turned on a lamp, followed by a massive boom from a thunderclap. The storm was right over him. Now was not the time to be in a forest with enormous trees. On the plus side, it would put the mercenaries behind him on edge.

He pushed forward despite having little visibility. His sunglasses made everything in his view even darker, but they kept the rain out of his eyes. There was another flash of light, and he was suddenly thankful for the glasses—where most would have been blinded, he saw perfectly, if only for a second. Then, his world fell into darkness once more.

Steel paused for a moment. His body was aching, and his wounds felt as though needles were being plunged into his skin. Anger welled up inside him. He had thought he had done enough training to return to his old fitness, but these past few days had told him otherwise. He was nowhere near in shape. He should be fighting fit by now, but then, he had never been shot and left for dead before. The doctors had been shocked by his recovery; they said, by rights, he shouldn't have made it. Yet, here he was. He knew the old man had injected him with something; however, nobody knew what, and frankly, Steel didn't want to know. What he did know was that it had saved his life.

He hadn't gotten special powers to rejuvenate like in the comic books—this was something more basic. It had somehow affected the clotting agents in his blood to work faster. The serum hadn't repaired him too quickly; it had just closed the wounds so he wouldn't bleed out. The rest was up to the surgeons and Steel himself.

Steel clenched his teeth and dug deep. He wasn't done yet —not while he was so close. He wiped his glasses with his sleeve and forced his body forward.

Unfortunately, his next step was cut short when he caught on a hidden tree root and was hurled forward, and things went black.

A few seconds later, Steel woke with a coppery taste in his mouth. He spat out a mouthful of blood and cursed his clumsiness. But then, he was tired. His body was at its limit. He hadn't eaten for what seemed like days, and he hadn't slept properly for just as long.

He moved his hands slowly, inching them into a position so

he could push himself up, but he stopped. The ground felt hard and flat. At first, it didn't compute. Where the hell was he?

Another flash of lightning lit up the area, turning everything into an icy blue tint—including the road on which he was lying. He smiled. He had reached the road, and the river wouldn't be far away.

The river was just the other side of the next forest. Steel knew that this part of the forest had several paths tourists used to get from the road to the river; all he had to do was find one of them.

He smiled. Finally, things were going his way.

CHAPTER SIXTY-SIX

THE LIGHTNING FLASHED, AND THE THUNDER ROARED LIKE an artillery barrage. The storm was right over the survivors, and the wind was straining the roots of the towering trees. The rain came down in sheets. Out in the open, visibility was down to feet, not yards, causing Sherman to rethink his idea when they stumbled onto the road.

The idea was to wait for a vehicle to travel towards Ridgeway Creek. Still, the poor visibility meant they wouldn't be able to see the vehicle in time, and the driver wouldn't be able to see them.

He feared that at the first glimpse of headlights, one of the survivors would get excited and run into the road, trying to flag it down and getting run down in the process. And, out here in the wild and with the shit weather, the driver might think it was an animal and keep driving. The driver might wait until they got home to check the damage or even wait until morning.

A deafening boom followed another flash of light; the storm was now right over them. The massive boom told him the lightning had struck something, possibly one of the trees. He smiled wickedly as he wondered if the mercenaries had been close to it. Then the smile faded—the stranger was also in there. He looked back into the forest. He couldn't do anything anyway; he had no idea where John would be. Sherman hoped the stranger had made it out and the mercenaries were now lost in the wilderness.

He looked over at the shivering group and at Debbra, who was still on the makeshift stretcher. They needed to follow the road, hoping the storm would subside and a vehicle would pass by.

He thought about looking at the map, but it would be pointless in this weather. He started to miss all the little things he had ever taken for granted, like plastic map cases and hotel rooms.

'OK, folks, we gotta keep movin',' he yelled over the wind.

The others nodded reluctantly, and they picked up the stretcher and headed down the road.

Sherman wondered how they had missed the train tracks and gotten to the road. Not that it mattered—they were now on a hard surface and not tripping over the foliage in the forest. On the other hand, if they couldn't see the mercenaries because of the weather, the chances were the mercenaries couldn't see the survivors... in theory.

However, as Murphy's law often reminded them, 'If you can't see the enemy, they can't see you.' Unfortunately, when Murphy wrote these laws, they didn't have thermal imaging.

The survivors followed the road but stuck to the verge to ensure nobody accidentally got run over or, if necessary, so they could drop to the ground at the first sight of the mercenaries.

Sherman stayed at the back of the group, turning around every few steps to check if a vehicle was approaching or if the mercenaries were.

The group's morale was low. They were tired, hungry,

and wet, and they were stuck in the middle of nowhere with a bunch of killers chasing them. The incident with Natalie had shaken them; they still couldn't understand why she had such a breakdown. Especially Laura—she had known her for years, or thought she had. But then, it had been a while since they had last spoken; perhaps her new job had taken its toll on her.

'What do we do?' yelled Karen.

Sherman glanced over at her; she had fear in her eyes.

'We follow the road, hope a vehicle drives past,' Sherman yelled back over the wind.

'What about the assholes following us?' Clarke barked, looking back over his shoulder, even though the rain was so thick they couldn't make out the trees.

'We'll just have to risk it. Getting to a town is more impor-tant at the moment. I just hope any drivers see us in time to stop,' Sherman yelled.

'In this weather! I'm just hoping the driver sees us before they run us over,' Clarke groaned.

Sherman stood, and the others followed. 'We have to go.' He bent down and grabbed one side of the stretcher. Bob, Clarke, and Laura followed suit. Then they started down the road, with Karen moving behind them, keeping an eye on the road and ready to grab the attention of a vehicle.

A bright light behind them caused them to stop and turn; a vehicle was coming, and judging by the lights, it was enormous —an eighteen-wheeler from the logging station, Sherman thought.

As they turned, they noticed the rain was beginning to subside, but the wind was still howling. Sherman was about to shout out to Karen to start waving when he saw the gunman on the other side of the road. He must have walked straight past them, unaware of their presence, but now he was staring straight at them, pulling his rifle slowly up to his shoulder so he could take aim.

The others stood frozen on the spot, fear gripping their muscles and holding them in place.

The gunman grinned as he nestled the butt of the assault rifle into his shoulder and closed one eye as he looked down the scope. However, he never saw a figure running towards him and the truck hurtling down the road towards all of them.

John Steel was about to head down the embankment and find his way to the river to wait for the logging boat; however, as the rain began to slow, he saw the others and the gunman. His first instinct was to call out and try to distract the mercenary. Still, the wind was blowing towards him, and his voice would have been carried in the wrong direction, so he decided to run.

Most people, especially trained soldiers, learn to have an almost sixth sense; they can feel when someone is near, and John Steel hoped this guy was one of them.

As he grew closer, he could see the truck's lights illuminating the road, but something was wrong. The road had a slight bend to it, but the lights were directly behind him. Had the driver fallen asleep? Steel risked a glance behind him and saw the truck was indeed heading for him and the gunman, who was too busy aiming his weapon to notice the immediate danger.

Steel dove out of the way, but instead of the sloping grass verge, he found himself falling straight down. He just hoped the next thing he felt was water.

The gunman was just about to fire an aimed shot when the bright light made him look over. He turned his head to see the bright glow of the headlights; he yelped and tensed his body, firing the weapon just before the truck smashed into him.

The sudden thump on the front of the truck caused the dozing driver to wake. He saw the bend in the road and pulled at the wheel, hoping to avoid ploughing over the side. There was a screech of tyres and a grind of metal as the truck began to tip onto its side.

The survivors gasped as the truck began to heave onto the left side, then shuddered before crashing down on all wheels. The brakes continued to scream until, finally, it came to a stop.

The driver got out, looked at the truck, and kissed his fingers before laying them on his truck as if to say *good girl*, then he threw up.

The survivors looked over at the truck, then over to where Steel had gone over the side.

They were about to run over to see if Steel was okay when they heard Debbra screaming and holding her right leg, which was bloody and had a large hole in the side.

Shocked, everyone dropped the stretcher and stepped back —all but Bob, who still held on to the pole, causing the stretcher to tip Debbra onto the road.

She screamed loudly as her injured leg hit the asphalt and shot a venomous look over at the others, but most of all at Bob.

'This wasn't the fucking plan, Bob! We were meant to slow them down so we could meet up with the others. Now look, you idiot!' She grasped her leg and whimpered.

Sherman quickly grabbed his belt and knelt next to Debbra, who went to lean back as if trying to escape.

'I don't know what the fuck is going on here, but you need to get a tourniquet on that leg, or you won't need to worry about whether you meet up with the others—whoever they are,' he growled.

Debbra nodded and leaned back on the stretcher as Sherman applied the technique.

She winced in pain as he pulled the fibre strap tight and locked it off using the fastening clip. He looked over at Laura, who had the medical backpack, and raised his arms as if to silently beckon her to throw it to him.

Laura waited momentarily, unsure if she wanted to use their bandages on her.

Sherman stayed in position; his eyes now glared at her, and his tone had changed as if to say, *Now, please.*

Laura slung off the pack and tossed it to Sherman, who began searching it for bandages, gauze, and tape.

'Karen, see if John is okay?' he ordered.

She nodded and ran over; Clarke went with her.

Sherman shot Bob an evil glance.

'So, Bob...' he began. '*You want to fill us in, or do you want to join your friend over there?*' He nodded to where the gunman had been slammed into.

Bob's face turned pale as the blood rushed from his cheeks, and his eyes widened with the horror of the situation. He was in deep shit, and there was no way out.

He went to say something when a cry from Karen made him look behind him

As he turned, Bob took to his heels and ran down the road. He had no idea what he was doing but knew he just had to get away. It was an interesting plan if you were in London, Paris, or even New York, but it was a bad idea if you were stuck in the middle of nowhere with no clue where you were running to.

Sherman watched him with dull eyes; he didn't have the time or energy to chase after him. However, he knew that at some point, Bob would stop, look around, reassess his situation and walk back to the group. At least his chances of survival with the group were better than with the mercenaries.

And Bob did. He stopped, put his hands on his knees—like a runner who had just finished a race—turned, looked at Sherman, and started to walk back.

Karen called over to Sherman again; this time, the cries were loud, desperate.

Sherman looked over at her, noting the panic in her voice, and ran over to the edge, leaving the whimpering Debbra.

He reached Karen and Clarke, who were looking over the embankment's edge, and found Steel hanging from a jutted-out tree root. The tree had long since gone, possibly cut down when they made the road, but the long root was still firm.

'Hold on, we'll try and get you up,' Karen shouted.

Sherman glanced at her as if to say, *Did you actually say hold on?* but she was too busy to notice.

Karen turned in circles as if looking for something useful. But they were on a road in the middle of nowhere.

'Try the truck,' Sherman called.

'I can't drive a truck?' she replied, stunned at the suggestion.

Sherman smiled and shook his head in disbelief. 'No, what I meant was, check the truck. It's a logging truck; there might be straps or something.'

'Oh!' she smiled with embarrassment. 'On it,' she said and ran to the idling truck; Clarke followed.

Sherman looked down at Steel, who was too far down for him to try and reach, and Steel looked back at him, but to his surprise, Steel didn't look worried—more annoyed.

Sherman was about to say something when Karen and Clarke returned with a lashing strap they had found in one of the side bins of the cab.

They lowered the strap and waited for Steel to grab it with his free arm. When he had a tight grip, he grabbed it with his other arm. Sherman, Karen, and Clarke grabbed the strap as though they were in a tug-of-war match and held on as Steel began to climb.

'Start pulling—slowly,' Sherman ordered, knowing that John might need the help after holding onto the root for so long.

The three of them moved back until they finally saw a hand appear, then an arm. 'Keep going,' Sherman ordered until Steel had heaved himself onto the asphalt and lay there, breathing heavily. His body hurt, and his wounds felt like red-hot needles were inching their way into his skin.

'You're outta shape!' laughed Sherman.

Steel just offered him his middle finger as thanks.

CHAPTER SIXTY-SEVEN

About a mile behind the survivors, Mr Jones and his mercenaries were heading north; then, they would double back to catch the survivors in an ambush.

Unfortunately, the men from the Trojan organisation were heading through the forest, close on the heels of the survivors.

The question was, who would get to them first?

Mr Jones was aware of the new threat; the Chairman had warned him, but even so, he had to wonder how they had found them so quickly when he and his men had been tracking them for days.

Was there a mole in their group? But then, the SANTINI organisation wasn't full of choirboys. The organisation was, after all, in the business of murder, assassination, arms smuggling, extortion, and blackmail. In fact, their business was about power and money.

He pondered the problem but knew it could wait until after the mission—as long as the mole didn't hinder the mission beforehand.

As soon as Mr Jones and his men hit the road, they began to

move north. If the survivors had managed to get to the road, they would have moved south, and then they would have run into Jones and his men. However, he was not so naïve as to think that the group might stick to the forest, so he left a couple of men moving parallel through the forest.

He hoped they would get to the survivors and, more importantly, the package. He didn't want to think of what might become of him and his men if they failed.

The Chairman was not a forgiving man. Nor was the person they all worked for—not that any of them had seen the main boss. All communication had been through a computer, and a distorted voice made the boss's sex impossible to ascertain. It also gave a very sinister illusion.

Mr Jones thought back to *The Wizard of Oz*, the voice behind the curtain. The all-powerful Oz. Perhaps the boss was just an ordinary person, maybe a little old lady. The fact that nobody knew was the frightening thing.

The fact the boss could be anyone, and when the shit hit the fan, he or she could simply disappear.

Mr Jones made his way down the road, the third man in the staggered formation. The rain had eased off, but the wind was still howling, bending the trees. In the distance, they could see lights from a vehicle, but they seemed to be stationary.

Maybe the driver had hit something—an animal? Or a person?

He smiled. 'Okay, let's pick it up. Our target is that vehicle.'

The mercenaries began to walk quicker but held off running. There was no point in risking slipping on the wet road or finding the vehicle had just stopped to answer his phone and was now setting off. The team wore all black, and the driver wouldn't see them until it was too late.

Mr Jones didn't need to order his men off the road; it was

almost instinctive. Seven men, armed to the teeth, heading for what they hoped to be the end of their mission.

Mr Jones was sick of this wilderness. What had been supposed to be a simple mission had turned out to be a shitshow.

He just hoped, before they went home, he got to meet the person responsible for killing his men. He needed a little payback.

CHAPTER SIXTY-EIGHT

THE CHAIRMAN HAD DECIDED TO FLY BACK TO NEW YORK, thinking Washington was not the safest place to be right now. The surprise visit from one of TROJAN's agents had made it all too clear they meant business, and the last thing he needed was to be looking over his shoulder—or worse, dead.

He wasn't a coward, just smart enough to keep his distance from possible harm. If push came to shove, he would have no problem putting a knife into her—after he had some fun, of course.

The Chairman had confidence in Mr Jones and his team. However, the past few days meant the teams had more to worry about than Trojan mercenaries. Someone in the group of survivors had been underestimated.

Of course, they knew about Colonel Mark Sherman of the SEALs. Still, he hadn't seen action in years, and none of the others had any military experience—except, of course, for the asset.

Like most of the other field agents, the asset had gone

through a period of training just so they could operate in the field or, in this case, survive.

However, the Chairman could not understand why the asset had not left the others and gone looking for Mr Jones as soon as they knew there were teams nearby. Unless, of course, the asset had been speaking with Trojan? It made sense and explained how the Trojan agent knew what the asset had.

He would enjoy hearing how the asset had been taken care of.

The Chairman settled into one of the leather seats in the private jet and sipped the champagne the steward had brought. He had things to plan and consider, and the thought of Trojan gaining access to the information made him shiver.

His organisation was about making money, whereas Trojan was about power and control. He dreaded to think of the fallout if they got hold of it.

If they had that much control, there would have been no end to the damage they could have done to America and other countries.

The Chairman sat, stared out of the window, and studied his reflection as the aircraft taxied. His greatest fear now was informing the head of the organisation—the mysterious voice from the computer.

The boss would not take it well, and he had no goat to tether for the sacrifice.

The flight back to New York would take just over an hour, much quicker than driving. He didn't have the luxury of wasting time, not when his life might be at risk.

The engines whirred, and the aircraft began to pick up speed. Soon, they would be in the air and heading east. Once they were, he had calls to make.

CHAPTER SIXTY-NINE

Down below, riding the river, pushing a mass of logs, was Old Man Burt in his lumber raft. The old tug was small and dirty, and black smoke billowed from the funnel, but she went on as if she had just come out of the shipyard.

The Merry Helen was made back in the seventies and was still going strong, just like Bob. In fact, *The Merry Helen* was Bob's first boat—or rather—the boat he did his apprenticeship on.

The boat belonged to his father, who took Bob on, and after he retired, Bob took over the business. There was not too much of a call for it now. However, the lumber firm still used him because he was reliable. The boat wouldn't get a puncture or run off the road, and it didn't matter if he fell asleep because the current would lead the way.

The trucks were expensive because they needed fuel, tyres, and frequent maintenance. *The Merry Helen*, not so much, and she never required tyres.

So, the firm kept him on in conjunction with the trucks,

which meant more wood flowed towards the city's lumber mills.

As Old Bob was steering the vessel, he noticed something large fall from one of the embankments. Curious, he leaned out of the side window and stared into the night, waiting for the next blast of lightning to illuminate the area. The wind had died slightly, and the storm was losing strength, but the lightning remained.

As he stared, the heavens erupted, lighting up the area like a football stadium. He found a man hanging from a tree root. He waited for the next flash of light and saw a man in a long brown coat; he smiled as he recognised the figure as John Steel.

As the boat cruised slowly past, Old Bob leant out and called to Steel, somewhat curious about what he was doing.

'John, is that you?' he yelled.

Steel cocked his head slightly and saw the boat with the logs, knowing instantly who had just called his name. 'Yes, Bob, it's me,' he yelled back, almost embarrassed at his situation.

'What the hell you doin', boy?'

'Oh, nothing much, hanging around, killing time. There was bugger all on television,' Steel said, sarcasm ringing in his voice.

'Oh, OK then,' Bob yelled back.

Steel gazed down in astonishment; he actually believed him. He rolled his eyes. 'God, I'm going to die here,' he said to himself.

Just as Steel was about to give up hope, he heard voices from above; it was Karen and Clarke. Steel gasped in relief, 'God bless ya cotton socks, Sherman.'

He felt the lashing strap hit him on the back and quickly grabbed it with a free hand. His body hurt like hell. His wounds were screaming; his muscles were on fire. Steel looped the strap around his wrist so there was no chance of losing his grip. Then, blowing out a lungful of air, he let go of the tree root and grabbed the strap with his now free hand.

On the road, Steel lay for a moment, breathing heavily. He thought all his training had given him some level of fitness, but then again, he never planned on falling off a caved-in embankment and hanging from a tree root.

He sat up and stared at the survivors and saw Debbra screaming and holding her leg; her husband, Bob, was kneeling, looking lost and scared.

Sherman nodded at Steel. 'You're outta shape!' laughed Sherman.

Steel flicked his middle finger at him, then stood up. 'We have a way out of here, but we have to hurry; our ride is leaving.'

The survivors looked at the truck, but Steel shook his head and pointed down towards the river. 'Old Man Burt and his log tug, but we have to go now.'

'What about her?' Clarke nodded towards the screaming Debbra.

'Fuck her,' Karen said.

Steel shook his head and rushed over to Debbra. 'No, she is coming with us. I want some answers.' He threw his pack towards Sherman. 'Take this.' Then he grabbed Debbra by the arm.

She winced in pain. 'No, stop, it hurts.'

'Oh, OK, tell you what, we will leave you here then. No problem. But then the question is, who gets to you first: the bears, the wolves, or the bloodthirsty mercenaries? Or you can shut the fuck up and live with the pain for a bit.'

Debbra looked at Steel, shocked. Not because of what he had said but because she was seeing him for the first time without his glasses. She stared at his dark, emerald, soulless eyes and shivered.

Steel had forgotten he had lost his glasses in the fall; now, everyone would see him, including Sherman. He would have questions, but ones that would have to wait.

Steel grabbed Debbra and hoisted her onto his back, ignoring her yells—despite bouncing her onto his shoulder a few times as if he was getting into a comfortable position, but in truth, he was just being a dick about it. Then, the group headed down a grass verge towards the river, hoping Old Bob was still there.

CHAPTER SEVENTY

Mr Jones and his team approached the truck cautiously. The eighteen-wheeler was sitting there idling, with no signs of the driver or anyone else.

He raised his closed fist, signaling the team to stop. They all knelt, alert and ready for instructions.

Mr Jones looked through the scope of his assault rifle, checking out the area to ensure it wasn't a trap.

He saw the driver; he was lying on the ground, his fat stomach rising and falling. He was alive, but there was no indication of why he was on the ground in the first place.

There was a low rumble; the storm was moving on. Now, stars were beginning to peep through gaps in the thickening cloud cover. A hazy, bright moon was lighting up the area like a searchlight.

Mr Jones continued with his search, finding nothing—only the driver. This was strange because the survivors should have at least gotten this far by now. He made a quick hand signal, and the team moved towards the truck, each man vigilant and ready for a possible ambush.

They approached the truck, and one of the team pointed to a bloody dent on the front grille. The driver had obviously hit something, possibly a wild animal, and had fainted after seeing the blood.

What Mr Jones found strange was that hitting wildlife in this part of the world was probably an everyday occurrence. He looked at the truck's rear; the whole thing was at a strange angle, as if it had swerved. Maybe the driver had fallen asleep and woken up at the last second to see he was heading for the verge and swerved. A shock like that would shake anyone up. However, it didn't explain the fresh blood. Unless he had hit something, and that had woken him.

One of the mercenaries called over, and the group followed his gaze. A combat boot, just like the ones they had on, was on the road, close to the verge.

Mr Jones looked around, curious. None of his men were missing. Then he thought about what the Chairman had said— a team from Trojan was there.

He smiled at the thought. Had one of their team made it to the road and gotten themselves run over? It would certainly explain the boot, and it was good news—fewer to deal with.

He thought about the Trojan team commander, trying to locate his man, wondering what had happened to him. Would he give a damn? Would he brush it off and continue on the mission, worrying about him later, if at all?

After all, that was precisely what he would do. All the men, except the ones in his personal team, were expendable.

Mr Jones stood, gazing up and down the road. There was nothing besides his team, the truck, and the driver.

One of his men sauntered over to Mr Jones and shrugged.

'Sir, with all due respect. Where the fuck are they?'

Mr Jones nodded slowly.

'That, Brian, is the million-dollar question. Where the fuck are they?'

Then, the shooting started.

The Trojan team made it to the road and found the SANTINI team. Their orders had been simple: retrieve the package. Also, eliminate any of the SANTINI team if you see or come in contact with them.

Two of Mr Jones's men had taken several rounds to the chest. However, he knew that because they were wearing ballistic plates, all they would have were a few broken ribs and sore egos.

Sparks exploded from the truck's trailer as the 5.56 NATO rounds ricocheted off the metal arms holding the logs.

'Give up the goods, and we'll let you walk!' came a voice from the tree line.

'Never!' yelled one of Mr Jones's men just as a burst of fire erupted from the forest.

Mr Jones stared at the forest, somewhat puzzled by the request. Not only was there no way in hell Trojan would have just let them go, but they thought he had the package.

'It's ya last chance. Give it up and walk away, or we'll take it from ya dead corpses after we've taken a dump on them,' yelled the voice.

Warily, Mr Jones stood up, to the amazement of his team, his assault rifle held in outstretched hands—a sign of a truce. He was taking a risk for sure, but he was also curious. If Trojan had not found the survivors, and they had not seen them on the road, where had they disappeared to?

'One question,' Mr Jones yelled into the darkened forest. He knew Trojan had the best vantage point; they were on higher ground, in cover.

'Sh...' the Trojan commander started, then cut himself off

from finishing the sentence. The last thing he needed was any of these hired hands to get the wrong idea after hearing the word "shoot."

'What's on your mind?' he answered after muddling through a response that would not end in a bloodbath.

'Do you see any of the survivors with us?' Mr Jones asked. He hoped the commander was a smart guy who would assess and figure out what he was talking about. 'We are alone; ergo, we don't have the goods.'

'Shit,' came a response from the tree line.

Mr Jones smiled. Good, he was working with a smart guy.

'Well, we can stand here all night and achieve nothing, or...?' Mr Jones started.

'What? Ya wanna team up and make nice?' came the voice.

'Something like that. Either way, we both have a problem because neither of us wants to go home without an answer. What are you going to do, go back to Trojan and say, "Hey boss, we found the SANTINI lot and killed them, but the package just disappeared, and we don't know where?" I'm sure they will be very understanding,' Mr Jones shrugged.

There was silence—except for the wind in the trees and the truck's engine ticking over.

'Look, we are both in the shit. We can do this together and find a middle ground, or we can... well, our best bet is to stay here, because I ain't going back without something. I might as well shoot myself now and be done with it—probably quicker and less painful,' Mr Jones thought about the psychopath they had working for them, Mr Williams or something.

Either way, he didn't need to be on that guy's list. Mr Jones had seen what Williams had done to people; hell, he had his own operating room, and it wasn't for making people better.

'So, what do you suggest?' came the voice from the forest.

'We head back to town and see if they made it back there,' Mr Jones yelled.

'And if they are?' the voice replied.

'Then, we bring back all their heads. After we've found the package.'

CHAPTER SEVENTY-ONE

JOHN STEEL AND THE SURVIVORS HAD CAUGHT OLD BOB'S attention at the last moment. They doubted the old man would have noticed them if it hadn't been for Laura's high-pitched scream.

The old boat wasn't meant for passengers; there was no lower deck or giant engine room, just the box cabin. So, everyone had to find a place on the deck and cover themselves with emergency blankets.

Debbra was still moaning in pain, but Steel and Sherman didn't really give a shit because both she and Bob had got them into this mess.

The question was, what was going on? What was this package?

Steel and Sherman walked over to Bob, who was lying next to Debbra.

She ignored Steel and Sherman, either out of pain or stubbornness.

'Talk, or you are both swimming,' Steel growled. He was cold, tired, and hungry.

Bob stared at both men and went to speak, but Debbra suddenly clutched his arm. Tears filled her eyes, a look of fear etched on her face.

'Look, we've had enough of this shit, start talking or so help me...' Sherman barked, swinging a fist back as though he was ready to punch Bob.

Silence.

'Who are they?' Steel asked calmly.

Bob stared into Steel's green eyes and shivered. 'It's you, the soldier from the mansion; they thought they had killed you,' Bob said, panic in his voice.

Steel wasn't sure who he was scared of—him or the people after them.

'Who are *they*?' Steel asked more firmly.

'We made a mistake; we thought we could get away with it, but Natalie got in the way. She had the data initially, she had discovered it and was going to take it to her boss in the organisation. We saw a way out. We found a way to make some cash and disappear,' Bob explained, his voice trembling from fear and cold.

'But you got greedy and tried to sell it to more than one party?' Sherman added.

Bob nodded. 'We thought if we let the first buyer know there was competition, they would raise the price.'

'Yeah, but why crash the plane?' Sherman asked, confused at the planning and execution.

Bob shook his head. 'That had nothing to do with us or Natalie.'

Steel and Sherman glanced at each other, but Sherman quickly looked away, unable to hold Steel's gaze. 'Are we looking at a third party?' they both asked.

'What's that?' Old Bob asked, trying to look as though he hadn't been eavesdropping.

Steel grinned; he could understand Old Bob's compulsion —this must have been the most exciting thing that had ever happened to him during his trips. 'That plane crash a couple of days ago; these are the survivors,' Steel explained.

'What, Frank Stubbs?' Old Bob asked.

'Yeah, that's the fella... or was. Why?' Steel asked.

Old Bob laughed out loud. 'His old lady poisoned him— found out he was making a packet and was gonna up and leave her. The trip you poor bastards took, she thought, was him leavin'. When she found out it was a tour and he wasn't alone, Beth went straight to the sheriff and confessed it all. Riddled with guilt, she was.'

Sherman shook his head in disbelief. He had wondered why Stubbs had mentioned a detour; now it made sense. 'Natalie's boss paid for the detour, didn't they? They were meant to do the drop-off in town; that was why Frank Stubbs talked about making a quick detour.'

Bob nodded.

Steel thought for a moment. 'What I don't get is, how do you know each other? You and Natalie, I mean?'

'We were all part of a research facility in North Alaska. We... Debbra and I were installed into the facility by another organisation. Double agents, if you will. When we were at MIT, we were headhunted and offered shitloads of money to work for the organisation. Still, we ended up staring at computers and digging for data on people.'

Steel knelt; Bob had caught his interest. 'As blackmail?'

Bob shrugged. 'Blackmail, leverage, weaknesses, ways to get to them for... well, you get the picture. These people are only after money, not power. Wealth and corruption are their game. The others, however, are the ones who are seeking power and control.'

'And the package? What is it?' Sherman asked.

Bob gazed down at Debbra, who shook her head, resolve in her eyes.

'Bob,' Steel barked, hoping to pull Bob from her control. 'Did you poison Natalie?'

Bob stared at him in surprise.

'I found Natalie's body. She had been taking some medication. On the bottle, it said not to be mixed with alcohol, and when I checked her canteen, it smelt of booze. Someone had purposely poisoned her; they knew about her tablets, and you had already admitted you had been working with her for a long time,' Steel explained.

Bob's mouth opened and shut like a fish, unable to speak, as though the news was as much a surprise to him as it was to any of them. Then Bob looked down at Debbra, who was now looking away, guilty and silent.

'Why?' Bob asked, astonished at the revelation.

'Because I was tired of you running after her. I saw the looks you were sharing; I knew what you two were up to,' she growled, turning to face Bob, hate burning in her eyes.

'So, you have the package?' Steel asked, hope in his voice, hoping it was finally over.

Debbra shook her head, her expression changed. 'I... I thought you got it from her,' she said to Bob.

'What? No... when?'

'That night she went nuts and tied up Sherman. I thought you two were in on it together?'

Steel asked Sherman, 'Does any of this make sense to you?'

Sherman shook his head, rubbing it at the memory of the surprise attack. 'Sorry, I was out cold. Damned woman nearly took my head off.'

Bob shook his head. 'What together? We are together. Me and Natalie were never a thing.'

'Yes... yes, you were. I saw you laughing and getting cosy when you could,' Debbra scoffed, not believing a word.

Then, a voice from behind them made them all look over. 'Debbra, Natalie was gay; she used to be my lover,' Laura said, tears running down her face.

'No... no... I know what I saw,' Debbra yelled.

'What you saw, or what you *thought* you saw? We were locked in that compound for months and years. The mind can play tricks on you, and you had been pretty nervous about this whole deal,' Bob sighed.

'Uhm... sorry to break up the heart-to-heart shit... but if you don't have the package, who does?' Steel asked, hoping they weren't going to say what he was thinking.

'Well. Natalie must still have it,' Bob shrugged, and they all stared back at the forest they had just fought to leave.

'Oh, bollocks,' Steel let out a deflated sigh. 'I was afraid you would say that.'

'So, what is it? This package?' Sherman asked, easing himself down beside Steel.

'Information, scandalous information on someone in the Senate. The organisation needs to sway a vote their way, and our—well, her—job was to find something on someone. And surprise, she did. And was going to use it to return to the world,' Bob explained. His voice rang with a hint of humour, as if something about it amused him.

'What's so funny?' Steel asked, finding nothing amusing about this whole business. Innocent people had died, some of whom he had known, and here this snake was smiling. It took all of his strength not to ensure Bob never smiled again.

'There was a time limit. She had to get the information to her bosses by a certain time, or both she and the information became... useless,' Bob shrugged. 'Tick, tock, time up,' he said, pointing to his watch.

A confused look came over Steel. 'If the information is now useless, why the bloody hell are they still after us?'

'Ah, yes, that might be our fault. We may have said we have the package. However, our organisation can still use the information for... another time,' Bob answered, the smug grin remaining.

'Okay, so what is the information on? What is the package?' Sherman asked, getting more impatient with Bob and his bullshit.

Bob paused for a moment before beginning to answer.

Steel watched Bob thinking. He knew the man would sidetrack the answer again, and he was out of patience with him. 'Bob, if you don't give us a straight answer right now, I'm gonna tie you to one of these fucking logs and see which kills you first —the current, other logs smashing into you, or the cold. Personally, I hope it's the logs, but hey, I'm fresh out of fucks to give.'

Bob stared into those cold, soulless emerald eyes. They seemed to bore deep into his soul; he shivered. He had seen green eyes before, and they had been beautiful. But these were almost like looking into the eyes of death himself. Perhaps he *was*. Bob swallowed hard, the sly grin replaced with one of fear. 'It... it's on a flash drive, a data stick.'

Steel and Sherman just stared as if willing him with their minds to continue.

'Trouble is, I don't know where it is,' Bob swallowed again.

'What?' Sherman grunted.

'I... we searched her things and found nothing, so we figured it had to be on her person—the one place we couldn't look,' Bob continued.

Steel thought for a moment. 'Unless you drugged her, made her feel sick. You slipped alcohol into her water bottle, thinking she'd throw up or something... or did you mean to kill her, but it went wrong?'

'We were running out of time, and this pussy wasn't gonna do anything,' Debbra yelled, more from the pain than wanting to be heard.

Sherman smiled. 'Did she figure it out? That's why she cracked you one? Good for her. Pity she didn't take your head off,' Clarke scoffed.

Steel thought for a moment. He remembered searching Natalie's body and backpack, taking the items, including her beloved keyring—the little unicorn. He smiled inside. Could it be?

'This intel you get on people... what sort of people?' Steel asked.

'Rich, influential government members. Anyone that the organisation feels is useful or a threat,' Bob shrugged.

'How about members of the aristocracy? Say... an Earl and Lady?' Steel asked, his voice cold.

Bob thought for a moment, as if thinking back. 'I think there was something... some Lord or something. He was also a member of the secret service, some clandestine version of MI6,' Bob shrugged again, as if it was just another job.

Steel nodded slowly, as if taking it all in. These people were responsible for his family's murder, for him being stuck in the middle of nowhere, looking over his shoulder. He found it strange—he actually felt nothing. No hate, anger, or sense of revenge. It was as though he was numb... no... dead inside. He found the lack of emotion both interesting and puzzling.

For so long, Steel had thought about what he would do when he found the people responsible, but now, looking at these two pathetic souls, he felt nothing.

Perhaps he would later, in the future, but at that moment, he couldn't give a damn about them. Possibly because they were nothing—analysts, people sat behind a computer, picking at people's lives. It wasn't their decision what happened after that. Did they even care? Possibly not. So, why should he care about what happens to them?

Of course, he would much prefer them to be shipped off to some nice interrogation centre, grilled for days until they broke. But what then? Sent to prison, given orange coveralls, and lost in Guantanamo Bay? Or worse still—flipped and working for the Secret Service as an analyst?

Either way didn't sit well with him. People had died because of them—whether they were good or bad, blood was on their hands—and all Bob could do was shrug.

Steel stood, and Sherman followed, causing Bob to stare at them in a panic. 'What you gonna do with us?'

Steel gazed down at Bob, then turned his gaze to Debbra, who wore a defiant look and smiled. 'Nothing, absolutely nothing.'

Bob shot Steel a curious look. 'So, we are free to go?'

Steel smiled. 'No, I said I wasn't going to do anything; I'm sure a few three-letter agencies will have a field day with you pair. How do you feel about the colour orange?'

Debbra glanced over at Steel's backpack and saw the hatchet lying underneath. It was close—a foolish mistake—but then, she wasn't going to leap up, not with that leg, and Bob... well, Bob was... well, Bob.

Debbra weighed up her options—a thousand thoughts in a split second. Unfortunately, there was only one outcome, but it turned out well—better on her terms than theirs.

In one swift movement, Debbra rolled, grabbed the weapon, and as she came back, her arm arched, slashing Bob's throat.

Bob rolled back, a look of surprise on his face. He touched his neck, but it was dry, with no blood. But as he went to speak, the slash on his neck opened up, and the blood began to flow.

Karen and Laura screamed and lurched backwards as the cascade of blood gushed from the deep wound.

As all eyes were fixed on Bob, Debbra sneered and then, in a final act of defiance, drew the blade across her throat and both jugular veins.

Everyone stood back in horror—all except Steel, who stared calmly.

Clarke leapt down and tried to stop the bleeding on Bob's wound. Blood gushed through his fingers as Bob's mouth opened and closed like a fish; no words came, only a gurgling sound. Then his mouth stopped moving, the wave of blood slowed to a trickle, and Bob's lifeless eyes gazed up in horror.

Clarke held Bob for a moment, then placed him down on the blood-soaked deck next to Debbra, who had died more quickly. She had already lost a lot of blood from the gunshot wound.

Everyone stared at Steel with looks of anger and surprise on their faces.

'You knew she'd do that... didn't you?' Sherman asked.

Steel said nothing; he just stared at the two bodies.

'Hey, answer me. Did you know she would do that?'

Steel turned to Sherman; his face was cold and expression-less. 'No, but then, she had no choice. I guess she thought she was dead either way, whether we took her in or left her here. If she believed these people were that connected, she would also think there was nowhere they couldn't get to her.'

'So, why did she kill Bob? Why not just herself?' Clarke asked, still trying to come to terms with what had just happened.

Steel thought for a moment. The answer was possibly simple. If this organisation was that secretive and powerful, wouldn't they have leverage on all their employees to ensure their loyalty and silence?

'I think if we checked, we would find there were family members, siblings that would have been threatened with harm if they ever turned. Maybe the organisation even told their employees that loyalty is rewarded—even to the point that if you die, instead of spilling your guts, your family will be looked after. Who knows? Either way, there was no fear in her reaction —well, possibly fear Bob would keep talking.'

'Who the hell are these people?' Laura asked, tears still streaming down her face.

Karen sat quietly, staring out across the water into the darkness. The rain and wind had stopped, and the clouds were starting to disperse. The calm after the storm? Or had the storm only just begun?

There was silence for a short while. No one felt like talking. A scream broke the sombre mood.

'Oh, for the love of... how the fuck am I meant ta get all that blood outta them planks?'

Steel looked over at Old Man Burt; he felt like laughing. It wasn't the fact that two bodies were lying on his deck that pissed him off—it was the fact that they were bleeding into his deck.

'Sorry, Bob, won't happen again,' Steel said.

Everyone stared at Steel and Bob with open mouths. Could these men be any more unfeeling?

CHAPTER SEVENTY-TWO

THE CALL THE CHAIRMAN GOT DID NOT EXCITE HIM. IN truth, everything about Mr Jones's report would have generally gotten him killed. However, he was one of the Chairman's best men, and as Mr Jones had explained, it would be a beneficial partnership in the end. He had plans to dispose of the mercenaries from Trojan at the first chance they got.

The Chairman had explained that the men from Trojan most certainly had the same idea, but then, it was a game of the quick and the dead.

The Chairman had reported to the head of the SANTINI organisation, who, despite the distorted voice, had been less than pleased. The whole operation had gone from bad to worse, and, most of all, the time to use the information had lapsed.

Unfortunately, John Steel's company had won the contract, which more than annoyed both the Chairman and his boss.

However, the organisation always had another scheme up its sleeve, and this was just a minor setback.

The Chairman was more thankful that someone other than Trojan had won the contract.

Mr Jones's job was to retrieve or destroy the information before Trojan got hold of it and the asset. The Chairman hoped his best man would not fail him this time.

CHAPTER SEVENTY-THREE

MR JONES LOOKED AT HIS WATCH AND NOTED THE DATE. Eight hours ago, the information had become useless, and the asset... expendable.

Mr Jones and a man named Brice, the team leader from the Trojan team, had formulated a plan: one team would stick to the treeline, and the other would remain on the road. Naturally, Mr Jones would have preferred the forest for cover but felt showing a little goodwill would go a long way. Besides, team two weren't far away and could take Trojan out in a pincer movement.

The only problem was that he had no idea how many teams Trojan had brought or where they were.

Mr Jones's team headed down the road in a standard staggered formation while turning to look at the forest. He didn't like the arrangement, but they had been caught off guard with no cover.

He had bought some time. Who knew, maybe they might make it out alive; after all, they were all professionals, all of them ex-special forces, battle-hardened warriors. But so were Trojan's team.

However, one thing was for sure: someone wasn't going home. Mr Jones just had to ensure his team made it home, and he dealt with the package one way or the other.

Earlier, as the two teams had broken off, Mr Jones had telephoned the Chairman to give him the unhappy news. Things had not gone as planned, that was for damned sure.

Unsurprisingly, the Chairman was not amused by the report but understood the situation. Mr Jones had made a tactical decision. It had been better to play nice and walk away than end up dead on the road; that wouldn't have solved anything.

He was ordered to continue as he felt necessary. After the Chairman had ended the call, Mr Jones contacted Sven and the other team to give them a situation report and tell them the plan. He also told him to keep an eye on things, not to rush into anything, and, most of all, to keep a lookout for support units.

He didn't need any more surprises.

As they marched down the road, he heard the sound of the river next to them and the cries of animals in the forest. The sky was cloudless, and the stars looked close enough to touch.

Mr Jones thought back to the patrols he had done when he was in the Army, the miles of dusty roads he had trodden. This felt no different, except the enemy was closer than he felt comfortable with. Mr Jones gently squeezed the front stock and pistol grip for reassurance.

He was scared, but that was okay; scared kept you alive, and complacency got you killed. Anyone who said they weren't scared in this situation was lying or dead.

'Okay, boys, let's pick it up a bit, keep your spacing, and keep your eyes open for trouble,' he said. There was no reply;

he knew there wouldn't be one. His men were well-trained. Of course, they were; he had trained them.

Mr Jones glanced over at the forest and the treeline; he could see the team from Trojan. They had both agreed to stay in visual range. If they had disappeared, it meant the deal was off. He would have preferred that, but he also liked being alive. Besides, he had a score to settle with the survivors, especially that fucking Navy SEAL.

He had killed his men. He had no idea how—the old man looked like he couldn't run anymore, let alone take out all his teams. But what other explanation was there?

It sure as hell wasn't the others; they were all office workers and a reporter.

He couldn't see Clarke Anderson going all *John Wick* on them; after all, he was only a war correspondent, not a combatant.

There had been reports of a stranger with them, but the description was more of a local than a soldier. The guy probably lived in one of those self-made shacks he had seen pictures of. He was probably used to shooting deer or trapping rabbits, and he probably grew up there and had never seen civilisation.

No, the person who had taken out his men was a professional. The only one was Mike Sherman, and Mr Jones was looking forward to having a conversation with him.

A painful conversation.

As they walked, Mr Jones began to plan. They needed the perfect place to dispatch their new friends, and a town was not the place to do it. There were far too many witnesses.

No, it would have to be on the road or, better still, in the forest.

He took out the tablet, which showed Sven's team's location; they were on the other side of the forest in a clearing, moving parallel.

His phone began to vibrate, and he retrieved it from his pocket. He looked at the caller ID—it was Sven. Mr Jones pressed the green icon and listened.

'Boss, we got a problem,' Sven said anxiously.

'What is it?'

'We just spotted two helicopters heading towards town; I think Trojan's backup just arrived.'

Mr Jones paused as he began to think.

'Boss? What do you want to do?' Sven asked.

Mr Jones glanced over to the treeline and saw Brice was also taking a call.

Mr Jones's grip tightened on the weapon. He knew if Brice had word they had reinforcements, this partnership was going to come to a sudden and bloody end.

Brice looked over at Mr Jones and smiled.

However, before Brice could do anything, Mr Jones had fired, and the bullet had taken the back of Brice's head off.

The rest of Mr Jones's team opened up on the other team, cutting them down.

Some had been lucky and had dived for cover and were able to return fire, while others had been shredded by a hail of bullets.

The firefight was quick, and even though Mr Jones had lost two men, the Trojan team had come off worse. Luckily, Mr Jones had surprised them despite the Trojan team's advantage of being next to the forest.

Mr Jones ordered the rest of his men to move up; they had to take out the survivors, and he couldn't risk word getting back to the Trojan reinforcements.

Shots rang out from the forest, but Mr Jones's men had split up, moving forward in an extended line, using fallen trees and large rocks as cover. Inching forwards. The far two would move forward first, then drop down and give covering fire while the next moved, and so on. A typical fire and manoeuvre—effective.

Eventually, the three men from Trojan were found and killed. Headshots. Clean and easy.

Mr Jones and his men searched the bodies, taking the extra ammunition and mobile phones; these would be a good source of information—plenty of numbers.

Mr Jones was down to himself and three other men. Not ideal, but that was war.

He pulled out his phone, found the Chairman's number, and pressed the call button. Time for some good news, he thought.

The Chairman answered on the fourth ring.

'This had better be good news,' the Chairman said, his tone angry and impatient.

'The Trojan team is down; we have mobile phones.'

'And I suppose there is going to be bad news?' The Chairman sighed.

'Team two reported two helicopters heading towards the town, so we must expect company shortly,' Mr Jones replied.

The Chairman paused, weighing up what to do next. The information was now useless, and the chances were that even if Trojan got hold of it, it would be months, even years, before they could use it—and that was dependent on whether the individual they had the documents on was still in office.

Also, they had no idea where that damned data file was. Without the asset coming forward, they were chasing their tails.

'Get your teams home. Abort the mission. No point losing any more on this,' the Chairman said with a deflated voice. He hated defeat. But then, nobody had won.

'And what about the asset?' Mr Jones asked.

'I found out who it was—well, one of three people, really. These three had left the compound at the same time, and after checking their names with the flight manifest of the tour, we got a match.'

'Okay, sir, can you send the photos to my mobile?' Mr Jones said excitedly—at last, a lead. If they had photographs, all they had to do was go to the nearest airport, namely the one in Talkeetna, and check all the people heading back to the States.

'They are on the way,' the Chairman explained. 'What's your plan?'

'Head to Talkeetna, check out the airport and see who is getting a flight to the US—not Canada. Catch them at check-in. There are eleven of us, so we can cover most of the US desks.'

Mr Jones glanced at his phone as it binged to alert him that he had mail. He opened the new post, flicked through the photographs, and stopped at Natalie's. 'Sir, this one—Natalie Childs,' Mr Jones said, his tone sombre.

'Yes, what about her?'

'We found her. She's dead. There were no wounds or bruising, so I'd say she had been poisoned. And another thing—by the look of things, someone had searched the body before us,' Mr Jones said as he thought back to the body in the woods. Even though Sven's team had found her, his description to Mr Jones painted a good enough picture. Sven had also sent a photograph using his phone, just in case.

A move which had proven useful.

'Damn,' the Chairman cursed. 'But we can't be sure who searched her, or why?' He thought for a moment. Maybe this wasn't as bad as they thought. 'The chances are it was the survivors, and they searched the body for useful items. If this Sherman fellow is in charge, I've no doubt they would have. There is no point in leaving items that they could use later.

Besides, we don't even know she was the asset.' The Chairman paused, assessing and planning. 'Go ahead with your plan. Get out of there and head for the airport. I've sent you pictures of everyone who was on that plane. If you spot one, chances are the rest aren't too far behind.' Then the Chairman hung up.

Mr Jones looked over to his men. 'On me!' he yelled, and the remaining men ran to him. Mr Jones pressed the number for Sven and waited. After the second ring, Sven answered, his voice seemed out of breath.

'Yes, Boss?'

'Sven, we are mission abort. Meet me in Talkeetna airport; we have some hunting to do.' And with that, he closed down his phone and smiled at his men. 'The beers are on me, boys. We're going home.'

Mr Jones and his men slung their weapons and headed to Ridgeway Creek. Their vehicles and hotel rooms were there. They would head back, shower, and change clothes before heading to Talkeetna.

They didn't expect to run into Trojan's backup squads just yet; they would probably use the forest as cover, thinking the road was too open.

Sven would be on the way back to the vehicles they had left at the lake, then head straight for Talkeetna airport. That way, they would have boots on the ground immediately.

The question was—how were the survivors going to get to the airport? And more than that, how the hell had they slipped past them now?

Something was off. They... no, he had missed something. Had the group doubled back and returned to the old couple's house by the lake, and now they were driving their trucks?

They might already be back in town; after all, they had all night to travel. They may have even gotten a ride with one of those logging trucks.

There were too many variables, too many what-ifs for his liking. But one thing was definite—they had to leave Alaska using commercial airlines, which meant they had to get to Talkeetna.

Where he and his men would be waiting.

CHAPTER SEVENTY-FOUR

As Old Man Burt eased his boat down the river, nudging the thousands of logs in front of it, John Steel sat close to the small pilot's cabin where Old Man Burt was steering and looked through his backpack.

He began to pick out some of the items he had confiscated from the mercenaries, all the while Old Man Burt was shouting, 'I'll have that, and that... what is it?'

Sherman sat near the back with the others, away from the blood. They had covered the two bodies with the emergency blankets.

Clarke had wanted to throw them overboard, but Steel had said no. Despite what they had done, they didn't deserve to become bear food, and the river provided the drinking water for the town. Also, whenever Steel had a coffee at Maddy Johnson's place, he didn't want to think about bits of Bob and Debbra floating in his cup.

As Steel waded through his pack, he came across what he had initially been looking for: Natalie's unicorn keyring.

He grabbed the head and the rear of the animal and pulled.

A smile cracked from the corner of his mouth as he looked at the shiny metal USB adaptor. He had found the flash drive.

Steel looked up and around; Sherman and the others were sitting at the rear of the boat; they hadn't seen anything. He put the two halves together and stuck the keyring in his pocket. The fewer people knew, the better.

Steel gazed at Sherman and the others, who were happily tucking into the ration packs they had received from the mercenaries.

Laura was eating a giant cookie as if it was her last; Sherman had one of the meals in the chemical cooker; knowing him, it was the breakfast menu. Karen was busy picking up one package and then another as if unable to decide. Up to a point, Clarke got bored of it all and told her to get both.

They all looked happy—possibly the happiest he had seen them. The thought that this was it, that they were home free, made them relax.

However, Steel knew that was the worst time. He had seen it on countless exercises, whether in Germany or the Brecon Beacons; the moment you were close to the end of an exercise, or as they knew it, ENDEX—that was when people relaxed, and accidents happened.

However, they were content, and he wouldn't ruin that. They had had an arduous journey and deserved some downtime, even for a little while. It was good for their morale. Because if this weren't the end, if the mercenaries were waiting at the airfield, they would need all the strength they had to make it home.

Steel looked at the group, laughing and eating; he felt happy for them. Then he noticed Sherman gazing over and nodded for him to join them. Steel shook his head.

Sherman stood up and carried a second MRE meal, probably the one he had opened but then decided he didn't want.

'Come over,' Sherman said, a spring in his tone.

Steel cracked a smile and looked past him towards the group. 'No, best not. Give them some time without me. They deserve it.'

'What makes you think they didn't send me over?'

Steel shot him a scornful look, causing Sherman to laugh.

Sherman offered Steel one of the MRE meals, which Steel took and sniffed at the open packet. It was chilli, or at least it smelled like it.

'Yeah, OK, you got me. But still, you're one of us,' Sherman said.

Steel shook his head. 'No, old man, I'm not. I'm just the one that got a lot of your people killed. I should have taken you to town straight off the mark. Instead, I looked for the best way for me.'

'Maybe, but you said you had seen the mercs in town. If that was true, you would have led us straight to them,' Sherman growled.

'Yes, and the mercs would have gotten their package, and nobody would have gotten hurt.'

Sherman shook his head. 'Yeah, they would have gotten the package, and then what? You heard what Bob said; they were using it as leverage, for God knows what. Hell, you might have stopped a major catastrophe. And who knows, they might have shot the asset anyway.'

Steel wanted to believe him and think that what he had done wasn't just out of selfish reasons. But something nagged at him. What had he become? He used to be a fighter for good, freedom, and justice. Put the bad guys in the ground for the right reasons. Now he was some loner who didn't give a shit about anyone else. Had the murder of his family changed him so much? Had he become wild and uncaring? Had he lost any reason to fight?

That was when Laura came over, knelt before Steel, and hugged him. 'Thank you.' Then she stood and went back to the others.

Steel gazed up at Sherman, who was grinning.

'Oh, fuck off, old man. Go and get some sleep.'

Sherman returned to the group and settled down, eating one.

Steel began picking at the meal Sherman had given him. It tasted like shit, not as good as the British rations, but food was food. The *eat when you can* rule popped into his head.

The army rules. There's an interesting set of instructions whose origin is still unknown: *Eat when you can, sleep when you can.*

Plan for the worst, hope for the best, and anything in the middle is a bonus.

There were many others, most of which were taken from some guy called Murphy.

However, army rules kept you in line. Alive.

Those two rules seemed apt for now: You should sleep when you can. Steel planned on doing both. They didn't need a sentry; they were in a log boat on the river. Nobody would swim in that river; they would freeze to death before getting close.

They had a long ride ahead of them, and in somewhat safer conditions, he hoped they would use the time to get some sleep.

Steel felt his eyes grow heavy. He couldn't remember when he had slept properly. He got comfortable, pulled his coat tightly around him, and then fell into a haunted sleep.

CHAPTER SEVENTY-FIVE

THE SUN WAS RISING AS OLD MAN BURT PULLED INTO THE logging station. The town was a good ten-minute walk from there.

John Steel was woken with a start by yells and screams; he went to reach for his hatchet, only to find it was the log worker foreman shouting orders to his crew.

Steel looked over to where the group had been and found them chatting with Old Man Burt on the riverbank.

With a groan from aching muscles, Steel heaved his body off the deck and joined them.

'Well, you are the most terrifying person to sleep with,' Laura laughed.

'Yeah, that must have been some nightmare you had,' Clarke added.

'Yeah, I dreamt I was stuck on a boat with some asshole reporter and his three annoying friends... oh, wait,' Steel stopped and gave a fake look of surprise.

'Yeah, very funny... dickhead,' Sherman laughed. 'Okay, so what's the plan?'

Steel looked at the road leading to town. 'Start walking, I guess.'

'No, I mean when we get to town? What then? We have to get to Talkeetna and get the first flight out,' Clarke said impatiently.

Steel shook his head. 'Too risky. Whoever these people are, they think we have what they're looking for; worse still, they might also be looking for the courier. Unfortunately, Natalie is dead. If it were me, I would go to Talkeetna and check out the check-in desks.

'I'm sure these people have your photographs, so they will know who you are and what you look like. All they have to do is spot one of you.'

'Okay, so what's the plan?' Sherman asked cautiously.

'Simple. We get the local pilot from here to fly us to Canada, and then we get to the US embassy; you can call someone there and get us a flight home,' Steel nodded at Sherman.

'Oh, is that all? Sounds great, but what if those assholes are staking out the airfield here?' Karen barked.

Steel thought for a moment. 'Even if they are, they can't do anything. I don't think they will murder an entire town—most of whom, by now, are tourists—just to get to us.'

'You seem pretty sure about that?' Clarke noticed.

Steel shook his head. 'I'm not sure of anything, but what I am sure of is that until you are back home and the package is handed over to the correct people, you aren't safe.'

Sherman shot Steel a look of surprise. 'You know where it is?'

Steel nodded.

'Wow, let us see!' Karen yelped in excitement.

Everyone shot her a grimacing look.

Steel shook his head again. 'No, the less you all know, the better.'

'But... you have it?' Clarke asked warily.

'I know where it is... well, I hope it's still there,' Steel said thoughtfully.

'What? You left it on Natalie's body?' Karen yelped in surprise.

'I didn't know what it was at first. It wasn't until Bob started babbling that I worked it out, and yes, I'm as pissed as you are because after I've gotten rid of you lot, I have to go back. Hopefully, it's a bear,' Steel grinned.

'Why?' Karen asked.

Sherman grinned. 'Hibernation, kiddo. The bear's gonna be sleepin' until next spring, and we're in bear country, which means hundreds of the damned things, so it's as good as gone, and so are they.'

Steel nodded, but a concerned look crossed his face. 'But I guess it all depends on how important this information was. If —as Bob said—it is time-sensitive, we won't hear from our friends again, but if it isn't...'

Sherman shook his head. 'Nah, waste of their time. They'd be better off getting someone else to try and look for whatever it was. The thing about information is it's always out there.'

'Alright, so we go back to town, grab this plane, and then what? I can't see Canada just letting us over the border,' Clarke exclaimed.

Steel smiled. 'And that is where I have to come in. I'll have to make some calls, but we'll be fine.'

Laura scowled suspiciously. 'And who the hell can you call that has that much clout?'

Steel paused uncomfortably. 'My mother-in-law.'

CHAPTER SEVENTY-SIX

An hour before Steel and the survivors docked, Sven and his men arrived at Ridgeway Creek. The plan was to get to the hotel, freshen up, grab their bags, and head for Talkeetna Airport.

It took fifteen minutes to shower, check out, and start heading out. That was until the SUV driver noticed a puncture in one of the rear tyres.

Sven had sent the driver to change the wheel for the spare. He looked at his watch; Mr Jones would not be happy to find them still in Ridgeway Creek and not at the airport in the city.

He was even less impressed when the driver returned, saying the rental had no spare.

Sven screamed and punched the man in the face. A loud crack sounded as his nose exploded.

The man fell to the ground and lay on his side for a second, dazed by the massive punch.

'Get up, you idiot. Go to the garage and see if they have a spare; failing that, see if they have a vehicle we can borrow.'

The man scrambled to his feet, his hand covering his bleeding nose, then turned and left.

Sven watched and shook his head in disgust. How could he have been put in charge of such idiots? They were just cannon fodder. Mr Jones had the best team; his were just last-minute hired hands. They weren't there to think, which was more the pity—this wouldn't have happened if he had his usual team.

'What now, boss?' asked another man.

Sven tutted, still pissed off from the driver's incompetence. 'Check out the airfield, see if they can fly us there.'

The man nodded and went down the street towards the end of town, where the airfield was located. It would take him a good fifteen minutes to get there, and he cursed the driver and himself for asking a question.

Sven turned to the remaining men and nodded to the diner. 'We'll wait in there; at least we can get some breakfast while we wait for the moron.'

The men disappeared into the diner, and as they did so, an average-sized man sitting on a bench pulled out his phone and pressed the green icon to call. He wore jeans, a thick dark jacket, and a ball cap. He looked like everyone else.

'It's Mitch. Ma'am, we got a problem.'

The man listened for a second, then responded as he continued to observe Sven and the others in the diner. 'The guys from SANTINI are here; I have eyes on seven men.' He paused as the person on the other end spoke.

'No, Ma'am, only seven; maybe the rest are en route.' He paused again.

'No, Ma'am, no word from team three. They had been dropped off near the lake, but there was still no word. The last contact was that they had engaged and then made a deal with the other SANTINI team.'

He paused as the person spoke. 'Yes, Ma'am, I thought the

same; team three is gone, and we are alone. Team two is in Talkeetna, at the airport; we are covering all bases.'

Another pause. 'Yes, Ma'am, we got the survivors' photos and know who the assets are.'

He paused, his eyes still fixed on Sven and his men. 'What do you want us to do about these men?'

The voice spoke, and he listened, nodding as he understood his instructions. 'Roger that, eliminate at the first chance. And what if the others get here?'

He listened and nodded. 'Will do, and we'll make sure there are no witnesses. It's probably best to get them while they are on the road. I think they will be heading for Talkeetna as well.'

A pause. 'No, Ma'am, I don't think they have either the asset or the information, or they wouldn't be hanging around.'

He waited as his boss spoke. 'Affirmative, Ma'am, there is no sign of the survivors. I figure they have already left or are at least en route to Talkeetna. Either way, we will get them there; it is the only way they can leave Alaska.'

The man's gaze switched to another man who had appeared on a corner next to the hardware store, and he nodded to the man, who tipped the corner of his ball cap in reply.

'Yes, Ma'am, all my men are in position. I'll give them mission orders later, so don't worry; we'll get that information.'

The reply made the man's face go white with fear. He already knew failure was not an option, but whatever his boss had said made it concrete.

There was a dead tone from his phone; his boss had gone, and he had his orders.

Time to go to work.

CHAPTER SEVENTY-SEVEN

JOHN STEEL AND THE OTHERS HAD MADE IT TO RIDGEWAY Creek just as the morning rush had started. People were heading to the train station to get to their jobs in Talkeetna, tourists had begun to gather outside the diner for breakfast, and others who worked for the logging company were heading for their shifts.

Steel had taken the group to the local hotel and explained the group's situation. He rented the only two rooms available for the group to shower and had told them to stay in their rooms until he came to get them.

Steel knew they would spot the group if any of the mercenaries were there. However, the chances were they had no idea who he was, so he could move about freely. Besides, he looked like a native, so anyone new wouldn't give him a second glance. He was, for all purposes, invisible.

Steel left his pack and weapons with Sherman—there was no point in wandering around town with them—and then he headed for Maddy Johnson's store. He needed to arrange new clothes for the group and trusted Maddy to do it discreetly.

John Steel left the hotel and looked up and down the street; there didn't seem to be anyone out of the ordinary. Definitely nobody wearing all-black tactical gear.

He sauntered across the road and headed for the hardware store, and that was when he saw the man sitting on the bench, trying to look casual, his gaze flicking around. Still, he was definitely concentrating on the diner.

Because of the sun's reflection on the diner window, Steel couldn't see what the man's interest was. He wasn't a tourist, and his clothes were too new for a local.

A sudden tingle at the back of Steel's neck gave him a bad feeling. He casually gazed around, hidden in the crowd of people he had lost himself in—human camouflage—and saw two other men, one on the corner near the hardware store and another further down near the doctor's.

John Steel broke away from the group and made his way to Maddy's store. As he reached the door, he greeted the man with a 'Mornin'' in a low baritone voice with a muffled American accent.

The man said nothing, just brushed off the greeting and continued to observe the street.

Steel smiled as he entered the store. This was his first confirmation—they had no idea who he was. Of course, if the man had reacted differently and started to yell to his team members, *I got one*, it might have ended with the man being pushed backwards and silenced.

However, the man had just looked at Steel as though he was a piece of shit. And to be fair, after the journey he had been through, he did. He was covered in dust, dirt, and blood. He might have looked better if he had been dragged through a hedge backwards.

Maddy heard the bell, which signalled a new customer, and

glanced over at Steel. Her mouth dropped open, and all she could say was, 'Jesus.'

'No, but walking on water might have come in useful,' he joked.

'What the hell happened to you?' she said, rushing over to him.

'I'm fine. It's a long story, but I need your help. Some people are in trouble. They need new clothes—don't worry, I'll pick up the bill.'

She poured him a coffee while he gave her a brief insight into which rooms they were in.

Maddy nodded as she took in the information. She explained that she would have to wait until the local girl who was helping with the store arrived before she could get away.

Steel nodded and drank, draining the cup of liquid. He was parched. Maddy refilled the cup.

'Anything else you need?' she asked excitedly.

'I need your phone; I have to make some calls.'

Maddy nodded. 'You can use the landline at my place. Get yourself a shower while you're there, and I'll bring you some clean clothes.'

Steel thanked her and headed for the back of the store to her place, which was built there. Maddy had her home built on-site, saying it saved time.

John Steel walked into the compact but beautifully furnished home. It had two bedrooms, a large area that doubled as a sitting area, and a kitchen. The spacious bathroom had a bath and a shower unit.

The home was all wood, with an old iron wood-burning stove. Steel noticed she preferred the old rustic look to some of the modern places built recently.

Steel found the house phone and dialled a number from memory; after the fifth ring, someone answered.

Steel waited for the usual greeting the senator's butler gave before saying, 'Senator Moira Kent, please. Tell her... it's John Steel.'

The conversation was brief—it had to be. After getting the pleasantries out of the way, they had gotten down to business.

Steel had explained what he could, but he was still in the dark about what was happening.

Senator Kent seemed to understand more than he did on the subject. She had explained that the right person could sway a vote, and if someone had damning information on them, it would be a good motivator.

Steel told her the plan was to fly out of Ridgeway Creek and head for Canada; from there, they would go to the US embassy.

Senator Kent paused as though she was checking through some telephone numbers. 'I have a friend who might be able to help. Also, you said you have the flash drive, so destroy it. If that information gets out, it could be used later,' she explained.

Steel agreed, but he had to have a backup plan in case they were forced to give something up.

They talked for a few minutes more before Steel said he had to go. People were waiting, and he had to shower and clean himself up. They said their goodbyes, and Steel let her hang up.

After a long and much-needed shower, John Steel emerged. He risked edging into the kitchen, hoping Maddy wasn't there, or worse still, the seventeen-year-old who worked for her. He would never live that one down.

On the kitchen table were new clothes, a fresh cup of coffee and, of course, the bill. He smiled; she hadn't billed him for the coffee—how sweet.

John Steel changed into the crisp new clothes. Of course, she'd have his size; it was the only place he had gotten new stuff.

He found a mirror in her bedroom and looked at the black jeans, shirt, and heavy-looking boots she had left. She had also left a pair of Oakley sunglasses and a heavy leather coat. His old clothes were gone, probably burnt instead of laundered. He hoped his long leather coat had survived.

He rubbed his chin; the bristles of his beard scratched against his hand. He thought about shaving, but the beard had served well as a disguise, so he decided to leave it for now.

The next call Steel made was to Derick Forbes, the CEO of Steel's company, letting him know all was well. Part of Steel's disappearance included a weekly check-in; this would put the board and investors at ease, knowing there was still a founding member. Plus, it was a hell of a selling point.

Strangely enough, ever since the story of the massacre and the idea that John Steel was alive, the stock had gone through the roof. Everyone loved a hero—not that Steel considered himself one.

But business was business, and he had made a bundle from it.

CHAPTER SEVENTY-EIGHT

STEEL PAID THE BILL, INCLUDING MONEY FOR THE COFFEE, and he bought a little souvenir: a keyring teddy bear that was also a flash drive.

He left Maddy's store and stepped out onto the busy street. Steel knew the roads would be empty in a couple of hours. Kids would be at the local school, tourists would be on their day trips, and people at the logging company would be at work.

That meant he only had a short window of time. If he was going to move the survivors, it had to be now.

The third call John Steel made was to Ken Henning's airfield. He explained he needed Ken to fly them to Canada. Everything was arranged, but he couldn't put in a flight plan. Their destination was Edmonton International Airport. The tower already had their details, so there were no problems. All he had to do was fly.

Steel promised Ken he would be handsomely rewarded, knowing that was the only sales pitch he needed. He had to be fuelled and ready to go.

So far, everything had been going as planned, which made

Steel nervous—not to mention the new faces in town, which meant the other organisations were there.

Steel had hoped they would all go to Talkeetna airport; it was the only way out unless you knew people. He had to keep watch on the three men. However, as he left the store, he saw five men exit the diner, one of whom he recognised as Sven, the other mercenary team leader.

Steel's stomach lurched. He had wondered why the man had paid so much attention to the diner. Steel continued walking, hoping he wouldn't be recognised in the new clothes. After all, he pretty much looked like half the men in town.

He crossed the street and was about to head for the hotel when he saw Sven and the others go inside.

'Bollocks,' Steel said under his breath. He could not get the survivors out with Sven or the others there.

They might not recognise him, but they would recognise Sherman and the others. He thought that if he told them to leave the hotel at a specific time, one leaving every fifteen minutes, it wouldn't look as suspicious as going together. Then, he would head for the airfield.

Steel went inside the diner, where he had a clear view of the hotel. His mind was racing. They were so close. He felt the anger swell up inside him. How was this fair? After everything they had escaped, only to be foiled by fate or just sheer lousy timing?

The young waitress walked up to Steel, smiled coldly, as if the owner had told her off for not being friendly enough to customers, and asked what he wanted.

Steel ordered a small black coffee. She rolled her eyes and waddled unenthusiastically back to the counter.

The number of people was thinning; his time was running out. He was beginning to think about going inside the hotel and taking care of the mercenaries individually—not killing them, just knocking them out. That was until an SUV pulled up and began honking its horn.

Steel smiled. There was some good news, after all. That must be the mercenaries' ride. He was just about to get up when the stroppy teenager returned and placed his coffee down; she was smiling as if she had suddenly recognised him.

'Hi, Mr Steel, sorry I didn't see it was you. Nice new clothes, better than that old dead carcass you normally have on. Black looks good on you—you should wear them more often,' she giggled and skipped away.

'Oh, for fuck's sake,' he groaned with a grin. 'Hit on by a teenager, as if I haven't enough problems.'

Steel took a sip of the coffee. Now he was interested. Unexpected things were happening. Sven's men were pouring out of the hotel, but only six of them. Where was number seven? Also, the three men he had seen observing Sven were rushing to their own vehicle.

Steel was slightly amused by this almost comical display, which reminded him of old TV shows like *Naked Gun*. As he watched, the three men left town, heading south towards Talkeetna, but Sven was heading north, towards the airfield.

As the vehicles left, Steel left a ten-dollar bill next to the empty cup and hurried across the road to the hotel. It was now or never; he had to get them out.

CHAPTER SEVENTY-NINE

It had taken only a few minutes to get the survivors out of the hotel, despite Karen's insistence that her hair was a mess.

They hurried out, taking the road north, and headed to the airfield. On the way, Steel warned them about what he had seen and the possibility of mercenaries at the airport.

Steel then explained that he had arranged for passage to Canada, and from there, someone would be waiting to rush them to the embassy. After that, it was the consulate's problem.

The group moved without a word. Maybe everything had been too much; perhaps it was the thought of being so close to the end but the idea of it turning to shit in a second if they got too hopeful.

No plan survives first contact with the enemy. This was sound advice, he had always thought, along with always having a plan B. Unfortunately, in this scenario, they were flying by the seats of their pants because nothing was certain.

The mercenaries weren't where they were meant to be, and

worse still, six mercs were heading where the survivors needed to be.

'You got a plan for these mercenaries if they are at the airfield?' Sherman asked.

'Yeah, kill them. Unfortunately, I have no ammo left for my rifle and revolver, and I would need to get really close to use the hatchet,' Steel admitted.

'And plan B?' Clarke asked.

'We could say you were the asset and give you to them; they might let us go after that,' Steel joked.

'Oh, yeah, and what about this flash drive with the info they are more interested in?' Karen barked.

Steel took the teddy bear keychain from his pocket and dangled it. 'I found it on Natalie when I searched her body.'

'Wow, you got it. Awesome, that's our ticket outta here,' Laura sighed.

Sherman shot Steel a wary look, unsure why he had done it but thinking he knew why. If things turned to shit, one of these would certainly give up the location of the drive.

Steel tucked the bear away, making sure he did it slowly so everyone saw.

Always have a plan C, Steel thought.

They were about a mile from the airfield when they heard the rev of a car engine. The SUV was coming back.

Steel and Sherman rushed everyone off the road and into cover, then watched in surprise as the black SUV drove past, heading south.

'What now?' Sherman asked.

'What do you think? We get the fuck out of here,' Clarke yelped and shot out of his hiding place.

Steel and Sherman shrugged at each other, grinned, and followed.

They found Ken Hennings in his plane; the engine was

running, propellers turning, and thick smoke billowing from the exhaust.

'Come on, come on, before those assholes come back!' Ken yelled from the plane.

The survivors clambered inside and took their seats. The end was near; they were going home.

'Did they give you any trouble?' Steel asked as he strapped himself into the seat next to Ken.

Ken shook his head. 'No, sir. They asked who this plane was for. I told them it was for a load of tourists on a glacier tour, and they were welcome to come along.'

Steel smiled; he had underestimated the old swindler. 'Nicely done,' Steel yelled.

'Remember that when you're tippin',' Ken winked.

Ken manoeuvred the plane and began to taxi, giving it some power until finally, they were in the air.

The survivors looked down at the view below—at the trees, the town, the winding road south. On the road stood a large red SUV, and heading towards it, a black SUV. The black car swerved, and tiny flashes became pinpricks.

Steel smiled. So much for Sven's team, he thought. Then, he turned his attention to the great blue yonder.

He wondered about what came next. He was heading for the US; he was back in the world. Would he return to Britain? Rejoin his regiment, start again? But what about the threat? The organisation was surely looking for him—the last survivor of the Steel family.

For the first time, he had no plan, let alone a plan B. His idea of rescuing these people and returning to the cabin was utterly destroyed. He was flying into the unknown, and he didn't like it.

He was a soldier, and he needed a plan and some structure.

He needed a clear routine: on this day, you do this; at this time, you do that. Now, he was without a plan.

They banked and headed east over the Tetlin National Wildlife Refuge. As the plane rocked slightly from the thermals, Steel opened the small window and let something slip from his fingers.

Sherman saw this and smiled; he knew exactly what it was. Now, the information would be lost—if not forever, then long enough that it no longer mattered when someone did find it.

He looked forward into the nothingness, closed his eyes, and slept.

CHAPTER EIGHTY

Mr Jones made the call he didn't want to make. He knew the Chairman was anything but forgiving, and this news was anything but good.

'So, Mr Jones, the survivors escaped, and your other team got ambushed by Trojan while they were on the way to do precisely what you were off to do. Stake out the airport?'

'Yes, sir,' Mr Jones replied, his voice cold.

'Is there any good news?' the Chairman asked.

'Sven survived with two others and managed to kill all the Trojan mercenaries.'

'And this is good news, how?' barked the Chairman, uninterested in whether the incompetent fools lived or died.

'Sven said that when he was at the Ridgeway Creek airfield, the pilot there was waiting for a tour, but after the incident, we checked again. The pilot had lied, and he had flown to Canada.'

'Again, I'm failing to see the good news,' the Chairman said impatiently.

'We waited until the pilot returned a few days later, met

him at the local bar, and got him nice and juiced up. I asked him about his trip to Canada, and he talked about helping some people in trouble; he didn't know that much,' Mr Jones continued.

'And?'

'He didn't know any of the passengers; in fact, three people were missing—the three analysts, to be precise—but he did know one of the passengers. In fact, he lived there and arranged for the flight,' Mr Jones said excitedly.

'Go on?' said the Chairman, growing weary of the tale.

'It was John Steel, sir. We found John Steel.'

CHAPTER EIGHTY-ONE

JOHN STEEL LOOKED OUT ACROSS THE SKYLINE OF Washington, DC. The sun was rising, bleeding a fiery orange into the morning heavens. Birds swooped and dived as if dancing to celebrate a new day.

He wore all black: jeans, a shirt, boots, and a leather jacket. He had also gotten a new pair of sunglasses. Steel rubbed his chin; not having a beard still felt strange, but he had to admit it was nicer.

Steel sat outside a café on Pennsylvania Avenue Northwest, sipping his black coffee and gazing at the White House.

People sauntered here and there, and others rushed to their places of work while he sat and watched the world go by. It had been a week since they had returned from Alaska, a trip that had been less than straightforward.

When they had landed in Canada, Sherman had made some calls, but they were all but smuggled into the US. There was always the threat from either organisation trying to stop them, but, strangely enough, none of them knew about the stranger who had aided the survivors. As far as they were

concerned, it was all due to Sherman and the survivors' deter-
mination.

Steel's gaze was interrupted by a man who had entered the
café. Steel smiled. It was Sherman, dressed in a dark suit and
looking less like a tourist.

Sherman ordered a coffee, waited for the beverage, and
headed over to where Steel was.

'Morning, John,' Sherman greeted.

Steel nodded in reply.

'Lost the beard, I see, and the Wildman outfit,' Sherman
smiled.

Steel sipped his coffee, wondering why the two were meeting. At first, when Steel had gotten the phone call in his hotel
room, he thought Sherman wanted to catch up and say thanks.
But now, the back of his neck was tingling; there was more to
this meeting.

'I was getting tired of people tossing loose change,' Steel
said coldly, waiting for Sherman to get to the point.

'I heard from the others; they are doing okay. Karen might
need therapy for a while, and I can't see any of them taking any
trips anytime soon, but they are alive. They said thanks, especially Laura,' Sherman paused momentarily. 'She asked me to
pass on her number, in case you wanted to... you know...
catch up?'

'Why would I want to do that?' Steel asked quizzically.

Sherman shot him a stunned look, then shook his head.
'God, you're such a fuckin...'

'Cold-hearted, green-eyed dickhead?' Steel answered,
remembering what Sherman had said to him when they arrived
in the US. While everyone hugged, he had just walked away
and disappeared into the crowd. Sherman quickly tracked him
down, but that was not hard. After figuring out who Steel was,

Sherman had someone ask all the top hotels if John Steel was staying there.

Once he had gotten to the hotel, Sherman had called John, greeting him with, 'You are the most insufferable, cold-hearted, green-eyed dickhead I've had the displeasure of knowing.' Then, he laughed before arranging the meeting.

'Yeah, somethin' like that. You are also one tough bastard, that's for sure. You also need a place to hide,' Sherman replied.

Steel raised an eyebrow, interested in how much Sherman knew.

'I know people who know people. I spoke to your old CO; we had done some... tours together. He said you were in the shit —that was why you were in Alaska. He told me what happened to your family... I'm sorry.'

Steel said nothing; he just drank from his cup.

'Some guy in MI8 then contacted me. I'd never heard of it, but it wouldn't be the Secret Service if I had. Anyway, he suggested I... help you disappear for a while. Apparently, they are interested in you—got a job for you when you're ready.'

'And how are you meant to make me disappear?' Steel asked.

'You, my boy, are gonna join my outfit,' Sherman said proudly.

'How? I'm a Brit,' Steel asked.

'And also half American, from your wife's side. Yes, I know. It's a massive stretch, but it's workable. Besides, her mother is a senator, so... well, you get the picture.'

'Okay, and how is this going to happen?' Steel asked, somewhat sceptical.

'You will come in as...'

'No. If I'm doing it, I'm doing it right,' Steel growled.

'What... as a recruit?'

'If I'm going to work as one of you, I must start from the bottom. Less suspicious that way.'

'And the cover story?'

Steel thought for a moment. 'Tell the truth: a serving British soldier wants to transfer to the SEAL teams. We don't have to go into the other stuff,' Steel shrugged.

'What? That a killer organisation murdered your family and is now hunting you?'

'Yes, exactly.'

'What about your family's company? How are you getting around that?'

'I have a good team looking after things, and the board knows my situation. And I was never really that involved anyway, so nothing has changed,' Steel smiled.

Sherman drained his Americano and stood. 'Well, John Steel, report to Coronado for your training, and God have mercy.'

'Why? I'm sure I will pass.'

'No, I meant the people who are after you.'

Sherman and Steel shook hands, and then Sherman left the café, leaving Steel to ponder the future. He was back in the world, but now he had a chance to train properly, and one day, when he was ready, he would stop running.

And then, he would do the hunting.

But for now, he had to disappear again.

Steel smiled. *God help them! I don't think so.*

ABOUT THE AUTHOR

Stuart Field is the author of the John Steel thriller series.

He's born in the West Midlands, Great Britain. Later, he joined the armed forces where after 22 years of fun and adventure, he left to start as a writer. Married with a daughter, he still hasn't grown up, which helps with the imagination. He loves to travel and experience other cultures. He loves to love life.

———

To learn more about Stuart Field and discover more Next Chapter authors, visit our website at www.nextchapter.pub.

Printed in Poland
by Amazon Fulfillment
Poland Sp. z o.o., Wrocław